Author's note: While this book is fiction, it was inspired by Romaine Tenney, an independent Vermonter who resisted the seizure of his land for the building of I-91 in 1964. Tenney projected a steadfast respect for Vermont and the land itself, for his animals, for his neighbors and for all those he came across.

The news briefs at the beginning of each chapter derive from *Wikipedia* and other news sources of the time.

JUST COMPENSATION

Verdant Books

(Independent Publisher since 2003)

Rutland, Vermont & San Francisco

Verdant Books

(Independent Publisher since 2003)

Rutland, Vermont & San Francisco

SHIRES PRESS

4869 Main Street

Manchester Center, VT 05255

www.northshire.com

JUST COMPENSATION

ISBN: 978-1-60571-543-3

JUST COMPENSATION

Richard Lechthaler

Chapter 1

THE FIRST SNOW

Friday - November 16, 1962

Los Angeles - *Cassius Clay defeated the world light heavyweight champion Archie Moore with a fourth-round TKO last night in Los Angeles. The 21-year-old Clay, known as the Louisville Lip, had predicted 'Archie Moore will fall in four.' Once again, his prediction was exact. The 49-year-old champ looked his age against the speed-fisted Olympic Gold medalist.*

He wasn't an old man yet, but working the farm alone on a wintery day sometimes made him feel like one. At 58, he was milking twenty cows, down from the sixty the boys had milked before his brothers moved on some years ago. Twenty. Sixty. Didn't matter much. It was the damn arthritics that bothered him. It always seemed worse when the weather turned raw. November can deliver raw. Not even Thanksgiving yet and snow on the ground.

The first snow always surprises. Doesn't matter if it's early or late, you're just not ready. There are lots of didn't do's that you just didn't get to. He knew without venturing outside that the bench by the pond was still out, the raspberry branches still uncut, and a siphon hose was now frozen hard to the ground. Gloves? He wondered where he had put them. The wheelbarrow was leaning against the barn. The wood he'd been splitting was now buried. Yep, the first snow always surprises because it sneaks up on you. Yesterday, he evaluated the signs of winter and concluded no, it wouldn't be today. And he was right; it wasn't. It was last night. As he looked out the bedroom window, he thought that it must have started as a light rain because the snow was stuck to the trees and the side of the barns. Just a little, but enough. When he looked out and up into the leafless woods he saw white branches and boughs with a pencil-thin line of dark tracing the branches out toward their tips and, elsewhere, just a slash of bark showing through here and there. Mostly it was white. White with thin pencil lines of dark. It was like an impressionistic painting. The mountains in the distance had a different look altogether, softer, like a down-filled quilt. A quilt on an unmade bed. Like his on the bed behind him in his little upstairs room. Peaks and valleys and rolling hills tucked in and around rolling hills. He liked to compare nature to something familiar and, because he spent the bulk of his hours alone, he freely talked to himself, often out loud, as he did now, considering how the extended branches were salt white with just a hint of pepper. He spoke out loud: "White outer fringe; darker toward the roots." It was a simple kind of poetry for him.

Rayland approached each day knowing that he'd know what the weather was going to be simply by reading the morning air or observing the signs evident to anyone who had paid attention for years. From the window, he could see that the snow wasn't deep. About two inches. He knew that it would be light and fluffy on top. Pretty to look at, easy to walk through. Flurries were spitting in the air but he knew they wouldn't last. After all, it was November and November was a time when the light was usually low and grey but the big storms lay ahead. Today the sun would be clear in between scattered flurries that would pass through. As the big white clouds raced across the sky, it made for a rapidly changing lightshow against the mountains. Off and on, the flakes hung in the air like feathers. It gave the appearance of a light fog or haze as he looked up across the land. Somewhere Rayland had read that a photographer would put a filter over his lens when taking a photograph of an old actress. The filter helped the actress look younger. And, because he was a farmer, that thought brought him to the old girls waiting for him in the barn. Ha! Old cows, that's what awaited him and that was fine. He knew how to take care of the old cows. Old actresses, not so much. Women? Well, he'd not had much experience there. And that was fine, too.

Early snow wasn't necessarily a bad thing. Late snow usually means no snow for Christmas. Might even be an open winter. He hated an open winter. All you could do during an open winter was cut more firewood. When there was no snow to insulate the house from the cold blowing through the stone foundation, you did two things. You threw more wood on the fire and you went ice-skating. That's all you could do. No one likes an open winter.

Rayland had put his old wool pants on over the long johns he'd slept in and then a baggy wool shirt on top. He stepped into a pair of comfortable slippers and headed down the narrow stairs to stoke the fire and get some heat going in the small kitchen. After a visit to the outhouse and feeding the dogs, there was enough heat in the stove to start his oatmeal. Oatmeal, my, oh my. He ate oatmeal a lot -- sometimes because that was all he could afford and sometimes because that was all he had on hand. But, mostly, he ate it because he liked it. Oatmeal with his own syrup on it and one of his homemade biscuits. That was his favorite breakfast. Sometimes his favorite lunch or dinner, too. After eating, he donned his barn coat and goulashes and headed to the barn. He plopped the old felt hat on his head on his way out the door.

The cold snap had firmed up the ground during the night. No wading through mud this morning. The air was crisp, clean, invigorating. The ladies were happy to go outside after the milking. He could always tell whether a cow was happy or not. He'd been around Holsteins all his life. He could read them better than people. They'll enjoy staying outside on a pretty day like this, he thought. They can watch the snow and the light show going on in the hills behind the snowy filter.

Rayland Jensen was a handsome man. Tall, thin and strong. He had rosy cheeks and a ruddy complexion from long hours outdoors. Deep wrinkles outlined his clear, blue eyes. Beautiful blue eyes. Eyes that seemed to sparkle when he talked to you. Especially when he laughed. And he laughed a lot. A faded old felt hat always sat on his head, in winter and summer. He had a long, well-kept salt and pepper beard and he always had a smile and a friendly word for those who stopped by. Big hands. Big strong hands and powerful forearms from years of milking and haying and working a farm. Hands that were rough looking but soft and kind to anything he touched. Rayland was a happy man. He'd tell folks he was as happy as a sunny day.

As he walked from the barn, a flock of geese, high above, caught his attention. They were honking instructions to each other as they changed positions in the V they formed against the sky. The change was a sharing of the burden of leading, plowing through the air on the long journey south. Hasn't been much sharing of the burden around here for some time, he thought. He followed the geese overhead. Being alone as much as he was, he lived with his thoughts lots of the time, as he did now. Doesn't bother me that I'm here alone, he thought. I get plenty of company and I really like each day as it comes. I do like it best when other family members are around enjoying the farm, especially the kids. I don't mean the work so much. Just the entire joy of farm life. You've gotta enjoy the work though if you want to enjoy a farm.

Just as he often talked to himself out loud, he also talked to the animals. The geese were no exception. "Better get going boys," he said, turning toward the horizon. "You're getting a late start on your trip south."

There was no doubt that an early winter was closing in.

"Probably a good day to get up to the wood lot and load the last of the split wood pile. Easier to load them logs now than to wait and have to dig them out from under a serious pile of snow later. Plus, I'll get an item off my didn't-do list." He smiled as he heard his own self-deprecating jest.

The Jensen farm had a large wood lot with plenty of maples for firewood and for sugaring. There were large open pastures for grazing, a small apple orchard, a brook and a spring that never ran dry. The sweetest water you ever tasted. The barn was raw wood, a bit worse for wear. The original pine boards were now streaked old barn boards with a splash of black here and there. An occasional knot of mahogany or a slight streak hinted of the original pine. Picturesque, yes, but working barns looked best from a distance. The closer you got, the reality of animals and hard work became obvious. Mud was the primary eyesore. Dung, rotted wood, busted hay bales, unfinished projects, old equipment and discarded odds and ends were hard to avoid up close.

At the moment, he had twenty cows for milking. He sold his raw milk through the local co-op and made enough to make ends meet. His two draft horses, Charlie and Max, were used for hauling and plowing, although there wasn't much plowing going on these days. Charlie and Max were big, black Percherons. They hauled milk to the co-op, wood from the fields, hay in summer and kids whenever the kids showed up.

There were two dogs. Star just up and adopted Rayland one day out on the road. Champ came as a favor to a friend who moved away after foreclosure. Tussle was in charge of the barn. The cat's favorite thing to do was catch a mouse and carry it around the barn to show it off. He'd carry it to Rayland, drop it and wait for a little praise. Then he'd eat it. The spectators paid no attention. That was his job.

It was always a family farm and now this was the family. Well, that's not exactly how it had always been. In fact, it was never exactly like anything. Too many of us, he thought. Five sisters. Three brothers. Seemed we always had a house full. Things were pretty normal growing up. At least until Pa passed away. Golly. Twelve years old. After that, things changed fast. If anyone had bothered to ask, he would have said that was when he became a real farmer. Was it a choice? What difference did it make if it was choice or necessity. Here he was.

The fact was that Rayland took excellent care of his ladies, his draft horses, chickens, dogs, and Tussle. There was also a barn owl. The owl showed no loyalty. Came and went as he darn well pleased. The other animals seemed to love Rayland as much as he loved them. The barns were old and always in a state of disrepair. He wasn't much of a carpenter, and his animals were more interesting than patching up that barn wall or shoring up the old woodshed.

He wasn't much for worldly things or modern conveniences either. He had no car. No tractor. No electricity. Right here, on these 90 acres where he was born and raised, Rayland had everything in the world he had ever wanted or needed. And, if you asked, and if you didn't, he'd tell you so.

Chapter 2

THE MAIL ARRIVES

Friday - November 16, 19

London - *Severe smog killed at least 106 people in London over the last several days and hospitalized many more. Most of those who died had pre-existing heart and lung problems. In 1952, similar conditions killed over 4,000.*

The old barn sat smack on the dirt road to town. Mud in spring. Dust in summer. Frozen ruts at the moment. Unless the ladies of the barn were acting up, you could clearly hear a car or truck coming down the road. Their speed announced whether they were just passing by or planning to stop. Rayland was grateful for the many friends who stopped to chat. Strangers too, often looking for a photograph of a farm and a real Vermonter. He always obliged. Hard to tell how many photos Rayland had posed for. He was such a handsome old Yankee; he must have made it into many, many albums.

"We got company, ladies," he announced. The car slowed to a stop by the open barn door.

"How you doing, Rayland? Those cows taking care of you, okay?" This was Jeep Perkins. He got out of his mail car and walked into the barn just as he'd done hundreds of times before.

"I've got some mail for you. Want me to put it in the house?"

"Anything interesting?"

"Nope. Same old stuff. Christmas mailers. A few coupons. Looks like maybe a letter from your sister in Springfield. The *Village News*. I'll stick it in the house."

"Yeah. And grab yourself a beer if you'd like, Jeep. Or a cider if you'd prefer. Cider's damn good this year."

"Nagh. Think I'll get a glass of water. That will be fine. Want one?"

"Yeah. Please, Jeep."

The kitchen was where Rayland lived. The main house was big enough to hold nine children and Rayland's parents when they were growing up. Since his mother died, however, Rayland rarely went into the main house. He lived entirely in an extension off the side of the house. It was a small ell with a kitchen down and his small bedroom up. The door opened onto a rough porch. The cow barn was across the way.

Jeep put the mail on the table and hitched up his pants before picking up two large mason jars. He went to the soapstone sink and pumped the pump handle a few times to get it primed. While he pumped, he thought, not for the first time, that farm houses smelled like barns. It was true. Didn't have much to do with cleanliness either. So many trips to the barn and back in those rubber boots. Back and forth, back and forth for decades. So many dirty overalls in the hamper over the years. How many manure-stained barn jackets hung on those kitchen coat pegs? Eventually, the smell of cow, manure mixed with hay, even the leather and the sweat on the horses' tack permeated everything. The barn had a slightly more acrid smell, of course. Probably from rat urine and mold under the hay bales. But the house and the barn certainly smelled similar. The farmers called it "fresh country air." Truth be told, the barn usually had a breeze blowing through, which made it smell better than the house on many days. Jeep had become used to the variations in aroma. He filled the Mason jars, hitched up his pants again and headed back to the barn.

Jeep was an interesting fellow. Brown eyes and wavy brown hair to match. He had an athletic build, was shy, but quick with a smile. When asked a tough question, he had a habit of tightening his lips and showing teeth. Some in town thought he looked like Humphry Bogart. There was something about him though that said, I can get this done. Because of his job, he stayed up to date on local events. That wasn't really his interest. That was his job.

He got his nickname during the war. After boot camp he was sent to mechanic school in West Texas. Upon graduation, he was assigned to some colonel as his driver. After only a few months, the colonel got shipped out to England to work on Operation Overlord. That was the build-up to D-Day. He must have liked Jeep because he set him up with similar orders.

In the Army, everyone had a nickname. Merwyn Perkins was happy to dump the Merwyn and become Jeep. For eight months, he drove the colonel to meeting after meeting at the assembly areas being set up across Great Britain. As the invasion approached, the colonel told Jeep they'd be headed to France. Jeep drove the colonel ashore onto Omaha Beach four days after D-Day. By the time they arrived, Omaha Beach had been built into a full-scale harbor with a floating breakwater, floating roadways and piers. Concrete caissons had been added for protection from the sea. It had become a massive artificial harbor that had been towed across the channel and assembled at water's edge. Only three days after landing, the massive harbor was in place. They called it Mulberry Harbor. The colonel had worked on the planning while in England. His orders now were to establish harbor security as soon as possible and then push on toward Paris. Jeep in the front seat, the colonel in the back.

The push to Paris was a two-month slog, but once Paris had been taken, liberated and secured, new orders arrived. The colonel got transferred to the Army College at the Presidio in Monterey, California. Again, Jeep got matching orders. However, after a few days in the California sunshine, the Army decided the colonel didn't need a driver. Jeep got shipped off to Fort Rucker, Alabama. From England to Paris to Monterey to dinkwater Alabama. At the end of his tour at Fort Rucker, he wanted out. He traveled a bit and eventually ended up as the mailman in Towsley, Vermont. Of course, he drove a Jeep.

No one had a better handle on what was happening in town than Jeep. You could get more out of him than the *Village News*. He was a man of facts. Not gossip. That suited Rayland just fine. He didn't have time for gossip. And didn't care.

The screen door to the house squeaked open, then banged shut.

"Pull up a bale and sit a spell. If we can stay out of the wind, it should be nice," Rayland offered. Jeep had two big mason jars filled with water. He handed one to Rayland. The meadow and hills looked beautiful with the morning light shining on the snow and, so, the two men sat and looked out onto the scene.

Then Jeep, apropos of nothing, commented, "November always remembers."

"Remembers what?"

"You know what they say. If you get a snowy November, the other months remember and you get a snowy winter. Looks like a snowy winter's comin."

After a long drink of the cold, spring water, Jeep looked at his jar. "Damn good water, Rayland. Best in town." He looked up. "Remember that batch of hooch you gave me a while back? I think you said your brother made it?" He sipped the water. "That moonshine was bitchin." He looked back into his jar. "It's because of this water." He sipped, then sipped again. "Why don't you ever make moonshine?"

"Cause I don't drink it much."

"Too bad." He swirled the water in his jar. "Where's your brother when we need him?"

Jeep's question was rhetorical, but Rayland didn't catch that. "He's working a steel mill in Ohio," he said, then became reflective. "Been gone a while now, as you know. Left right after Ma died five years ago." His brow wrinkled. "Wow. Five years. Funny thing is I was just remembering how Greg came to me soon after she died and he told me he wanted out. 'Let's sell the farm,' he said." Rayland rubbed his forehead. "I gotta tell you, Jeep, I thought he was crazy."

He took a sip of water, looked deep into the jar as if some information were in there.

"He had a lot of pressure on him after Pa died. I don't think Ma meant to put it all on him, but Greg was the oldest. Maybe he just took all the responsibility on his own. I think it became too much. She relied on all of us. Had to. But I never felt the pressure the way Greg did."

Rayland got up and walked over to a cow, scratched her behind the ear and adjusted her tether.

"I told him 'Damn if I'm moving. This is where I belong. If you want to go, fine. I'm not going to try to hold you back. But I'm not leaving.'" He retied the tether and patted the cow on the rump. "I told him 'If things don't work out, you can come back. You'll find me right here.'"

Rayland moved back to the hay bale and sat.

"He was the last one to go." He looked at the cow. "They all slipped away. The girls got married. My brothers just didn't want the farm life, I guess."

He looked at Jeep then added as if needing to offer more explanation, "Being here with my cows and horses and the farm and all seems like the natural order of things to me."

Another long pause. Then, looking out into the meadow, he said, "Too bad Greg is so far away. Everyone else is close enough to come back and use the farm any time they want. And they do. It's always been a family farm. Still is." He looked at his boots. "I'm proud of that."

Jeep took off his black watch cap and rubbed the top of his head. "It fits you, Rayland." He took a last drink. "You're sure good with these animals."

Lightening things up, Rayland changed the subject "What's going on in town these days?"

Jeep bowed his head slightly but looked up at Rayland as if he were looking over bifocals. "Not much. Never is." He paused. "You going to go to the Christmas party? It's on the 20th, I believe. At the Trout Club again. Arrive late and let them warm the place up or you'll freeze your ass off. I guess that's the big news." He set his mason jar aside.

"There's something going on in Asia that I don't really understand. Seems like another war getting started. The commies in North Vietnam are sneaking into the south. Kennedy is sending advisors to help. I guess we're trying to stop them. It's hard to say, not knowing. What do we care about Vietnam? Hard to tell who wants what. That little fat Russian guy is the one to keep your eye on." Jeep tried to recall the name. "Khrushchev. Yeah, Khrushchev. That little son of a bitch is a handful. He's the one who tried to put intercontinental missiles in Cuba last month. Seems we're okay in Cuba for the moment."

He lit a cigarette. "Kennedy says he's going to put a man on the moon. Maybe. But he's having a heck of a time just getting a black kid into the University of Mississippi." Taking off his cap, he scratched his head. "Can't get a kid into school, but he's going to put a man on the moon," he chuckled. "The kid went to enroll, and, well, the good ole boys didn't care much for that. All hell broke loose. Riots. Fights. Burning cars. It got ugly. The president called out the National Guard and federal officers to quell the riots. Finally, the next day, I guess, things calmed down."

There was a long pause as they both pondered the changing times.

"Must have been one hell of a first day in school for that kid." Jeep said. After a long pause, he added. "That's pretty much it." He blew a smoke ring and proudly watched it float out across the barn.

"Any news on the highway?" Rayland asked what was clearly uppermost on his mind. At least, that's what Jeep had been thinking, but avoiding.

"It's coming, that's for sure," he said, surprising himself with his own bluntness. "They just keep pushing forward. I heard they opened a strip in Montpelier a few weeks back. Several hundred cars lined up to drive three miles. Three miles for crying out loud. People are excited about this, I guess."

Along with the cows, they both looked up when they heard a car coming.

"You've got company. I gotta go anyway. You know what they say, 'When the buds are the size of a squirrel's ear, it's time to plant the corn.' Gotta go or the mail will never get delivered."

"Squirrel's ear? Plant the corn? What are you talkin' about?"

Jeep ignored the question. As they walked out of the barn, a pickup pulled in. Ford T 100. It was Norman, Rayland's neighbor. He parked next to the snow bank and got out.

"Hi, Jeep. Hello, Rayland. How you boys doing on this fine day? You got any mail for me, Jeep? I'll save you a stop." Jeep looked through his bundles as Norman announced, "I'm going over to Leo's, Rayland. Can I pick up anything for you?"

Leo's Market was six miles away across the bridge and up the hill almost to the town square in Claremont. There was Tanner's General Store in Towsley, but it didn't carry much. Gasoline, beer and candy bars. They had an old meat cooler. A nice looking piece of marbled beef might sit in the corner one day. A week later, it might still be there, but it was no longer the same color. There were also hot dogs and baloney and a few canned goods. Tanner's sold newspapers, too, and coffee and sometimes donuts. The maple glazed were actually pretty good. There were bundles of kindling, boxes of ammo and worms. That was about it. Well, maybe not everything. There was always a rumor that Albert Tanner, the proprietor, had a box of sex toys in the back room. They were for sale if you were interested. No one ever admitted to being interested even though Albert would boast that sales were brisk.

Rayland had the choice of walking to Leo's for provisions or eating oatmeal from Tanner's. He ate a lot of oatmeal, but he seldom walked to Leo's. At least, not all the way. Someone always gave him a lift, or stopped by like Norman had to offer to pick up groceries for him.

"Mind if I ride along, Norman? Let me get out of these boots and change overalls. I'll grab a ride with you. See you later, Jeep."

Norman Cairns was an interesting guy. He owned and worked the neighboring farm with his wife Aud. He always looked like he'd just come from a business meeting, not straight from the barn. He was wearing his canvas field jacket with the zip-in liner, made for days like today, and a corduroy Tractor Supply Co. ball cap. The jacket had big pockets so that a hunter could stuff a dead grouse or two into them, but Norman used the pockets to hold a tape measure, a large pocketknife, his eyeglass case and a note pad and pen, things he considered essential. Snow or no snow, he wore LL Bean boots that came up to above his ankles. The laces were never tied to the top.

He was neat, trim, and well groomed. He had an Ag degree from UVM and he looked the part. Wire rim glasses. Almost professorial, but with an Ag business comfort. And he ran a pretty smart farm. Milked about sixty cows. Did a little sugaring in the spring. Thirty or so of the trees grew on Rayland's woodlot. He and Rayland worked the sugaring together and shared the results. Norman liked to tell how he met his wife in the cow barn at the Tunbridge Fair. It was true.

Vermont fairs were where families brought their best livestock, produce and needlework for competition and blue ribbons. Back then, Norman was 21 and fresh out of college. Aud was 19. He still laughs at himself remembering the time he first laid eyes on her. Aud had just been handed the blue ribbon for having the top dairy cow at the fair. She walked by, blue ribbon in hand and headed back to her stall. Cow. Blue ribbon. All he saw was a beautiful young blond girl in the prettiest dress he'd ever seen. Blue eyes.

Creamy complexion. She was a knock out. Two short pony tails bobbed on either side of her smiling face. The dress she was wearing was quite unusual, maybe a costume. Colorful suspenders that ran from the waist over her shoulders held up a colorful green apron with black piping and little flowers on the hem. Underneath the suspenders was a white, puffy blouse with a low neckline that every young man in Tunbridge must have admired. The costume was stunning.

Vaguely pretending interest in the cattle, Norman sidled toward her stall. Aud was hanging her ribbon for display. When she turned back toward him, she offered a pleasant smile. It stopped him in his tracks. He started to speak, but felt nothing but a stammer coming out. He stopped and started over. The only thing he could get out of his mouth was "What's the name of your cow?"

What's the name of her cow? Golly. He wanted to kick himself. That must have sounded so stupid. He couldn't believe it himself. Stupid. And immature. What's the name of your cow? Golly, Jeez.

"LilyBelle," she smiled. He just stood there, empty-headed.

The next thing out of his mouth was the best he could do. "What's that thing on her head?"

Golly damn, you dope, he berated himself in silence. What's that thing on her head!? Holy camoly. How dumb can I get? She's going to think I'm the biggest dope in the county.

"It's a garland of buttercups and Queen Anne's lace. I'm from Switzerland. When I was a little girl in the spring our village would hold a cow fight. The winner got a crown. A garland of flowers. She got to lead the herd up to high pasture for summer grazing." Aud casually scratched the cow behind the ear. "It really wasn't much of a fight. More a pushing contest. We tried to pick Miss Bossy to lead the parade. La Reine des Reines. Queen of the Queens. The cow fight was more of a sweet way to say goodbye to winter. There was more wine drinking and laughter than fighting."

Norman just stood there and watched her. Several folks stopped by to offer congratulations. She chatted with them while he stood and watched. The crowd was filing out. The barn was shutting down. "Can I give you a ride home?"

She continued scratching Lily Belle and, nodding toward the cow. replied with a soft chuckle, "Do you have room for both of us?"

Dag-gone-it. I am a Bozo. Total Bozo. Stupid. Stupid. Stupid. He wanted to die, standing there feeling like a nincompoop. Yet, on the other hand, it couldn't have gone too badly. They got married three month later.

Aud worked alongside Norman on the farm. She planted a tremendous vegetable garden. A flower garden. too. Most dairy farms didn't have flower gardens. Too much work. Aud tended her gardens with regularity and with pride, often wearing one of those pretty dresses. He had learned that it was called a dirndl.

Norman and Aud and the three kids were wonderful neighbors. And Norman was always good for a ride to town.

Leo's was a small-town, rural grocery store. It had most of the basics plus a few treats that were hard to pass up. Large brownies with walnuts, Apple pies, and a tray of deviled eggs that always sat near the cash register. They smelled so good you had to have one. There was bread, meat, and occasionally fish. Cereal, coffee, dry goods, beer, sodas and a few vegetables. No dairy except ice cream. Dairy was delivered to your door if you didn't live on a farm or have a neighbor with a cow.

"Treat you to an egg, Norman?"

"Yeah, sure, Rayland." Rayland looked over the tray of eggs, picking out two nice ones. There must have been thirty egg halves on the tray. They appeared identical to most people, but Rayland knew his deviled eggs and wanted two of the best. He looked them over carefully.

"Ten cents apiece, Rayland. Two for a quarter." Leo joked.

Leo was a short, heavy-set man with a happy face, a dark complexion and always a white butcher's apron that hung below his knees. He had just the slightest accent and some in town suggested that he was a foreigner, but no one really cared. He was very friendly and had short pleasant conversations with everyone.

They bagged their provisions, paid the bill and headed to the truck. Once they were moving, Rayland unwrapped the egg halves and handed one to Norman. They ate as they rolled back toward the river.

"What do you hear about the highway, Norman?"

"Well, they're in business down in Brattleboro. In one summer they pushed from the Massachusetts border all the way through Bratt and a couple of miles north. They pushed that thing right through town. Well, not right through the center of Brattleboro, but not far from the center. They took out houses, farms, filled in wet lands, leveled hills. You name it."

They ate quietly. "I hate to hear that stuff, Rayland, but the drivers down there are loving it from what I hear."

"What do we need it for?"

“Need it or want it? Ike got this started when he was in office. Remember when he came to the Addison County Fair a few years back? He did some fishing and some politicking.”

“Yeah. I remember. They gave him a cow.”

“Sure did. I guess he was just checking out the political climate.”

“And George Aiken gave away the house!”

“I don’t know if you can blame old George. He’s been pretty good for the state overall. But now, Ike’s plan is to have highways crisscrossing the country. It’s all so that commerce can get from here to there quicker. Anything that gets in the way of speedier travel seems to get run right over.” Norman finished his egg. “Aiken is a cheerleader for the road. No doubt about that. El Mouton, do you know him? He’s the salesman. He’s in charge of economic development for the state. He’s out selling everything that Vermont’s got. Skiing, syrup, lumber, tourism. According to El, this new road is going to open up Vermont and cure all our problems. It’s going to get us out of the sticks. Progress. my friend. Progress is the new religion,” he paused. “They’re buying that in Bratt.” Again a long pause. “We’ll see what happens as it comes north.”

Seemed like nothing but a faster way to get New Yorkers through here and gone, Rayland thought. While Rayland was unsure of what the road would mean or bring, he knew that local people would pay a price for that so-called progress. As they drove, he worried that local people were getting a sales talk but, in truth, all they had gotten so far was a lot of uncertainty. Still, he kept his thoughts to himself. The future would get there soon enough, highway or no highway. All he said was, “Not sure I see the reason for it," then turned to look out the window and watch the trees pass by.

"Maybe Jeep can help," Rayland mumbled. "He says he met Ike when he was stationed in England,"

"Jeep? Jeep and Ike? I'm not buying it. No sir. I'm not buying that." Norman slapped the steering wheel with both hands. "Hanging out, were they? Toolin' around together? Holy camoly. What are you saying, Rayland?" He laughed out loud.

Rayland thought for a few seconds and then he laughed, too. Mostly at himself. "I don't know that they were toolin' around England together, but I think he met him. Or maybe he saw him." They had a good laugh at the absurdity of the thought.

As they crossed the Connecticut River, Rayland spoke again, "Norman, if there's no traffic, would you stop on the bridge for a spell? We can get a pretty good look at Towsley from out here."

Norman obliged. From the bridge you could look several miles upriver to where the bank rose gently into the small village of Towsley. The church steeple gave clear indication as to where the village sat. The best thing about the town was that the road was paved. As Vermont towns went, it was small but it could boast a community church and a general store.

"Now look at this, Norman," Rayland said, bringing his neighbor's attention to the lay of the land. "Where's that highway going to go? You've got some land along the river. But not much. Might be quarter of a mile, perhaps a little more, before you start getting to Route 5 and then the town."

"They aren't going to knock down the village, right?." He looked at Norman. "They'd destroy the community. It would be a tight fit to get four lanes between the river and the village. On the other side of Route 5, you've got a nice shoulder of farm land rolling up to the foot hills. Then there's the mountains. They aren't going to build in the river. They aren't going to bulldoze the village. They're going to avoid the mountains if they can. That puts them right through our farms, Norman."

"Yep."

Chapter 3

A TOWN HOLIDAY CELEBRATION

Friday – December 20, 1962

Edwards Air Force Base, CA. - *NASA research pilot Milton Thompson, after making a weather evaluation flight for an impending X-15 mission, made a simulated approach at Rogers Dry Lake, but experienced major problems. Unable to resolve the situation, he ejected while inverted at 18,000 feet after four complete rolls of the airframe. The fighter plunged nose first into the dessert while Thompson descended safely by parachute.*

"Hey Rayland, you headed where we're headed?"

Thomas Lumstead and his wife pulled over to give Rayland a lift. Just about everyone was headed to the Trout Club for the town party. Once the darkness of winter set in, any event that brought people together was looked forward to. Especially a party.

"Want a ride?"

"Hello, Thomas. Hi, Freddie. Don't mind if I do." Tom's wife's name was Fredericka, but everyone called her Freddie. The Lumsteads had been in town for five years now. He practiced law while she stayed home running the house and raising the kids. Freddie was a small, energetic woman who got involved with many town activities and committees. Tom had attended Dartmouth College just up the road in Hanover. After law school and a short stint at a law firm in New York City, Tom returned to the rural area he loved. He put out his shingle in the village. They were in their late-thirties.

"Whoa-ee. Cold one tonight," Rayland said as he climbed into their vehicle. "Hope you got your woolies on, Thomas." Once the temperature went anywhere near zero, wool pants were the fashion. "How those two little ones of yours doing, Freddie?"

"Not so little anymore, Rayland," she said with a big happy smile. "Sally is in third grade and Tommy Jr. is in sixth. No more babies left at home."

"Might be time for you to step up to the plate again, Thomas."

"Might be. But might not be, if you know what I mean. Let's just say two is a good number. I had two older brothers, and someone was always fighting with someone else. I remember the time Howard took my sled and left it at his friend's house. Then the friend claimed it was his. I had the damnedest time getting it back. It was one of those classic Flexible Flyers. Best sled on the hill. I missed half the winter because Howard's friend had my sled."

Tom Lumstead could talk. As the only lawyer in town, he knew everyone's business. Most were of the opinion that he was a pretty good lawyer, but he sure could talk. About anything. People say he talked so that he could pad his bill. No one really believed that. They knew he was honest but, as Jeep liked to say, he could talk the leg off a mule.

The Trout Club was a mile and a half out of town, up on the lower shoulder of Mount Towsley on a 192-acre pond. You were in the club if you lived in town. In 1859, when the club started, it had rules and regulations. Those old timers were fishing purists. Trout were the sport fish they wanted to catch. You had to use a fly rod and little fake insects and flies. Over time, things changed. Now there were no trout.

Seems someone introduced bass several years back. The bass ate the trout. No one really cared. In fact, the locals found that bass put up a good fight, and were fun to catch. Pretty good eating too. The pond was also loaded with perch. They're kind of boney, but sweet. Perfect for a fish fry. It was a fine place for summer outings or special occasions like tonight. The membership was particularly proud of the two nesting loons that crooned through the summer evenings on the far end of the pond. Everyone was protective of the loons. If one came near your boat, that was fine, but do not row over to the loon. That is a no-no. Don't mess with our loons.

As they hit the straights on the access road they could see the club ahead. It was a funny little clapboard structure with a big wraparound porch sitting under an extended overhanging roof. The porch could accommodate several long picnic tables where families enjoyed their catch after fishing. There were wood and charcoal grills on the lawn for grilling your fish. Or your hot dogs and hamburgers if you got skunked out on the pond.

Sitting there on that snowy little hill, all lit up, the club looked warm and inviting. Inviting it would be. Warm? Not so sure. The old forest green clapboards leaked enough to blow out a candle when the wind kicked up. The windows were worse. Leaky panes and no storm windows. Those screens might keep out a mosquito or two, but they weren't much help against the winter wind.

A big stone fireplace was built into the long middle wall. A wood-burning stove stood in the corner. The wood burner was about four feet high with a chimney pipe straight through the roof. You could get a big fire going in that stove. Problem was, if you didn't fire it up well in advance, it didn't do much good.

John Hurley, the local real estate salesman, lived out on Trout Club Road. Because he didn't have regular hours, he could pretty much do what he wanted when he wanted. He was a jovial fellow, and his face always expressed exactly what he was thinking. His bushy eyebrows bobbed as if they were keeping time to music.

John always volunteered to get the fire going. For a 6 o'clock party, he would stop in around 3 o'clock and get two fires going, one in the fireplace and the other in the wood burner. By 6, the room would be getting comfortable. By 9, that old woodstove was belching out heat. The levers to damp down the fire had broken long ago. Instead, the doors to the cabin would be left ajar for comfort. By 9:30, the windows were being opened.

Everything in the cabin was hand-me-down. Used and unmatched chairs. A cushioned couch and an old card table in the corner. The ladies always wanted to sit on the couch. Took forever for those chairs and benches to warm up. The cushions of the couch kept the seats, theirs and the furniture's, from feeling like a block of ice.

In the far corner, there was a small kitchen area with a stove and a sink. No water in the winter, of course. Next to the kitchen was the ego wall. That was where you posted your photograph showing off the big one you'd landed. Some of the photos went back years. The clubhouse hadn't changed much over the decades.

A dining room table stood near the front windows that looked out onto the pond. Once it had graced some significant nearby home. Now, one drop leaf, the one closest to the windows, was broken. It drooped down several inches off horizontal. Not only could you not sit to eat on that side of the table, but you took a risk if that's where you set your casserole dish, dinner plate or beer.

More than once someone's chicken potpie ended up on the floor. Didn't matter. No one was there thinking this was the Woodstock Inn. It was just a good old town party before the Christmas holiday.

The room was filled with neighbors and friends and the energy that comes with not having seen one another for a time. Loud chatter. Happy greetings. Good cheer. And a bowl of Ron Davey's secret punch.

"Ron, you didn't let your dog sit in the punch again this year, did you?" Norman asked.

"I did, but it doesn't seem to be slowing you down." Ron, an easy-going local builder, laughed at the thought, and then added. "That's your third cup, isn't it, Norman?"

Everyone was in party mood. They joked and kidded, giving each other grief about practically anything. Rayland walked in and through the crowd, greeting and being greeted. "Hello, Norman. Hello, Aud. Feels like I haven't seen you, Aud, since berry picking a few months back. Thanks for having Ralphie drop off some jam. Tastes mighty good on a crust of bread. Hello, Doris. What are you going to surprise us with at dinner tonight?"

"Well, after last year's mess-up, maybe I'll just sing." Doris Reguiska was the person in town who volunteered for everything. She might mess it up, but her hand always went up first. Maybe it was because she was a widow and wanted the company. More likely, it was because she was so good-hearted. A bit of a ditz, but a lovely person. Doris was always well groomed, usually with a new perm to boot. She had a good word for everybody. Except for John Hurley when he teased her.

"You know, if I hadn't left the pecans out of the pecan pie, you would have thought it was delicious, Rayland

Jensen. I remember you didn't have any trouble getting it down anyway."

"Doris, it was delicious. We just didn't know what to call it."

"Call it pie, Rayland. Call it pie."

Doris had a habit of standing close to you and tugging on your sleeve if what she was about to say was important or funny. She pulled on Rayland's sleeve. "This year I've got scalloped potatoes with cheese. And I put in potatoes and cheese. What did you whip up?"

"Well, I read about this in the *Rutland Herald* a few weeks back, before Thanksgiving. You know how they run all those recipes right before a holiday? This dish is really catching on in high society. So they say," he added shyly.

"Sure is good to hear that we are high society," chimed in Mazie Davies, Ron's wife. After a few cups of punch, Mazie could start an argument with an empty house, but she was in a good mood tonight. "Rayland, you treat us too good. Can't wait to try whatever it is. What is it?"

Without a lot of confidence, he stood there with his potluck offering in hand and mumbled, "Meat balls with grape jelly."

"Meatballs with grape jelly? Sounds like something we ate at Boy Scout camp." Norman was leery. "How did you find high society in Rutland?'

Rayland grinned and said, "Just find the folks with the indoor plumbing,"

While they laughed and chuckled, a friendly voice leaned in and asked, "May I try one?"

"Sure, Kathleen." Rayland replied. Kathleen Elliston, known to all as Kate, was the elementary school principle. Attractive, with auburn hair that she often wore in a bun. But, when she let it down, like this evening, men noticed.

She was a little younger than Rayland. And almost as tall, which he found a little disarming.

Kate had been in town three years. Everyone knew she'd been suddenly widowed a few years prior to taking her current position as principle. Her husband's car hit some black ice and then a tree on his way home from work. Tragic. Rayland had been a little sweet on her since she arrived.

Lifting the lid from the pot, she peeked inside, "Hmm. Looks safe," she smiled. Everyone watched as she picked a single meatball out with her fingers. "Smells good." She put it into her mouth. Everyone watched for her reaction. "Oh my. That's good, Rayland. Those society folks really know their meat balls." She licked her fingers. "Better try it, folks. These aren't going to last long."

The buffet table, at least the three quarters that didn't slant toward the floor, was filling up fast. Rayland found a safe spot away from the broken drop leaf where he set his creation.

"Rayland, I hear you're hanging out with society folks these days."

"Hello, Ulmer. Actually, they hang out with me. In the barn," he joked. "You still hang out with those famous political folks in Montpelier? Anything going on up there these days?"

"Somebody always has something they think is important. They take you to lunch, twist your arm and try to get this or that. Always looking for something." He took a fork, speared a meatball and popped it into his mouth. He savored it, rolled his eyes up and back down and said, "Yum. Damn good." He went back for seconds. "Don't repeat this, but it's usually a bunch of bullshit up there, if you know what I mean. I'll bring everyone up to date when we do the announcements. One more for the road? Damn good, Rayland. I suggest you keep hanging out with those society folks. Damn good."

John Hurley piped up. "Somebody drag Anna away from the punch bowl and let's get this dinner started." Anna's response was to thumb her nose at him.

"Jennie, would you and John help me move this card table?" Doris asked. "Over near the food. I think we'll need the extra space." John had the best vegetable garden in the county. You knew there'd be beans and squash and tasty parsnips in whatever Jennie was adding to the feast. She was a wonderful cook. Jennie and Doris moved the table while John refreshed his drink then moseyed over.

"John Hurley, you move slower than a Sunday afternoon," Doris admonished.

"Whistle and get their attention, Doris." John's eyebrows bobbed as he pantomimed with fingers to his lips. "Two fingers in your mouth and blow."

"John, if I tried to whistle like that I'd probably spit out my uppers."

"Well, maybe better to just go around and get 'em headed toward the table then. I'll get Pastor Sherman thinking about a blessing."

The pastor was a tall, quiet man, well-liked and well - respected. He moved to the center of the room and stood quietly until he had everyone's attention.

"Nice to have you all here on this pretty winter evening. From the sounds and the laughter, I think everyone is well and having a good time. God bless us. Let's bow our heads for a moment to give thanks. Heavenly father, we thank you for this bounty before us, for the warmth of our homes, and the warmth of our friendships. We humbly ask you for peace, well-being and charitable kindness to others who are less fortunate. Especially during these holiday times. Amen and amen.'" He looked up. "Let's eat."

The buffet table looked delicious. There was venison stew, scalloped potatoes, noodles with broccoli, squash, corn fritters, corn chowder, fried chicken and Bratkartoffeln. Bratkartoffeln was a dish Helma Struckin had made. She loved to cook, and loved to have others enjoy it, too. This was a recipe from her homeland. Otto, her husband, explained that it was made with potatoes, chunks of bacon and onion. "Ja, ja." Helma added. "You will like it. Ist gut."

In addition, there were many, many deserts.

The din of conversation quickly turned into the clink and clatter of plates along with small talk. John was the first up for seconds.

"Karl, did you shoot the deer for this stew? It's delicious," he called out.

"Nope. I shot the chickens." He waved a drumstick for emphasis. Karl Zalewski and Agnes ran an 'I'll-get-it-done-for-you' business. Karl was a Jack-of-all-trades kind of guy. He did excavation work, pumped septic tanks, did mechanical repair and buried large animals with his backhoe. When he wasn't doing those things, he hunted. Big game or small, Karl liked to hunt. Agnes kept the books and did the billing.

Well, Karl's joke got things going again. There was lots of laughter and joking bouncing back and forth across the room as others helped themselves to seconds.

"Doris, you forgot the pecans again. There were none in my scalloped potatoes," Thomas teased in a rather lame fashion. Doris chuckled recalling her pecan-less pecan pie.

Eventually things settled down. Coffee was poured. All was well.

"This might be a good time for our announcements." Doris moved in front of the fireplace. "I've got a few town announcements and then I'll turn things over to Ulmer. He can tell us what's going on up in Montpelier. For starters, we will have a new moderator at Town Meeting this March. Thomas Lumfield has offered to fill in for our last moderator who, by the way, did a wonderful job. Me," she beamed. As Doris chuckled at her own dumb joke, she was surprised to receive a standing ovation. "Oh my. Thank you. Maybe I shouldn't give up the job." She quickly raised her hands followed by, "Only kidding. Only kidding."

"Tom, would you like to say a few words?"

"Doris, let's just say I've never said just a few words in my life, but let's see what I can do." He smiled to the gathering. Tom had on one of his snappy bow ties, black with green holy leaves and red berries, along with a V-neck sweater. He looked good in a bow tie. Younger men with flat stomachs usually do.

"Thank you. Thank you. I hope to see you all at Town Meeting. First Tuesday in March. Nine o'clock. Don't be late. It's the day you should also get your tomatoes started indoors. That's how you know it's Town Meeting Day. See you there."

"Okay. Thanks, Tom. That's a good reminder."

"Next, I want to thank the Ladies of the Green for the beautiful Christmas tree they put up. Thank you, girls. Wonderful job. Thank you. We will need help getting boats into the pond again as soon as the ice goes out. Fishing season gets underway mid-April. Also, the town ball field needs some cleaning up and patching. Seems once the season is over the teenagers like to hang out there and do all kinds of things. At night. If you know what I mean."

"No. What do you mean, Doris?" John asked, "You've never been to a passion pit?"

"You hush up, John Hurley. Wasn't that long ago you were hanging out down there yourself. Drinking beer and who knows what." That brought hoots and catcalls from the gathering.

"Hush up. Hush up. This is important. We got notice from the Highway Department that starting in May, the surveyors for 91 will be coming through town. If they're going to survey on your property, they are supposed to come to your door and tell you so. If you're not home, they will leave a notice that they've been there.

"Now, it is my pleasure to turn things over to our state representative, the honorable Ulmer Winslow. Maybe he can get into some details. Ulmer, I yield the floor." Ulmer Winslow had been the county rep to the state senate for years. He was an older, dignified gentleman with grey hair and white sideburns. He always wore a nice sport coat and tie. Not much ever happened in the county making Ulmer the perfect man for the job. All show and no go.

"Give 'em hell, Ulmer," someone shouted.

"I do, boys. I do." Ulmer relished the limelight. "Well," he said, then paused and cleared his throat for effect. "You know we've got a new governor, Philip Hoff. A young man. Thirty-five, I think. I know him well. I know him well. We worked closely in the legislature for the past few years. He's a Democrat. We haven't had one of those in the State House for some time now. Even though he's a Democrat, he's very smart. Book smart anyway. You don't want to sell him short. His plan is to bring our state into the twentieth century. Even if he has to bring some along kicking and screaming.

"He wants to clean up the environment, and change how education is organized. With the success of that IBM plant up in Essex Junction, he is gung ho to get Route 91 completed and the 89 extension out of New Hampshire up to Burlington ASAP. IBM brought in a lot of new folks, and Phil wants to bring in more. Route 91 is coming, folks. Let's get ready to welcome the future. I know you all have questions. I'll open the floor for discussion."

Norman, looking every bit the successful country businessman in his Woolrich vest and twill shirt, got the ball rolling, He took off his glasses before speaking. "Ulmer, I thought the original plan was for the road to come up through Chester and Ludlow. One road right up the spine of the Green Mountains. Is that plan still alive?"

"I'm afraid it's not," Ulmer said, thumbing his suspenders and looking at Norman. "Money. It's always money. The department thinks it's cheaper and easier to go north from the east side of the state. Then at White River Junction, the highway will split. Route 91 will continue north. Route 89 will come in from across the river and head northwest to Montpelier and Burlington."

He looked around for the next question. "Yes, Anna," he said recognizing Anna Jaffe.

"Hi, Ulmer. Thanks for coming." Anna stood. "Where's the Highway Department looking to put this road?"

Everyone thought they knew the answer, but Anna wanted to get it out in the open.

"Right now, it appears two different options are on the table. Go up between the river and town or go up along the shoulder of the mountains to the west of town. The surveyors will work both sites starting this spring."

"If they come onto our property, are we allowed to shoot them?"

That slayed her husband. Preston was a big, loud man with a big, loud laugh. He couldn't hold back. She cracked him up. Anna and Preston had a small farm up on Cobble Hill. Anna had purchased it before she met Preston. She'd been fixing it up forever. Amazingly, the work went much faster once Preston's money was behind the project. Anna milked six cows. She also had an artificial insemination business that she started a few years back. Late summer and early fall she visited farms up and down the valley. Then, about nine months later, she'd be back to help with the birthing process. She got along well with the farmers. She was well respected. She could hold her own at the Dairy Co-op or over a beer celebrating a newborn calf.

Preston stood up, "Now hang on, honey. Before anybody shoots some college kid laying out a road, think about what's coming our way." He paused and looked around before. "Progress," he said, with a kind of reverence in his tone.

Preston was a financial guy from Boston. He managed a mutual fund portfolio, and he looked a little like Mr. Monopoly except he was taller and didn't wear a monocle. He had a square jaw and prominent chin and fancied himself a snappy dresser. He wore pressed overalls and high-end boots with rubber soles and leather booting up to mid-calf. He liked telling you that he got them in Canada when he bought the company. Anna was his younger wife. Full-figured with curly red hair and freckles, she was every bit the country girl. She was a handful.

"This road is about the future," Preston continued. "Why, at my firm, we are already seeing signs of what these highways can do to stimulate business. As we eliminate dirt roads, inefficient crossings and wandering byways, businesses can get materials to market faster. The manufacturers can get their product back to the consumer faster as well." He took off his wire rim glasses and poked them in the air to emphasize his points. "They can truck in steel beams from Gary, Indiana, baby clothing from Oshkosh, Wisconsin, and furniture from the Carolinas. Everybody is going to be a winner."

"Wait a minute." Rayland rose to speak. "Everybody is going to be a winner?" Rayland was a man of few words. He measured them carefully, and he had the ability to punctuate his concerns with a disarming grin and his sparkling eyes. "It seems to me that there will be some winners, and some losers. Who is it that decides?" He looked around the room. "Preston? Ulmer? Who is it that decides who wins and who loses?'

"Well," Ulmer cleared his throat again, gaining time while he thought how to answer.

Preston preempted him. "Rayland, it's the future," he said. "It's economic development. It's progress. Nobody is going to be the loser. You know the problems small farmers are facing. Why the milk haulers themselves are putting some of you out of business. It's tough to make it with a small herd. The government knows that." His strong jaw jutted out when he made his point. "When they come through, it'll be good for some of those farms that are struggling. If the highway affects your property, the government will pay you a fair price. It's called just compensation. No losers."

"Seems to me," Rayland continued, "this progress you're so proud of is something imposed on us by, well ... well ... by people from somewhere else. They don't know us. At best they're unaware." He looked around the room. "Maybe they're self-serving. Or worse. We don't know."

Preston wanted to move on. "You've got a point, Rayland, but it's already been decided. There's no holding this back. Isn't that right, Ulmer?

"Senator Aiken will be bringing home the bacon. He says we are on the verge of the greatest economic boom in Vermont history. We'll all benefit."

"Are we allowed to shoot them?" Anna asked again. Again Preston roared with laughter.

The discussion of pros and cons on the new highway continued. Continued longer than needed. "It's the answer to most of Vermont's problems." "Don't take my land!" "This'll get Vermont out of the sticks." "I like Vermont the way it is." Friends and neighbors had lots of differing ideas on how to proceed, how to accommodate the future. How to fight or accept the changes that were coming. The lines were being drawn,

Rayland slipped outside after a few moments to gather his thoughts. He was alone in the middle of the snowy one-lane road looking at the stars. From the porch, Kate asked, "You okay, Rayland?'

"Oh, hi, Kathleen. Yeah. Yeah, I was just out here looking for the North Star."

He turned and noticed how elegant she looked in her black wool coat. It had some sort of fur around the collar and snowflakes settled on it for a moment before they disappeared. He'd never had a friend quite like Kathleen.

"Kind of a strange thing to do in the middle of a party, isn't it?"

"I was feeling kind of lost in there. Whenever I feel like that, I try to find the North Star. Then I know where I am again."

"What made you feel that way?"

"To my way of thinking, when that road comes through, it's going to be good for some, but it's going to bring some kind of loss to most of us. Maybe loss we can see. Maybe loss we can't see. I don't know." He looked at her. "When you run a super highway through a village like ours there's going to be change. What happens to simple folks when you take away their land, their livelihood, their house and you give them money to...?" He paused to choose his words. "And you give them money to just ... to just .... What? Go away?" Again, he stopped to catch up with his thoughts. "There are going to be winners and losers. I'm not sure everyone understands that."

He looked away, then said softly, "I'm not sure everyone cares, Kathleen."

"Do you think it will affect you?"

"There isn't any way that road is going to make me any happier than I am right now. Might not seem like I've got a whole lot, but I've got everything I want." He looked at the stars. "What's that road going to bring me? Baby clothing from Wisconsin? Or a chair from the Carolinas?" Turning to her, he added, "And what's it going to take away?" He looked back at the stars. "I don't know, Kathleen. But, I'm concerned."

For a long moment, they gazed up at the night sky.

"Which one is the North Star?" Kathleen finally asked, breaking the awkward silence.

Rayland's mood lightened. "See the Big Dipper?" He pointed.

"Yes. It's easy to find tonight."

"Now, look at the dipper. Those two stars that make up the outside of the dipper cup, they point directly at the North Star." They concentrated on the Big Dipper. "Now find the Little Dipper."

She took a moment. "Got it."

"The end of the handle of the Little Dipper is..." He paused for emphasis, "Is the North Star. Once you can find the North Star, you will never get lost. It's directly over the

North Pole. Always over the North Pole. So, if you know where north is, you can figure out where you are, and which direction you're headed. Kind of neat, isn't it?"

"You know, you're the only one who calls me Kathleen?"

"I know. I like calling you Kathleen. It's a pretty name."

"I like it, too." They both stood looking at the stars enjoying the clear night and the crispness of the winter air. They were very comfortable with one another. It was a pleasure to be in such a lovely place with someone you were comfortable with.

"Rayland," she said, pausing until he turned in her direction. "If you don't get lost, would you like to come to my home for Christmas dinner?"

Quickly his demeanor changed. "Kathleen, I'd really like to. I really would, but I can't. I spend Christmas with Emory and his family. My brother's family is the closest family I've got. I love his kids like he does. It's where I belong on Christmas. Thank you though. I don't get any offers nicer than that, Kathleen. Thank you."

Their gaze turned back toward the night sky. The comfort and friendship they shared were very much present at this quiet moment.

"Maybe we could do something New Year's Eve," she suggested. The question hung in the air. "What do you think?"

"I'd like that, Kathleen." He looked skyward for a second, then back at her, "What do you usually do on New Year's Eve?"

"Well, in Grafton, we'd have a nice dinner and then welcome in the New Year with a toast and a kiss."

"Kiss?" He looked into the woods, then back to the sky. Turning to Kathleen he said, "I guess I'd better go home and practice."

Chapter 4

POWER OFF – POWER ON

Tuesday - January 15, 1963

Washington D.C. – *In his State of the Union address at a joint session of Congress, President Kennedy called on Congress to pass legislation to lower income taxes as a means of stimulating the economy. Kennedy called for individual tax rates, ranging from 20% to as much as 91%, to be cut to a range of 14% to 65%, and for the corporate rate to be cut from 52 to 47 percent.*

"Good morning, ladies." Like most farmers, Rayland got up early and went to bed early. No matter how early he got to the barn, the cows were ready and waiting to be fed. "Okay girls, food is on the way. Brrr."

The temperature must have been in the single digits and the wind was blowing. January is a tough month. The days are short and grey. They aren't getting longer yet. They don't even seem to be trying. Icy winds blow through the barn and rattle the tree branches. Birds hunker down and stay nestled in. There is always a stretch when the temperature hits -18 or -20 and stays there. But, once past the frigid days, perhaps mid-February, by golly, you've broken the back of winter. Spring is coming. This winter, however, still had some anger left.

"Let's get you ladies some breakfast, and then we'll get started." Rayland opened a bale and pitched hay into the trough at the head of each corral. The cows ate while he milked.

"Alright, Ida Mae. You're up."

Rayland sat on his stool and started the rhythmic milking process. The milk would ring off the side of the stainless-steel collecting bucket making a distinctive sound like shinggg with the g ringing in the air like a bell.

Shinggg Shinggg Shinggg Shinggg.

He also liked to sing while milking, and the cows seemed to like it. At least they never complained. It made the whole process go faster.

"I got up one Sunday morning, how hungry I did feel," he sang.

Shinggg Shinggg Shinggg Shinggg.

The rhythm of milking continued.

I went down to Grandma's house to get a good square meal.

She called me in the kitchen. She said there was a treat.

There was plenty on the table, but be darned if I could eat.

The buns were on the floor. The hog behind the floor.

The coffee pot was on the chicken coop.

There were insects in the air, 'cuz the butter had grey hair

And the baby stuck her foot right in the chicken soup."

Shinggg Shinggg Shinggg Shinggg.

So, it went. Lots of rhyme but no reason. Just the way he liked it.

"Next," he bellowed just like the barber in town. "Your turn, Daisy."

Rayland moved to the next stall. Star, his man's best friend, moved with him. Star never got far from Rayland, especially when he was milking. The dog would lie down behind the cows, hind legs under him with his paws together in front. Occasionally Rayland would squirt a spray of milk at Star, which the dog licked off his whiskers with great relish.

Shinggg Shinggg Shinggg Shinggg.

Star was his buddy. One summer afternoon about six months back, while walking back from Leo's, a half pint mutt tagged along. They walked and talked. Well, Rayland talked, but they enjoyed each other's company. Karl came by in his truck. "Want a ride, Rayland?"

"No, thanks, Karl. We're enjoying the walk. "

Otto and Helma Struckin, neighbors to the south, honked and offered, "Come on, Rayland. Hop in."

"No. Thanks, Otto. We're getting to know each other, but stop by when you have a chance and we can catch up."

Aud came by.

"No thanks, Aud. I've got a new friend I'm looking after."

She offered to take them both, but they were in no hurry. The mutt was a shaggy little fella with a bent tail broken near the tip. "Let's call you Shaggy." Rayland enjoyed having the dog tag along. He could tell this little fella hadn't had an easy life. He was frayed around the edges. You couldn't see his ribs because of his curly black and brown coat, but you could easily feel them. He stopped to eat anything that came before him – grasshoppers, flowering weeds, even an old Tootsie Roll wrapper.

Rayland turned to his new friend. "We're not going to call you Shaggy. I'm going to clean you up. We'll brush you out and by dinnertime you will be looking like a movie star."

They walked further. "That's it," he realized. "Let's call you Star. I like that. Yeah. Star. Hope you like it, too."

When they reached the farmhouse, Rayland made a pot of oatmeal and shared it with his new friend. Then he gave him a bowl of milk. Then a biscuit. Then another. It was obvious the dog hadn't eaten in a while.

After downing everything Rayland offered, Star lay down in a sunny spot on the kitchen floor and took a nap. Rayland cleaned up his dishes and was about to leave and finish his chores. The dog jumped up to go along. Did the dog think, Don't leave me? Or, did he think, Of course, I'm coming along. Get used to it.

Rayland easily got used to it, and Star seldom left his side.

Champ was a recent addition. Billy Jackson and his wife had to auction off fourteen cows and put their house and farm up for sale. That or face discloser. They were moving to New Jersey. Hell, about a third of the dairy farms in the area had disappeared in the past ten years or so. The Jackson's dog needed a home. Champ would be good company for Star.

"Wish I could help you more, Billy, but I'll look after your dog," Rayland had told him. The dogs got along fine. Star kept track of Rayland, but Champ was an adventurer. Rayland was convinced that Champ had some sort of herding dog or hunting dog in him. He was shorthaired, medium build, and loved to run. His buddy Star was short-legged and built like a satchel. He loved hanging out with Rayland in the barn. Champ preferred to run a circle around the cows trying to herd them up, barking and running, running and barking. Once he realized the cows didn't care, he'd go find something else to do. Dig a hole. Sniff a frog. Chase a car, or just play in the woods. But the routine became set. Rayland and Star worked the barn. Champ kept track of what was going on in the fields, meadows and woods.

Rayland and Star moved down the line to the next cow.

Shinggg Shinggg Shinggg Shinggg.
And Rayland resumed his accompaniment:
"I'm looking over some dog named
Who I never seen before.
One dog likes pizza.
The other does not.
I like my dogs and I like them a lot.
Now there's no need explaining
Why it's not raining.
The weather is not so hot.
But I'm looking over some dog named Rover
Who I never seen before."
Shinggg Shinggg Shinggg Shinggg.

Applause broke out behind him. "Whoa, Rayland, you might be the Elvis Pressley of the dairy business. Original compositions, too, I note."

"Yeah. People get emotional when I sing. Emotional one way or the other. Maybe I'll work on some wiggles and thrusts to see how far I can go. How are you, Norman?"

"Who's your new friend, Rayland?"

"Well, this is Billy Jackson's dog Champ. You know Star."

Norman took a moment to pet the dogs and scratch their heads. He dug into his big coat pocket and rooted around until he found what he was searching for. He gave Star and Champ each a small dog biscuit. "Darned if Star isn't the ugliest dog I've ever seen." Star beat his tail against the wide board floor at a quicker tempo loving the attention.

"Do you know about the highway meeting coming up in two weeks?" he asked.

Rayland looked up with interest.

"Several highway commission members are coming down to tell us what we might expect in the next few months. Ulmer arranged it. It's a meeting to put some facts on the table. Monday night the 4th at the school. Seven o'clock, I think. I'll check. Want me to pick you up?"

"Sure. Thank you, Norman."

"Yeah. It's about time we get some details," Norman said as he sat on a bale of hay against the inside wall. "But that's not the reason I came by. I 've got an idea, Rayland. I want to bounce it off you." He watched Rayland milk.

"I'm making some big changes at the farm this spring. We're pretty excited. Wanted to tell you about it. New milking system, refrigerated storage tanks, a larger milk house to accommodate the bulk tank, and new hay barn. I'm going all in, Rayland."

"Phew. That's going to cost you. How you going to pay for all that?"

"Efficiency, I hope. I know you read those dairy journals and magazines. You know what's going on in the industry. Small dairies are disappearing like to beat the devil. Scares me."

When Norman had something important to say, he had a habit of looking down before looking back up and directly at you. He looked down at his half-laced Bean boots and then back up, catching Rayland's eyes.

"I believe I've got to modernize and grow so I don't go with them. You see it right here in Towsley. Jeez, the creameries won't haul your milk anymore. Their cost to haul depends on how far you are from the creamery, and how many farms are on that route. If you're really out in the sticks, you're screwed. Traveling backcountry dirt roads to pick up milk from small farms, well, there's just no money in it. They want the big farms on decent roads. The little guy hauls it himself or, if you're lucky, you find some small-time hauler who overcharges because he can't make any money either."

He removed his glasses to clean them with his handkerchief. Leaning forward, he pointed, glasses in hand.

"Look at you. First, you milk. Then you pour it into a five-gallon can, carry it to the milk shed, and strain it into another can. Once that can is full, you carry it up to the icehouse to keep it cold. What's that can weigh? Eighty, ninety pounds? For all that, you get $4.27 per hundred weight for your milk even if you haul it yourself." Putting his glasses back on, he looked down again. You knew there was more coming.

"Seems the bigger farms are all getting refrigerated bulk tanks. It's almost required. Shoot. Wilcox Brothers will put in a refrigerated bulk storage tank and system for me and let me finance it over seven years. I figure if I can get about eighteen to twenty more milking cows, it will pay for itself over time."

He paused and scratched Star's head again.

"These bulk tanks are mighty slick. The milk goes right from the teat to the tank. It gets strained. Then it gets stirred as the cream and milk cool. Wilcox sends in their big rig tanker truck to pick it up once a week. That's it."

He became less enthusiastic.

"Well, there are a few requirements I'm not so keen on. If I use their storage tank, there are procedures. Cleaning and sanitizing procedures. No more washing the automatic milkers in the kitchen sink. You need a barn sink. A USDA-approved barn sink." Catching Rayland's eyes again, he added, "Required. A washing and sanitizing facility. Right in the barn. Federal regulation, they say."

"Aren't you taking a big chance, Norman? Not knowing where the highway is going to go and all?"

"Yeah. A bit of a chance, but Ulmer set up a meeting for me with the state highway commissioner. He told me the state is going to do everything it can to save the bigger farms. So, it seems an expansion might work in my favor. Wilcox Brothers agreed that if I get closed down by the new road, they'd take back their refrigeration and bulk tanks and cancel out my loan. So, yes, I'm taking a chance, but I'm feeling pretty good about it. It's a chance I have to take."

Rayland took a moment to digest that and then said quietly, "Norman, I've got a pretty simple operation here. I milk a few cows, make a few bucks, and live the way I want to live. Sometimes it might appear to be hard, but if you love it, it's not hard at all. In some ways it's easier than changing. I don't think I'm a candidate for one of those refrigerated bulk tanks."

"No. Maybe not, but I've got something I want you to have, Rayland. Let's call it a present from my cows." He got up. "Follow me." They walked to his pickup truck. In the back were boxes. Lots of boxes with tubing, and wires, motors and suctions for the teats. Rayland had seen this kind of equipment in action on many farms. But automatic milking machines were foreign to the Jensen farm.

"Good Grief. Is that for me? Come on Norman? What am I going to do with it? I don't even have electricity."

Norman nodded and laughed. "That's the best part. I ran this all by Sparky over at Ed's Electric. He's coaching me on how we can get you some electricity right into your barn. Free. The power company will never know." He looked back. "Probably never know. Come here."

He pointed up and walked over to the nearby utility pole.

"See how close those wires and that transformer come to your barn. Sparky says we can climb up there, shave that small wire a bit, not the big one. Got to be the small one. Then we can splice right in and you'll have electricity in the barn. Just like that." He pulled up his leather collar against the wind. "Sparky would do the job himself, but if he got caught, he might lose his license. So, it's us, Rayland. Me and you. A little ingenuity and you will be all set."

"Or dead. I'm not climbing up to play with those wires."

"Yeah. Aud says she'll kill me too if I climb up and play with those wires. Don't worry. I've got a plan. Safe as can be." Banging his gloved hands together, he continued, "We get everything lined up in advance. First, we need a ladder that's long enough. I don't think your loft ladder will work. We'll need to extend it by three or four feet. We need some electric tape, insulation tape, splicer, electrical box, switch, good electrical wire, electrical conduit and we are in business." He sat down on a bale of hay. "Then we wait."

Rayland was patient, but the answer didn't come. "Wait for what?"

"Ha. I thought you'd never ask." Norman liked to tease a bit. With the joke out of the way, Norman went straight to the point.

"We wait for a power outage. Shouldn't need to wait too long at this time of year. The power is always going out around here. A heavy snowstorm. Branches fall across the wires. A tree comes down. The power goes out. Up we go. While the power company is walking the lines, pulling branches and trees off the downed lines, we'll have plenty of time. We clamp onto that live wire. When power comes back on, it's lights, camera, action as they say."

"What in Sam Hill, Norman? Have you lost your mind?"

"Rayland, you've got arthritis. Correct?"

Rayland nodded.

"Now you've got an electric milker. I know you know how to use one. Plug it in. Put the suction cups on the teats, and away you go. Not only will this help with your arthritis, but it'll free up your time. When you're in here milking by hand, you can't do anything else. Two teats at a time. That's all you can do."

"And what happens when I get caught?"

"I thought of that. First of all, there is nobody in town who would turn you in. I hate to tell you, Rayland, but everybody likes you. Everyone I've told this to thinks it's a great idea."

"Dag-gone Norman. How many folks have you told?'

"Lots. Lots and lots."

"Oh, for crying out loud. And what's second?"

"Second? What do you mean?"

"You said 'First, nobody would turn me in.' What's second?"

"Yes. Second. If they did turn you in, we'd run them out of town. Like a skunk at a picnic. We'd run them right out of town." He paused hoping he'd sold his idea. "Come on. Let's put these boxes in a dry place until you can use them."

They started stacking boxes in the far corner of the barn.

Rayland wasn't sure about the idea. Or maybe he was sure but didn't want to tell Norman. While Norman was excited about his gift, Rayland was apprehensive. His friend noticed the lack of enthusiasm.

"Rayland. I can tell you don't give a rat's ass about this equipment, do you?" He removed his TSC hat and scratched his head. "Sometimes I wonder, what is it you want from this farm? What is it about being a farmer that you really like?" The last box was off-loaded. "If we were sitting here three years from now, and you look back on these years, what is it you want to accomplish? "

"Heck, I don't know. You see, you're a good farmer, Norman. And a good businessman. I respect that. I really do. But that's not me. I'll tell you what I'd like out of the next three years? I want to milk my cows. I want to hitch up my horses and work the fields or drive them over to the co-op. I want to cut my fields by hand. That's what I want. If I'm still alive three years from now, I want to look back and know that I'm still farming the way I like to farm. Still chopping the wood. Still boiling the sap. Still making cider. And still milking my cows, damn it."

"You know. Rayland, the Stone Age didn't end because they ran out of stones." Norman let that sink in. "The future gets here. Sooner or later, it gets here." He stood in front of Rayland with his jaw clenched. "What are you going to do when you're too old to do all those things? You can't do them by yourself forever."

"Well," Rayland thought a bit. "Maybe I'll slow down and follow in the footsteps of Saint Isidore."

"Who?"

"Saint Isidore." Rayland looked at his friend. "Patron saint of farmers." He stacked the last box on top of the pile. "He took care of animals and the poor."

Norman was dumbfounded.

"According to him, if you have your spiritual life in order, everything else will fall into place."

"Where the hell did you get that tidbit?"

"Readers Digest," Rayland said. He raised his eyebrows as if to add, gotcha on that one, didn't I, big boy? "Anna gives me all her old copies. Want to borrow that issue?"

Norman fumbled in his jacket pocket again. He pulled out a pack of gum and they each took a piece. They chewed for a bit, not talking until Norman said, "Rayland, you are an original. You really are an original."

He put on his hat and turned up his collar. "Gotta go, buddy. See you soon.

Rayland stayed outside as Norman pulled away in his pickup. As he watched, he thought, Norman's right, of course. And I know it. They'd both watched as neighbor after neighbor sold his herd and took a job in one of the mills across the river, or like Billy Jackson, someplace else. It was so sad to watch a man sell off his lifetime of work and just move on. Is that what's going to happen to me, Rayland thought as Star come over to lie down before him.

"Just move on? Is that what I do, Star? That's what my brothers and sisters did. I never asked them if it was easy or not. The girls mostly didn't have a choice. They moved in with their husbands. I think Jeremy missed the farm after he left, but he wanted more than milking and mowing. I never did understand why Greg moved on. He was actually anxious to go. I think he was angry. Too much responsibility. I was glad to take the responsibility, Star, but I wasn't the oldest so it was easier. It was a choice."

He gave Star good scratch.

"I miss Greg, but I like running the farm." He stopped and pondered his situation while he abstractedly petted the dog, talking to him in his usual rambling, thinking-out-loud manner.

"I sure hope my family doesn't think I'm a failure because I didn't become a businessman farmer like Norman. Heck, I'm not an ag-business guy. I'm just a farmer. Give me a patch of dirt and a cow or two and I'm a happy man. I hope they don't perceive that maybe my staying is a failure. Just move on is an option, I guess. Just like it was for Billy. But it's not something I want.

"Yeah, there are jobs across the river. The mills are slowing down, but they're still employing. New Jersey has even more jobs." The more Rayland talked to Star, the more his tail wagged. "A man has to feed his family, but everyone hated that auction when your neighbor and friend sold off the herd. Usually one cow at a time. If you bought one, you felt guilty.

"How did this all happen so fast?"

It was true: There were fewer farms and, of those remaining, fewer had milk cows. Ten years ago, a farm with six to twelve cows was typical. There were family farms up and down the valley. Not now. Herds were getting bigger. The cows were getting healthier. They produced more milk per cow. By a lot. Farmers were getting smarter, too. But the haulers kept putting the squeeze on us, the little guys. Ten years ago, a cow produced about a gallon of milk. You could milk her twice a day. That's all you got. One gallon. Some farms get twice that now. Specialization. Modernization. Sure, modernization was the answer. Rayland just didn't care to hear the question. It was almost as if the future wasn't in his future.

But come on, he thought, isn't there a place for someone like me? He didn't speak that question out loud, though. He and Star walked back into the barn and over to the milking equipment. He looked at it and said aloud. "Damn, if this doesn't remind me of the Army, Star. In France, there were thousands, maybe millions of horses. War horses, horses to pull supply wagons or haul bodies. Horses to ferry artillery and troops to the front. There were horses everywhere. Some healthy. Some lame. Some wounded. I told the Captain, 'Captain, I'm good with horses. Raised and cared for them and worked with them all my life.'" He paused and shook his head. "He assigned me to drive a truck. I'd never driven a truck in my life."

Yep, he thought, these milking machines remind me of the Army.

By the time Norman and Rayland arrived at the meeting a few days later, the gym was already three-quarters full. Chairs were set up facing the stage, and a table had been set up in front of the stage for the town select board. To the right was an easel with flip charts. The gym was filling quickly. A basketball hoop hung at each end of the room, and the floor was painted with a foul line on both ends. The gym was small enough that the foul lanes almost touched at the tip. The dimensions of the court went to the wall making the walls the out of bounds. The only place for spectators to stand was on the stage or in the doorway. The room was too small for anything but an elementary school basketball game, but it was perfect for a town meeting.

Kathleen was there talking to the selectmen. He caught her eye and waved, then noticed the state presenters organizing their flip charts. The selectmen moved toward their seats ready to get the meeting started. Norman, Fred Schmidt and Anna Jaffee made up the current board. Anna despised being called a selectman. Selectwoman, damn it. Selectwoman.

In the absence of a gavel, Norman wrapped an ashtray on the table to get everyone's attention. "Good evening. Good evening, everyone. Thank you for coming. As you know, we've got a community outreach group from the state highway commission here tonight to give us the details for the new highway and answer questions. Any questions before we start?" He looked around. There were none. "Okay, then we'll get started."

"Let me introduce our quests. El Moulton heads up the state economic development agency. El." Moulton stood and signaled hello to the gathering. "And Matteo Phister who sits on the board of the commission. Matt." He also stood and acknowledged the group. "And our presenter will be Lawrence Malloy, chief engineer of the Route 91 highway project. Larry, I'll turn things over to you."

After an introduction about the overall reasoning for the new highway, Malloy broke the project into five phases of road development.

Phase I was Planning. This included a discussion of common adverse impacts to animal habitat, air and water pollution, noise, damage to natural landscape and the destruction of a community's social and cultural structure. Can the necessary property be acquired to build on? Can the project be designed to be an asset to the community?

Phase II he called Surveying the Area. It included important items like accessing the location, the terrain and the soil properties. What were the drainage capabilities and potential problems? What was the current traffic volume in the area?

Phase III Malloy named Earthworks and it included how to establish a stable foundation for the road to sit on for years to come, where to build the embankments and other items like drains and sewers, screened soil and the amounts of crushed gravel and stone needed.

Phase IV, of course, involved paving, whether asphalt or concrete.

Phase V he called Open to Traffic, involving a loose time frame that might or might not be met.

And, finally, as the audience was getting restless, Phase V was brief. The thorough presentation left the audience a bit overwhelmed, but satisfied. From animal habitat to open for traffic had taken two hours. The town knew that Phase II was upon them.

On February 7, twelve inches of snow fell and gusty winds did their usual job. The lights at the Cairns house flickered around 6 p.m. They flickered again fifteen minutes later. Then the power went out. Dark. Night. No crews on the secondary lines until first light. Norman was up, though. He knew the crew would be working on cutting downed limbs at least all the next day, maybe longer. Perfect, he thought.

Two days later the power came back on. The Jensen barn had power for the first time since being built in 1892.

Chapter 5

EASTER DINNER

Sunday - April 14, 1963

Da Nang, South Vietnam - *U.S. Maine Corp Seahorse transport helicopters airlifted 435 South Vietnam troops to attack and destroy a Viet Cong mountain stronghold along the Thu Bon River. For the first time, the transports received an escort of U.S Army UH-1B gunships.*

He heard the car pull up outside the barn, and he was ready to go. Rayland always loved spending the holidays with his brother and family.

"Hey Ricky," he yelled before the car had come to a full stop. "Seems I haven't seen you in a dog's age." Ricky was quickly out of the car and at Rayland's side, his smile as big and disarming as his uncle's. His blue eyes sparkled with excitement. Emory was coming right behind. Rayland couldn't hide his affection as he gave his nephew a big hug. "I'm so glad they let you out of the institution."

"It's the University of New Hampshire, Uncle Rayland," Ricky said, grinning in appreciation of his uncle's humor.

"Tell me what you've been doing? Are you still studying civil engineering? How many years now? Seems like about ten or so."

"Only four. Actually, it's only been three and a half. I graduate in May. Hope you'll come to the graduation."

"I'd be honored, if your dad will give me a ride. What do you think, Em? Will that old Chevy handle another passenger?"

"It's only three years old. Runs like a dream." The brothers shook hands. "How you doing, Rayland?"

"Good. Good. I'm doing good, Em. Graduation. Wow. Then what, Ricky?"

"I've applied to Officers Candidate School to become an officer in the Navy. I figured with the draft and Vietnam and all, I'd be better off picking my own path instead of taking a chance. If I get drafted, I'm just another grunt in a foxhole somewhere. If accepted to OCS, I go to Newport, Rhode Island, for four months. When I graduate, I get commissioned an ensign. What do you think?"

"Holy camoly. Ensign Ricky Jensen, United States Navy. Sounds impressive to me. You've always been a leader, Ricky. Even as a little squirt taking charge on the ball field. Officer in the Navy. Seems to fit. Way to go."

"Thanks, Uncle Rayland."

"You know Ricky, if you're old enough to be in our military, I think it's okay for you to call me Rayland. No need to call me Uncle."

"You kidding me? You're not getting rid of being my uncle that easily. You're probably the best uncle in the world. I'm keeping you ... UNCLE Rayland," he emphasized. "Like it or not. Come on. Let's get going. Marcy can't wait to see you, and I want you to meet my girlfriend."

'Whoa. Graduation from the institution, then officer in the Navy, and then marriage? I can't take all this."

"No. She's just a friend from school. For now." He turned to go. "Come on, Dad. If we can't get Uncle Rayland moving, let's pick him up and throw him in."

Rayland walked to the car beaming with delight. Em too, loved watching this exchange as he was standing by the open car door, his face filled with pride.

"Well, Ricky, remember what your Grandma J always said. 'The best time to pick a wife is in the morning,'" Rayland said. "Remember that, Em? She said that to all us boys. I never did quite figure that one out. Probably the reason I never got married."

Emory was Mr. Middle Class and proud of it. He and Alina had a comfortable four-bedroom house on a tree-lined street in Claremont, New Hampshire. Nothing fancy, but lovely, especially with the bustle of cooking and the chatter of family catching up with one another. Em had a good job at D&J Hoover Machine Tool and Die, He was several years younger than Rayland, thirteen in fact. But the two had always been close. After Pa died, it seemed that Rayland took Em under his wing to help him along on the farm and in school.

Emory and Alina invited Rayland to every family holiday dinner. And he always went. In fact, he looked forward to the visit well in advance. Ricky would be home. Marcy and her new husband Frank would be there. His younger sister Rho and her husband Ed would be there also. Then too, this year there would be the new girlfriend.

It seemed everyone was in the kitchen. Everyone talking to everyone. All at the same time. A happy holiday gathering.

"How do you like living in Hartford, Marcy?" Rayland asked. "Kind of a big city compared to Claremont, isn't it?"

"It sure is, but we aren't right downtown. We aren't quite in the suburbs either. We're in between, but we both work downtown." She was dishing parsnips and the first asparagus of the season into serving bowls. "Frank is now the assistant editor of national news for the *Hartford Currant*. He got a big promotion right after we got married. I work for Aetna. In claims." She looked up from her chore. "It's a big insurance company. Not my dream job, but it's a good company with really good benefits. We already have pension plans. Someday, maybe, we can come back to Vermont and buy your farm from you so you can retire."

"If I retired, you know what I'd do?" He paused. "I'd get some cows to milk, and a dog to throw a stick for, a few chickens, and a horse. Gotta have a horse." He thought for a moment. "Maybe two horses. I don't know what that will cost you, but that's what I'll do with your money." Everyone just looked at him as if to say, Yep. That's Rayland.

"Okay. We're ready to head to the table," Alina implored. Eventually she got the family moving toward the dining room.

Dinner was traditional. A big baked country ham and, of course, Ma's scalloped potato recipe with cheese, cream and onion. One Easter Alina served roasted potatoes. Well, she took some grief for that. It had been Ma's scalloped potatoes ever since. The food was good and the conversation lively. It was a splendid Easter dinner.

"How did you end up at UNH, Hannah?" Em asked, moving the conversation to the guest who had been the quietest.

"My family lives in Newton, Mass. It's a suburb of Boston. I always enjoyed New England, especially rural New England, and I wanted to get to know something other than the city."

"What are you studying?" he asked.

"I'm a poli-sci major." There was nodding but little acknowledgement of what poli-sci might be. "Political Science," she answered their unasked question. "I hope to work on a political campaign after I graduate. From there, maybe I'll go into politics. We'll see where it goes."

Hannah looked every bit the young coed. Thin and pretty, long straight hair, skirt a little above the knees and flats. She had a pleasant manner about her and she exuded a quiet confidence. On the surface she appeared quite conservative except for her necklace. It was a thin rope of red and blue thread woven together with a metal charm about the size of a fifty-cent piece hanging from it. Alina noticed it with interest and ask about its origin.

"It was given to me at the New Moon Commune up in Wynlett, Vermont. That's up in the Northeast Kingdom. It's a hippie commune." She let that sink in. "The symbol is made up of the letters P, L and G. If you look closely, you can see the letters intertwined in copper." She held it out away from her neck for those who were interested. "It stands for Peace, Love, Groovy."

"Oh," Alina muttered softly. For a few moments, the table reverted to quiet eating.

Ricky got things back on track. "Hannah is an activist, Dad. She's a real leader on campus."

Feeling a little behind the times, Rayland asked, "What does an activist do?"

"They protest, Uncle Rayland. Or they organize protests."

Rayland sat for a moment, cut a bite of ham and, as he started to pick it up, he asked gently, "You're in college. You're twenty years old. You're smart, and I might add, quite pretty. What do you have to protest, Hannah?"

"No. I don't protest for myself." She smiled. "It's always for some cause. We organize and protest to help others improve their lot in life. I'm very fortunate for all that I have, but not everyone is as fortunate."

"She's organizing protests in Durham against the Vietnam War," Ricky chimed in. "Why are we sending our boys to Southeast Asia to fight in a civil war between a corrupt government that we support and Ho Chi Min in the north? People are starting to catch on to just how dumb that is."

"If you get your Navy commission, will Hannah be protesting you?"

"No. I don't think so." He looked at his uncle. "The protests are aimed at the people who send us to war. Not the people who fight them. She's big on the civil rights movement, too."

"What do you do when you protest?" Rayland asked.

"In Durham, we have rallies and marches." She put her fork down and looked up. "Students with placards march in the streets and stop traffic, or they meet in front of a movie theater at show time. It's all about creating awareness." She paused, not wanting to dominate the conversation, but everyone seemed interested. "The civil rights protesters in the South can really teach us a thing or two. Just a few days ago in Birmingham, Alabama, protesters had sit-ins at lunch counters around town to protest segregation. They got yelled at, punched, spit on, ketchup squirted in their hair. I guess it was really awful."

Rayland was feeling lost. "Who got punched and yelled at?"

"It was primarily black students who want equal rights. They got backhanded freedom after the Civil War. In the South, the blacks are still very repressed. Just can't do the things that whites do. They drink from 'blacks only' water fountains. At the movies they must sit in the balcony. They can't eat at the same lunch counter as whites, and they have their own schools. Separate but equal, they say. It is separate, for sure, but it's not equal."

Silence.

"Next they're going to boycott local merchants and stores."

More silence.

"Are these the causes that you hope will end segregation?" Rayland asked.

"No. Segregation is the cause. Getting rid of segregation is the cause. Sit-ins, protests, boycotts are done to create awareness. We hope that one day soon, enough people will be outraged by how these people are treated that our politicians will do something."

Still confused, Rayland asked, "So, if I don't like this new highway coming through our town and farmlands, should I protest?"

"Well, you can't really protest just because you don't like something. Is it unfair? Does it do anything detrimental to the area? Is it unjust? Is there something inherently wrong with the highway?"

"Well," he started, "as I understand it, when the road comes through, if you've got something and the government wants it, they take it. You name it. Farms, houses, pasture, meadow, woodlands. And you don't get a say. Nothing. If they want it, they take it." He paused for a second. "Doesn't seem fair to me."

Hannah thought for a long moment then carefully articulated her thoughts as best she could. "The government can take the land because they need it for the project. The project is supposed to be for the betterment of all. That's called eminent domain. I really don't know much about eminent domain." She stopped to think. "Do you think others will rally around your cause? How do most people feel about the highway?"

"I don't know. Some like it. Some don't. My guess is there are too many on the other side of things from me, people who see some goodies in the basket for themselves. I'm not sure they're looking at what we might lose. Only what they might get."

"Not everything we face can be changed, but nothing can be changed until we face it." She looked at Rayland. "That's my philosophy."

"Wow." Rayland chewed on that for a bit. He became pensive. Alina and Rho started clearing the table.

Finally, he looked up. "Alina, that's the best baked ham I ever had."

"You said the same thing last year, Rayland," she smiled. "You're a very good guest. Hope you saved room for dessert. Would you like some more ham?"

The ladies hustled about clearing the plates and making room for the dessert. Em sat back well satisfied, Rayland quietly picked at his last piece of ham. Marcy and Ricky began telling stories to Hannah about the Jensen farm. Frank had heard all the stories before, but he enjoyed hearing them again.

"When we were kids, Hannah, we went to the farm every chance we got. If Dad said we were going to visit Rayland, Ricky and I got ready in record time," Marcy started. "We'd pack lunch and a bathing suit and pester Dad to get ready, too. Once we got to the river, we knew we were almost there. " She looked at her brother and asked, "Remember that old bridge, Ricky? You could look through the metal grate we were driving on and see the river below. Ricky would always try to spook me out by saying 'We're going to fall in, Marcy, we're going to fall in.' But it was so stupid. No one paid attention to him, even though it was kind of scary to look through a bridge into a river you were driving over.

"When we got to the farm, we were out of the car and running before the car stopped. Rayland was always in the barn. Usually Jeremy and Greg were with him. Aunt Rho and Grandma J were usually in the kitchen. Grandma always had hot squeegees waiting for us. We could eat them all day."

"What's a squeegee?" Hannah asked, laughing as she thought of those things you use to wipe a window dry.

"It's like the fried dough that you might get at the fair," Frank said, happy to add his two cents worth. "Fried dough with powdered sugar sprinkled on top. Or maple syrup. It's a four-star grandmother treat. No nutritional value, but very tasty."

"I think Grandpa J named them squeegees," Ricky remembered. "Not sure why, but the name stuck."

"After a quick hello, a hug and a squeegee," March continued, "our shoes were off and we were running through the fields. We'd play tag or hide and seek in the barn, or we'd go for a swim. We'd ride one horse and take the other on its harness over to the Cairnes' farm and pick up Eben and Liz. Then we'd all ride back together. Sometimes even little Ralphie tagged along. So, there were usually four or more of us running in and out of the house, up the hills and around the barn. If we ran through the barn while Rayland was milking, he would squirt us with milk."

She laughed at the sweet memory.

"Of course, that just slayed everyone. Especially Rayland. He just smiled and milked. On the farm you had to find your excitement where you could, and we found it everywhere. No matter what we did, all the brothers and sisters were so kind and happy. I know they really liked having us around. Those are my very favorite childhood memories, Rayland.

She was on a roll now, the memories coming back as they always did when she took the time to think about them. "Even how we helped with the farm chores. Well, we tried to help. It took two of us to lift a bale of hay, so I don't know how much help we really were. But we tried. I remember raking behind Rayland while he was cutting hay. He'd tell us the cutting was all about rhythm, not power. Rhythm and a sharp scythe." She faked a deep male voice. "'And don't lose your stone. Don't lose your stone. You've got to keep that blade sharp or you won't get home in time for dinner.' Then he'd pick up that scythe and go out on the hottest days of summer and swing that long handle back in a sweeping arc and then bring it down with a full cutting swing along the grass. Rayland could go for hours. It was a repetitive rhythm that I couldn't keep up with. And I was only raking. Rake and fluff. Rake and fluff. Get it into windrows for the baler." She looked at her uncle. "You'd only stop to get a drink of your switchel. Remember the switchel, Ricky? That stuff was awful. It was something like water and cow urine wasn't it, Uncle Rayland?"

"Mine was actually water with ginger, vinegar and a little maple syrup, but I always put a little cow urine into yours, Marcy."

Ricky and the others laughed at her. Marcy laughed, too. "I can still hear that scythe swishing back and forth. I can still smell the fresh cut grass, too."

"It was really a happy place. Still is." Ricky added, nostalgia making him speak quite softly. "Uncle Rayland, do you remember when you and Dad and Mr. Cairnes were cutting ice for the cold house and you all fell into the pond?"

"Hard to forget that one. I get cold just remembering it."

"That was such a funny afternoon." Ricky turned his attention to Hannah as he told the story. "We were sledding up on the hill above the pond. It was a beautiful March day. You know: Blue sky. Comfortable temp. No wind. And great snow. Marcy and Liz had sleds, and Eben and I were sliding in cardboard boxes. Those boxes weren't great for sledding, but they sure were fun. You got in and started downhill and you had no control. None. The box would get going fast, but it invariably caught an edge and dumped you face first into the snow. Really fun. We were laughing and pranking around. But then we heard the ice break."

"Jeezum crow, what a day," Rayland said. He remembered it as clear as yesterday but just sat back with a smile and let Ricky tell the story. It was fun to hear it from his nephew's point of view.

"Rayland and Em and Norman were on the pond with a couple of hand saws cutting strips of ice for the cold house. They'd haul them out to the side of the pond and then cut them into blocks. It was a warm day. Their jackets were on the back of the wagon when the ice gave way. I guess the three of them got too close together. There was a loud crack, and in they went.

"We heard it loud and clear even up on the hill. It was really scary at first. The roars and yeows of them hitting the icy water sure caught our attention. We rushed to help. Turns out that where they were cutting was only about four feet deep."

Everyone found that to be quite funny.

"Didn't matter. Didn't matter." Emory piped in. "That water was just as cold as the deep end."

"Must have been." Ricky became more animated. "They were hooting and yelling. Yeow! Damn it! Jiminy and maybe other words we didn't get to hear too often. Bet you coulda' heard them in town. They rolled up onto the bank, looked at each other, and raced to the house. The girls, Eben and I got the ice into the cold house. We grabbed the coats and hurried to the kitchen. By the time we got there, Rayland had a fire going in the cook stove. The stove had a big chamber that warmed the grills on top, and heated the room as well. All Rayland was wearing were his long johns and rubber goulashes. Dad had on a pair of Rayland's overalls with no shirt, and Norman was sitting on a stack of newspapers over by the bookshelves wearing just an old wool sweater and a towel.

"Their wet clothes hung everywhere! From lamps. On the handle of the water pump. On the firewood rack. Any place they could find to hang something. Socks and underpants were being dry grilled on the low burn side of the stove. It was a mess. A wet laundry mess.

"We all piled into the kitchen in the ell," Ricky continued, Hannah hanging on every word. "Seven of us packed into that little space. Wet laundry. A warm fire. The window steamed up. Rayland heated some cider and made oatmeal. We got out of our sledding clothes, but the only place to put the coats was outside on the porch. We didn't care. It was such fun.

"The room smelled like a wet dog, all that wet wool hanging around. 'Who wants hot cider?' Rayland asked? Everybody. We were starting to get comfortable in that little space. 'Who wants some oatmeal?' Norman and Em took some. 'Who wants a day-old biscuit?' Nobody. 'Who wants a day-old biscuit with Norman Cairnes' famous maple syrup on it?' That sounded pretty good. Seven takers on that offer.

"What a day. We joked and laughed and told stories. We argued about maple syrup. We quizzed each other. How many gallons of sap to make one gallon of syrup?' Rayland would ask. 'Easy one.' Liz knew the answer. 'Forty, plus or minus.'

"'Give that girl a biscuit,' Norm said. We were laughing with one another and just being kind of silly, but it sure was fun. I'll never forget it. Then Rayland asked out of nowhere, 'Is it possible to stand an egg on end?' It was agreed that you could not. 'Yep. You can. I read it in the Farmer's Almanac. The Chinese say you can only do it on the first day of spring.' Everyone hooted and booed Rayland's notion of an egg standing on end. It didn't pass the smell test, but Uncle Rayland is the master of obscure facts. It might be true. I'll be darned if I know where he gets the stuff. "

"You remember too much, Ricky. I'm not taking you the next time I fall through the ice," Rayland said, his face a picture of pure joy.

"I think it's a good time for Aunt Rho and me to head to the living room and watch a little TV." Alina said apropos of nothing other than she'd heard these stories many times before. "Help yourselves to another piece of pie and come join us."

Em and Rayland sat and talked for a bit as the others moved from the table. "Want a shot of Wild Turkey, Rayland? Helps the digestion. Helps you sleep, too."

"Don't mind if I do." He smiled as his brother got up to find glasses. "You must be doing good, Em. A big crowd for dinner. Wild Turkey in the cabinet. Doing good."

"Well, you know, Rayland, I got a little business of my own on the side. I change oil, do lube jobs and minor repairs on neighbors' cars. I don't make much. Just some extra Wild Turkey money, you know."

"You keep changing the oil, Em, and I'll keep helping you with the Wild Turkey." He took a sip. "Deal?"

"Deal." They clicked glasses and relaxed in each other's company. "Reach back, Rayland, and get that TV Guide behind you. Up there with the magazines."

Rayland picked up the little magazine and thumbed through it. After several pages he asked, "Do you get all these television stations, Em?"

"No. I think that's for the entire northeast region. We get channel 3 and 10. Sometimes 31 if the weather is right. Look and see what's on the Ed Sullivan Show tonight. Eight o'clock, I believe."

"Let's see. Today is the 15th, right?" He looked for the Ed Sullivan Show. "Here it is. Tonight, he's got Teresa Brewer and Liber-ace."

"That's Lib-er-ach-ee." Em enunciated, sounding out each syllable. "I've got to get you a TV, Rayland. You're missing out on a lot." Em gently shook his head. "Liberace. He's your kind of guy, brother," he joked. "What do you say, Rayland? Want to watch some TV?"

"No, Em. Thank you for everything, but I've got to get on home. Not even finished with all the chores yet. And I've got to start planning my protest. Ricky and Hannah said they'd give me a ride."

Chapter 6

JUST COMPENSATION

Sunday - May 12, 1963

New York - *Folk singer Bob Dylan refused to perform in his television debut on the Ed Sullivan Show after the censors at CBS network would not allow him to sing "Talking' John Birch Paranoid Blues" on the popular Sunday night variety show. Dylan has become a strong voice for young activists.*

Jeep arrived with the mail and entered through the barn, as he always did. No Rayland. He continued toward the ell and saw him working on the porch. Doing laundry.

"Well, if it isn't Mother Hubbard," Jeep teased.

"Knock it off, Jeep. You might get hit in the puss with some wet long johns."

Rayland was bent over a washtub, scrubbing a garment on the small washboard. "Of all the jobs on the farm, this is the worst," he grumbled. "I had five sisters, you know. I never, never did the laundry. They'd do laundry every week. I didn't even think about it. When they got married and then Ma died, me and Gregory we'd put off doing the laundry until we ran out of clothes to wear."

Laughing at the thought, he took the garment he was working on and ran it through a wringer attached to the side of the tub. "We finally decided that once a month we'd wash everything. He'd take one month. I'd take the next."

He inspected the garment, a shirt, and gave it his approval.

"Now he's long gone and I got the damn job every month."

He hung the shirt on an overloaded line that ran from the house to a nearby tree.

"Rayland, if you don't mind me saying, you doing laundry looks like a three-legged cat in a sand box. Why don't you buy a washing machine? You've got electricity in the barn. Put it in there. Sears will deliver. All you need to do is plug it in and use it."

"I don't think the cows would like it. Too much noise." He adjusted the makeshift clothesline pole to keep everything up and off the ground. "But damn if I don't hate this. Especially in the winter."

He dumped the washbasin. Then he dumped the rinse basin and picked up his empty laundry basket.

"What have you got today, Jeep? Let's go inside."

"They're coming, Rayland. I've been delivering these letters all day. I don't know what it means, but they're coming."

Jeep put the mail on the kitchen table, placing the letter from the Vermont Highway Department on top.

Rayland dried his hands and looked at the letter. "It makes me angry. I feel so damn helpless. I've got to figure out what I can do." Rayland picked at a callous on his hand. "I've got to figure out what I *can* do."

Seeing the concern on Rayland's face, Jeep said, "Why don't you go talk to Ulmer or Thomas Lumfield? They might have some advice."

Rayland looked at the letter again, picked it up, but put it down unopened.

"It's about the surveyors coming. It's the rules and protocol and stuff. Everybody says it's nothing, but," he hesitated, "it's hard to say, not knowing." He poked through a pile of Rayland's magazines as he spoke. "What are you reading, Rayland?"

"Whatever folks give me. I'll read just about anything."

The small bookcase held magazines, farm journals, paperbacks and hard covers, all in no particular order.

"I wasn't much in school," Jeep offered. "Oh, I can read okay, but just not very fast. Driving a jeep in the Army, you didn't need to read fast." He looked through the books on the shelves. "Were you good in school, Rayland?"

"I don't know if I was any good or not. Had to drop out in seventh grade when Pa died. My sister Roslyn was the smart one. She's the oldest. She was just about to graduate from high school and go to a junior college in Mass., but Pa's passing put the kibosh on that." He looked through the rest of the mail. "She got a good job with an accounting firm in Claremont. Worked her way up. She did good. Between Ma and Ros and school, I learned to read." He put the mail back down. "I like to read. If you can read, you can learn."

Pointing to a book near Jeep, he said, "See that yellow cover? Next to it is one I think you'd like. *The Ox Bow Incident*. It's a good one. A law and order western. Take it."

Jeep continued looking through the books. "What's this? *A Plain Introduction to the Art of Astronomy*?"

"Oh, it's about the sky and the stars, the planets the galaxies."

"What's a galaxy?"

"It's a large collection of stars. Billions of them. You've seen one and you don't even know it. Ever seen the Milky Way?"

"Sure."

"Galaxy." He looked at Jeep. "That's the galaxy that our earth is in. It's pretty interesting stuff. Want to borrow that book, too?"

Jeep thumbed through it, looking at the pictures. "Did you ever think about working in an office? Like your sister?"

"Are you serious? You ever seen bull riding like they do at a rodeo?"

Jeep nodded.

"Those big old bulls come out of the shoot with a cowboy on their back and they buck and they jump and twist and buck again. There's a strap around the bull's flank, and they tell me the strap somehow binds their genitals. That's why they buck so much. That's what I'd be like in an office. Like a bull with my nuts tied up and somebody on my back."

Jeep started laughing. Rayland grinned. Then he laughed a little. Then he laughed harder. Then Jeep laughed more. Before long, tears were rolling down their cheeks.

"Ho, man. That's a good one, Rayland. That's a good one. Guess you won't be working in an office, hey?" He blew his nose. "That's a good one." Rayland wiped his face with his hat.

Eventually, they turned their attention back to the books.

"Can I take these two? I'm a slow reader. Might take a while to get them back to you."

"That's fine, Jeep." They walked out to the car. "Look at that mud, will ya? Not sure how you get around in that stuff."

"Not very fast, that's for sure. I can understand why the haulers are reluctant to build their business on the dirt roads picking up a few cans of milk here and a few there. Can't be any money in it for them mucking around on these roads."

"Did I ever tell you the tall tale I tell to tourists when they complain about mud season?"

"Don't think so."

"Well, it goes like this: One time, right here, I saw a hat lying in the middle of the road. Right about over there." He pointed a short distance away. "A good looking hat. So I eased over to pick it up. Wouldn't you know, there was a head under the hat. A man's head. 'You okay?' I ask. He says he's fine, but ... he's worried about the horse he's riding." He smiled and his eyes lit up. "Get's 'em every time, Jeep. Gets 'em every time."

Jeep snorted, rolled his eyes and smiled. "I'll keep that in mind, but I've gotta hustle. Mail to deliver. Take care, Rayland."

Rayland was still chuckling to himself as he walked back into the barn with Star tagging along.

"Mud season sure isn't the prettiest time of the year around here, is it, Star? Just a natural part of the cycle, I guess. Can't get from winter to summer without some mud along the way. Now in France, that was a mud season." He reached for the scythe. "We fought in the mud, ate in the mud, slept in the mud." He picked up his sharpening stone and sat on a hay bale. "When I came home after the war, I told Ma I'm never leaving again. I did. And I meant it."

The sharpening stone sang on the blade as it swiped back and forth.

"We'll be cutting hay soon enough, Star."

The dog stretched out at his feet.

"Feels a little different this spring though. Too much uncertainty."

The stone made another pass on the blade. He looked up at nothing in particular.

"Too much uncertainty. You can feel it throughout the valley."

Back and forth the stone slid as he thought about his current situation.

"Star, I'm not much on planning for the future, but it seems this time the future is coming to find me. Could be I'm in the way of something and I've got no way to stop it. Worst part is I see no favorable alternatives." Back and forth the stone slid. "Probably a good time to have a visit with Attorney Lumfield to see what kind of rights I have."

Star looked up and yawned.

A few days later, Rayland knocked and opened the kitchen door to the Lumfield house. Freddie was busy cleaning up after lunch. "Hello, Freddie. I brought you some eggs."

"Hello, Rayland. That's very nice of you. I can always use eggs." Freddie took the eggs. "You know where the office is. He's expecting you," and she sent Rayland off through the house to Thomas's office in the back.

It was just a separate room in the house with a large, polished table for Tom's desk, several faded wildlife prints on the wall, two wingback chairs across from Tom for the clients, and lots of reference books. To the side of the lawyer's desk stood an antique wrought iron lamp that looked older than light bulbs. But it worked and it was very interesting. File cabinets filled a small adjacent room that might have been a closet prior to conversion.

Thomas was expecting Rayland and greeted him with a friendly handshake. Today's tie was Dartmouth green.

The two men chatted about nothing for a moment before getting down to the important stuff. “How are the Phillies going to do this year, Rayland?”

Rayland was a known Phillies fan. It had more to do with atmospheric conditions than with Philadelphia.

“We’ve got a new pitcher. Jim Bunting. Picked him up from the Tigers. I think he’ll help a lot down the stretch.”

The Phillies were the team Rayland could pick up on his little transistor radio on a summer’s night. Cities with 50-K watt stations bounced their signal off the upper atmosphere and around the country. The only problem was you didn’t know which station was going to come in or when. If the Phillies game didn’t come in, he might have to settle for the Pirates all the way from KDKA in Pittsburg, or perhaps the Cleveland Indians.

Tom settled back and offered Rayland a cigarette. He declined. Tom lit one for himself. He was a Chesterfield man. They moved on to business.

“What can I help you with, Rayland?”

“Thomas, Preston Jaffe always says when it comes to this new highway ‘Everyone wins. Everyone wins.’ I’ve been thinking about that. Thinking a lot. Seems to me maybe everyone loses. Remember when you were a kid, Thomas? Remember how excited you got at Christmas? Santa is coming. Anticipation. Excitement. Santa is coming. You could hardly sleep you were so excited. Remember?”

“Sure do.” He inhaled deeply. “Let’s just say my younger brother Timmy used to wet his pants.”

“Yeah. And then some older kid in the schoolyard told Timmy there was no Santa Claus. It’s your parents, you dummy. It’s your parents. Well, that little kid will grow up and he will still enjoy Christmas, but it will never be the same. The kid knows he lost something. What he lost might be hard to describe, but it's still a loss. It will never be the same."

"I remember it well, Rayland. I suppose I was in second or third grade and Elwin McClore, a big old playground bully, told me and Willy Herzog. I'm not sure I believed him, but Willy did. Willy cried all the way home that afternoon. It was a painful loss of innocence." He paused. "I think in a way, I still believe in Santa Claus. But you're right."

Tom rubbed out his cigarette in a too-crowded ashtray.

Rayland moved to the issue that had eating at him for weeks. "Seems to me to be the same thing here in Towsley. We're a simple little farming community. We're more like that little kid than the bully. We're not going to be the same once that four-lane road comes ripping through."

He sat for a moment. "You never miss the water until the spring runs dry, Thomas." He looked across at the attorney. "It's true. You don't miss it 'til it's gone."

They both sat quietly for a moment. "You're right, Rayland. We won't be exactly the same, but that doesn't mean bad."

"It doesn't mean good either," Rayland replied quickly.

Thomas lit another cigarette. Rayland asked, "What is eminent domain?"

Tom paused and gathered his thoughts. "Eminent domain," he said, using his most authoritative attorney voice, "eminent domain allows the government to take private property and convert it to public use."

"How can it be stopped?"

"Well, you can always file a grievance, but unless you've got a fortune to spend fighting the state, the short answer is, it can't. The general benefits to the community from the furthering of economic development are enough to qualify the taking of the land. With just compensation, of course. The government provides just compensation to the property owner, meaning you will receive a fair price for your property, no matter what type of property it is."

"Pardon me, Thomas, but that's bull shit."

Tom Lumfield sat back.

"Thomas. Thomas, how can they call it 'just compensation?'" He looked at Thomas with hopefulness that the attorney wished he didn't have to dispel. But, before he could respond, Rayland continued. "They're trying to take away land that I've lived on all my life. Land that my Pa owned forever. Shouldn't a son be able to continue with a farm that his father built from dirt and stone? His dirt. His stone. And it's now my life." He paused. "And it's my livelihood. It's my roots. They want to take it because they don't want to bend a road this way or that? Look. Look at these hands, Thomas."

He held out his big calloused, weathered hands.

"These are the hands of a farmer. I'm not a man of books like you. I'm a farmer. See those dark lines in the knuckles and in the creases? I can wash my hands all day long and the lines don't come out. That's over fifty years of ground-in dirt and cow shit from the farm. See the bent finger? I broke that finger working on the farm. On my farm, Thomas. Not their farm. It's my farm, damn it. That farm is my life. It's in my heart. How can they call it 'just' to take a man's land right out from under him? Take his land so that some city slicker can zip right past us and get to Canada faster."

Rayland took a deep breath, then continued. "We were all born on that farm. All nine of us. Ma and Pa built the farm, lived there, worked and died there. That seems to me to be the natural order of things. Why's the government messing with that?"

He paused. Looking away, he took a deep breath, repeated the question: "Why's the government messing with that, Thomas?" He slumped forward, tired and saddened, but he wasn't done. He had come for a purpose. "I don't need much, Thomas, but don't let them take what little I have," he said, holding his head in his hands and letting out a slow, long exhale. "You've got to help me, Thomas."

"Don't go borrowing trouble, Rayland," Thomas said, unnerved by Rayland's plea. "Nothing has happened yet. You're worrying about something that hasn't happened yet."

As soon as Thomas heard himself repeating the phrase nothing has happened yet, he knew he had nothing to give Rayland, no assurance, no explanation that would assuage his friend. He just sat there looking at Rayland. He knew he was looking at a man facing something he didn't understand and couldn't embrace even if he did. A friend. A neighbor. The attorney hoped he could help but he didn't know exactly how. Finally he broke the silence. "I'm sorry, Rayland. I'm truly sorry."

"I'm not leaving, Thomas." Rayland said as he gathered himself and headed for the door. "I'm not leaving."

After the door closed, Freddie stuck her head in. "Is he okay, Tom?"

"I think Rayland just left his heart on my desk. I'm worried about him, Freddie."

Rayland started his walk back to the farm. His mind was blank, his emotions drained. He gazed up at the mountains in the distance, and he could see the curtain was about to rise. That was the way he thought about this time of year. Every year he watched in amazement, day by day, as the color crept up the side of the hills, then up the side of the mountains. Looking at it now lifted his spirits.

The meadows and fields are the floor for this natural theater, he thought. The seats of the theater were filling quietly with hay sprouts, and grasses, and wild flower shoots. Look up from the floor toward the stage, bushes and fruit trees were coming to bloom. White apple blossoms. Yellow forsythia. Pink honeysuckle buds. Above them, the main stage, the mountains. And the curtain was about to rise. Spring is a great word for it, he thought for the umpteenth time.

Having lived all his life with the seasons, he knew that the vernal pool was the orchestra pit where it all started. The little ponds of ground water seepage and snowmelt were the first to come to life. Tender green spears pricked upward. Ferns and grasses, trillium, pennywort and skunk cabbage – each in turn pushed their heads above ground. Yellow green first, almost chartreuse, then a brighter glassy green, then darker green slowly spread across the forest floor. The days warmed and the wood frogs appeared and readied themselves for their matting song. These spring peepers sang in the warmth of the afternoon sun. The grasses and pucker brush, and curly ferns all had their distinctive shades of green. So many shades of green. Next the birch trees got into the act. Their leaves were tiny, but the birch buds hang in clumps. You can't see the buds from a distance, but up close, they looked like fuzzy caterpillars, yellowish green caterpillars hanging from the tips of branches.

It quieted his mind to observe this natural transformation. It was calming. He wasn't much used to saying these things out loud although he had kind of done so with Thomas a few minutes ago. He spoke quietly to himself as he walked along, the way a man who lived alone tended to do. Had Thomas heard him? Would anyone understand what it meant to him to live in this place, in this way? A place where he could watch the seasons come into themselves. Watch each of his animals come into itself. Look around, he thought. This is the only place I've ever been part of. And that's just fine. This is a part of me, and I'm glad to be a part of it.

Sometimes his conversations were like a catalogue of information he had accumulated over the years. The observation unfolding in his mind, point by point, seemed to calm him. Looking up into the woods, he observed what he already knew, that there were few oak trees in the mountains here. Maples predominated, budding out in red or yellow green. Soon enough the sugar maple leaf would turn green and the red maple leaves red, of course. Beech trees were the easiest. They were reluctant to shed their leaves. The few clinging brown leaves that had held on through winter helped give them away. The new deep green leaves pushed the clingers to the ground as they emerged

Depending on temperature and sunshine, the emerging leaves came out on trees higher and higher, moving color up the mountain a few feet or yards every day. The colors were variants of green -- dark green, pea green, lime green, bottle green, sage green, olive green, lemony green, apple green – all of which made for Vermont green. The yellow and the light green leaves shimmered and danced. The dark pines stood tall and dignified. The white pines looked on, deep green at their core with a yellow fringe on the end of branches. If the color green could assault the senses, this was the time and this was the place.

The curtain was rising on the wonderful show called springtime in the Green Mountains, and Rayland was happy for the moment just to see it again. Rayland had seen the show many times in his years, but he stood there and marveled just the same. The show erased any winter weariness that might remain after the long dark months. The show renewed hope and lifted spirits. He stood and looked. He took in the wonder of the natural show getting started right before him. No wonder he loved this place, this state, his farm, his life. No wonder.

Chapter 7

IT IS WHAT IT IS

Monday – June 3, 1963

Charlotte, NC - *Fred Lorenzen won the World 600 NASCAR race yesterday despite his car running out of gas on the final lap. Junior Johnson had been leading the race until suffering a blown tire with three laps left. Lorenzen's win brought his earnings to "just under $80,000," making him the biggest money winner in stock car racing history.*

"Baaack. Baaack. Baaack," Rayland repeated in a soft, low voice. The b came quietly followed by a long, slow breath of an a and an almost silent k. "Baaack. Baaack." He put his palm on Charlie's barrel chest, touching it lightly and backing the horse closer to the wagon.

"Good boy, Charlie." He patted the horse on the neck and gave him a piece of carrot.

"You ready, Max?" He moved in front of the second horse and backed him to the wagon with the same soft command. "Baaack. Baaack."

The horses stood patiently chomping on their carrots. They were already harnessed. The pole straps still needed to be connected from harness to wagon. Then they were ready to go. Rayland climbed up onto his seat, made a tck tck tck sound with his tongue against the roof of his mouth. The big animals moved out. It was just yards up to the cold house.

"Whoa," he said and they stopped where it would be easiest to load the milk. Twelve five-gallon milk cans.

Someone once told him that a full milk can weighed 90 pounds. He had no idea, but it sure felt like 90 pounds. The older he got, the heavier they got. By the time number twelve was loaded, he'd rolled up his sleeves, removed his hat, and was headed to the pump for water.

He came right back and climbed aboard. “Okay, boys. We're ready.” He slapped the seat next to him and Star jumped up and occupied it. Again, the tck tck tck sound. The horses headed down hill toward the road.

“Hoooo. Hoooo” He slowed their progress not wanting to spill any milk. “Hoooo. Hoooo.” When they got to the dirt road he made a clicking sound with his tongue against his teeth on the side of his mouth. “Click. Click. Click.” The horses picked up a comfortable, steady pace.

They all rode along enjoying the day. Rayland looked for wild flowers on the forest floor and other signs of summer. A few trilliums were still in bloom in the wet woods near the streams. Blue irises were a welcome splash of color in the swampy low areas. Daylily shoots were poking up, but no flowers yet. As they passed the Sullivan farm, he was hit with a sweet perfume.

“Smell that, Star? That's honeysuckle. See it? Over there on the side of Sullivan's barn.” He slowed the wagon. He inhaled deeply. “Wow. Now that smells like summer.”

Someone in a jeans jacket, riding jodhpurs and cowboy hat came riding toward him. He stopped. The red curls fluttering out the back of the hat were a dead give-away. It was Anna on her Morgan horse.

“Hi, Rayland. Everything okay?”

“Honeysuckles. Take a whiff.” He inhaled. She did the same.

“Oh my. That's lovely. I've got a honeysuckle, but mine is so overgrown it doesn't bloom much. I don't get that beautiful scent." She noticed his cargo. "Headed to the co-op?"

"Yeah. You headed somewhere, or just out for a ride?"

"We've had so much rain this spring, it's just nice to get out." She smacked her neck. "How the black flies treating you?" She smacked another one.

"I made peace with the black flies years ago. But you, you're waving your hand around and all trying to shoo them away. They think you're saying 'Come here. Come here.'"

"Could be. Or maybe I'm just sweeter and more tender than you." She smacked another. "I don't mind getting bit now and then, but when one flies in my mouth..."

Before she could finish her sentence, a car came around the curve behind her horse. The driver hit the brakes and the horn at the same time and skidded to a stop. The horse reared and nearly threw her. Wide-eyed, it lurched its head and neck forward, set to bolt. Before the animal could launch off its hind legs, Rayland dove from his seat and grabbed the horse's bridle strap. As soon as his feet hit the ground, he started driving with his powerful legs. He wanted to force the horse's head to the side. The horse bucked and threw Anna into a graceless dismount that landed her on the seat of her pants in the middle of the road. Rayland continued to drive his legs and push the horse's head to the side. *Drive your legs. Drive your legs. Get her head turned. Don't let her get her power lined up behind her.*

The horse wasn't calming easily, but once it realized it wasn't going to go straight, she reluctantly let Rayland push her to the side of the road. He held on to her tightly and with concern. His face was pressed to her neck. He was talking to her as they half walked, half hopped and skipped over toward the Sullivan's lawn. The horse calmed slowly and Rayland walked her back to the meadow behind the house where she had more room and felt more comfortable. The two of them stood in the meadow, Rayland still talking to her.

The driver was out of his car and rushed over to help Anna to her feet. Before he could help, she looked up and accosted him, "What kind of dumbass are you?" Her face was as red as her hair. "You're lucky you didn't kill somebody." She got back on her feet on her own and got in his face. "Me. You could have killed me!"

"I'm sorry ma'am. I guess I was going too fast."

"Don't give me that ma'am stuff. Of course you were going too fast. You flatlanders are always going too fast. You don't seem to get it."

"You aren't hurt, are you?"

"Just my dignity." She dusted off the back of her jodhpurs. "I have ample dignity. I'll be alright. You on the other hand might have a terminal case of stupid."

"Should I go help that fellow with your horse? What's he doing?"

"I'd just leave those two alone." She looked across the way. "He's talking to her. Calming her down."

"He tackled your horse." He too was looking across the road. "That was amazing. And. now he's talking to her?"

"He's a horse whisperer. He talks to horses." Picking up her cowboy hat she added, "Cows too."

"Is he an Indian?"

"Where are you from? The moon?" she asked, thinking Heaven help us from these fools. Rayland and the horse were slowly making their way back from the meadow. As they walked back onto the road, he said, "She going to be fine." He rubbed the horse's neck. "Aren't you, Buttons?

You're going to be fine." Turning to the stranger, he said in a quiet yet stern manner.

"Mister, there isn't anything in these parts that you need to hurry to get to. Slow it down. Wherever you were headed will still be there later."

"I'm sorry to cause such a scare for you folks,"

He loosened his necktie and tried to explain. "I have a meeting with the state road commissioner. I'm trying to sell traffic and road signs for your highway. I'm late. I really misjudged how long the trip would take on these back roads."

He looked at his watch.

"In fact, I may have missed it by now. But everyone's okay. That's the important part."

Turning to Anna, he said, "Sorry again, ma'am." Then he turned and got back in his car and pulled away. Slowly.

"Your horse, ma'am." Rayland handed her the reins. "She's ready to be ridden."

"Rayland. I don't know who to hug. You or Buttons." She kissed the horse on the cheek. "These flatlanders don't learn quickly, do they?"

She climbed up into the saddle.

"There are more and more of them coming every day it seems," Rayland said as he returned to the wagon. "Just check the license plates. The new ones aren't like the tourists. The tourists are here to enjoy what we've got. These people are always in a hurry to get in and get out. Not much we can do about it." His voice had a tinge of futility in it. "As my big brother always says, it is what it is, Anna. It is what it is."

He got up into his wagon. When he was seated and ready to go, she looked across at him with smiling eyes and said, "Thank you, sir."

She winked and headed down the road. “Tck. Tck. Tck.” The horses started to move. “You know, Star. Sometimes you get an animal you’ve got to hit in the head with a board before you can talk to it.” He gave the dog a scratch on the neck. “I guess some people are like that, too.” He pulled an old biscuit out of his pocket. “That fellow might be one of those. Not a bad person. Just needs some learning to face up to what’s what. That’s all.”

“I remember when Emory was a kid. About six. Maybe seven. He’s the baby, you know. Thirteen years younger than me. Born the same year Pa died. So me and my brothers were like his Pa. Em was put in charge of the chickens. He couldn’t do much more. He tried, but he wasn’t much help. Too little. Well, one day me and Gregory and Jeremy were up trying to divert a drainage stream. We heard this racket coming from the hen house. Out runs Em and hot on his tail is the rooster. That rooster always gave Em fits. He’d chase him. He’d peck him. This time he flew at him with his talons out. Hit him in the middle of the back and knocked him down. Before he could peck him, Em scampered away.”

“We laughed, but not so Em could hear us. He’s just looking out for his hens. I can remember it now, Star. Gregory wiped his brow and then gave us all a lesson. ‘It is what it is. Nothing more. Nothing less. Em will grow up. Then one day he’ll kick that rooster’s ass.’”

Rayland gave Star a piece of biscuit. “Anyway, a few minutes later, Em comes plodding up the hill and asks to borrow a shovel. He takes the shovel and walks back down the hill. We’re leaning on our shovels watching to see what’s up. Em walks straight to the chicken coop and stands in front of it.”

Rayland scratched the dog's ear then continued the story. "The rooster comes flying out and he swings the shovel and hits the rooster like it was a baseball. The dumb bird is stunned, but tries to get up. Em raises the shovel and brings it down on the rooster's head. Whap! That old cock got up and scurried under the coop. Didn't come out for two days. We're up on the hill hooting and yelling and cheering Em on. Calm as can be, he walks back up to us and hands Greg the shovel."

He turned to Star to make sure he was still listening. "We're mussing his hair and banging him on the back and shaking his hand. Oh my, oh my, did we laugh." Star was busy with his piece of biscuit.

Rayland smiled at the memory. "We're standing there together, the four brothers. Em looks up and says, 'It is what it is. Right Greg? 'You betcha, Emory. You betcha.'"

After dropping off his milk and checking his account, Rayland, Star, Charlie and Max headed home. Everyone was enjoying the afternoon sunshine as they came across Wethersfield Flats. The flats were a long stretch of meadow with a shallow brook meandering through the fields. The mountains framed it on both sides creating a picture waiting to be painted. Up ahead he could see a work crew getting ready to knock off for the day. He slowed the horses then pulled them to a halt.

"Howdy, boys. Are you the surveyor crew they've been telling us about?"

"Probably. But we're just assistants." Three young fellows in jeans and T-shirts were putting equipment away. They looked like they'd had a full day. "What's up? Can we help you with something?"

"Just wondering what is it you fellas do."

"That's a good question. Seems my job today was to follow Mr. Potter. That's him out there." Mr. Potter was out about a quarter of a mile or so. "I follow him out there and he says, 'Josh, run back to the truck and get the other transit.' So, I run back to the truck. When I return, he says, 'Oh darn, I'm out of surveyor's tape. Josh, run back to the truck and get some surveyor's tape.' And I get to run back to the truck again. That's pretty much what I did all day."

His comrade in the Red Sox hat teased, "That's cause you're his favorite, Josh."

"Yeah. Well, Potter had me running my ass ragged while you two were probably goofing off and having a smoke somewhere."

"Sounds to me like you boys have quite a job. Are you college boys?"

"Yeah. Just a summer job." Josh's sidekick said as he put a box of small tools in the back of the truck. "A good one though. We're outside and we're earning money and we're doing something important. Mostly we plot elevations." He sat down on the running board. "Ole man Potter shoots the angles and triangulates different locations, but we help build the contour maps. They need the contour maps to figure out where the highway will go." He dusted his pants with his Sox cap. "It's pretty interesting."

"How do you figure out elevation?" Rayland waved his hand toward the meadows and mountains. "There's a lot of elevation out there."

"See that hay shed out there? Past Potter?" Josh pointed to a broken down old hay shed out in the field. "We use a barometer and figure out how far above sea level it is. Let's say it's 800 feet. Now the trick is to find a lot of places in this valley where the elevation is 800 feet." He swept his index finger to point out where they might be. "Once we have that information, we have our first contour line. Think of that first line like the perimeter of a pancake."

Josh, that is the dumbest analogy, and you just love it, don't you?"

"Yeah. I do, Bobby. It makes sense to me. Think of all the 800-foot elevations as the outer edge of an uneven pancake. That's our valley floor. That's our base elevation. Then you shoot 1000 feet and that's the second pancake. Stack it on top of the 800. Then 1200. Each pancake is getting smaller as we climb up. Keep going – 1400, 1600, and so forth. We're building a stack of pancakes. That's our mountain."

"What do you do with these pancakes?" Rayland asked.

"They become contour lines on a map. The engineers back in Burlington, or wherever they are, can see exactly what they have to work with. Sleep terrains here; shallow slopes there." He looked at Rayland who still seemed interested, so he continued. "They can see that the road can go here." He pointed across the flats. "But, not over there." Josh pointed to the rising mountains. "See what I mean?"

"Yes. I think I do. Is that what Mr. Potter is doing?"

"No," the third assistant chipped in. "He's shooting angles and figuring out distances. If you know the distance from Point A to Point B. and if you know the distance from Point A to Point C you can figure the distance from Point B to Point C. He's into math stuff. We're trying to find lines that work. At least that's what we've been doing the first few weeks. Let me show you."

He picked up the transit and flipped the triangle legs out to form a base. Then he pointed the lens down the valley.

"See that barn way down the valley? Way down there?" Rayland nodded. "If I shoot a line two to three degrees off to the right, I'll miss that barn by a quarter of a mile, but look what's off to the right."

"Mountains to the right. You can see that on Josh's pancakes, if I've got this right."

"Yeah. You've got it. So, if we can't go that way ..." He swung the transit slightly left. "If we go two to three degrees left, I miss that barn by plenty. That's the way to go."

"But with all those trees, you can't see what's down there." Rayland knew full well what was down there. The village of Wethersfield lay beyond those trees.

"Doesn't matter. The facts tell us what we've got to do. We've got three lines here, but only two work – straight at that old barn or to the left. We can tell that from here. You don't need to go look. You can call that shot from Burlington or anywhere."

"Heck, the first time a survey team shot the height of Mount Everest they had to shoot from almost 100 miles away," Bobby jumped back in. "Nepal wouldn't let them into the country. I think they shot from India. The important thing is, from 100 miles away they came within 28 feet of being right on."

"You seem like pretty smart guys. Do you care what's down there?" Rayland asked, turning to look into their faces, to see their reaction. "Or whose barn that might be? What if that farmer has three or four kids? Does that matter?" He looked from one to the other. "Is it okay to make that decision from Burlington? Or from India? Or wherever?"

Rayland pointed left. "It's a pretty sure bet that if you go through those woods you're going to come out on this same dirt road where we're now sitting. There are houses on that road. Does that matter?"

Nobody spoke.

"Knock down somebody's house. Kick a farmer off his land. Who makes those decisions? Is it Mr. Potter?"

"No. Not Potter." Josh thought for a moment. "Not Potter. Probably the engineers in Burlington." He figured. "Maybe politicians in Montpelier."

"How do they make that decision?"

"Money. That would be my guess," Bobby mumbled. "What's the cost to go here? What's the cost to go there? It's always money."

Rayland could tell they were feeling uneasy with the way this was going.

"Mister, there's not much we can do one way or the other. We're just building a map. Earning some beer money."

The conversation was pretty much over. "Okay." Rayland said with a smile." I guess that's honest enough." Tipping his hat, he said, "Thank you gents for the lesson. I've learned about building a map, stacking pancakes and shooting Mount Everest from India." He lightly tapped the reins. "Tck. Tck. Tck. Thanks again, boys. Enjoy your beer."

Bobby shook his head, not sure what to think.

As the wagon pulled away, he petted the dog absentmindedly. "Star, I don't know. I guess it is what it is."

He looked out onto the field where Mr. Potter was starting to pack up his equipment, and he thought about things.

"No, Star. It isn't what it is. This is different. It's what they're making it. Two degrees here. Three degrees there. It's what they're making it." He looked at the dog. "That doesn't seem to be a reasonable way to change the entire path of a man's life. Lives are going to be changed, changed a lot, based on some engineer 80 miles away drawing lines on a map. Something is really wrong with that."

They rode along in silence.

"It isn't what it is, Star. It's what they make it."

Chapter 8

A SUMMER BARN DANCE

Friday - July 19, 1963

Houston – *An artificial heart pump was placed inside a human being for the first time, at the Methodist Hospital at the University of Houston by a team led by Dr. Michael DeBakey. The unidentified patient survived for four days before dying of complications from pneumonia.*

Albert Tanner was the worst square dancer in the county. He was known as wrong-way Albert. Albert's problem seemed to be that he just didn't know his right from his left. He was a big man who'd eaten too many of his own donuts. His hair was greying and he moved around his store without energy. On the dance floor, however, his pace quickened and his face expressed joy, and, some said, confusion. Albert had lost his left eyebrow to a piece of shrapnel during the war. When he became surprised or startled or pleased, he'd raise his good eyebrow and it appeared to throw his face out of balance, hence the appearance of confusion to match the actual befuddlement.

Square dancing is not difficult. If you can walk and pay attention, you can square dance. Just do what you're told. You don't need to memorize or learn anything. The caller tells you what to do. Most callers walk the square through the dance prior to getting started. After that, just do what you're told. Albert had difficulty with that concept. It's just the way it was. Albert didn't get it. If you were in the square with Albert, you laughed a lot. Even Albert laughed a lot. It was all in good fun, and with Albert in your square, it was both fun and funny.

Norman's new barn was magnificent. Large and clean and solid. The party was Norman and Aud's way of showing off their new expansion. Party lights were hung across the beams. There was a long table with food and goodies. A large tub of beer and other drinks were outside under the nearby maple. Aud wore a colorful dirndl, and somehow it fit in at a barn dance. Norman looked like the country gentleman that he was. He had on a beige shirt along with a lightweight leather vest and the requisite blue jeans with a big shiny belt buckle.

The Cairnes had hired the Cider Hill Apple Smashers, a local square dance band familiar to everyone. John Caulder played the fiddle, Harold Tanner on the accordion, and Billy Weststock was the caller and played guitar. The Smashers played Little Liza Jane to get the music going and start the party. Once they had everyone's attention, it was time for a square.

"Okey dokey, folks. Who's ready?" Billy asked the crowd. "Thanks to Norman's beautiful new barn, we've got room for two full squares. Who's up first?"

Rayland and Kate joined John and Ginnie Hurley and Tom and Freddie and Albert and Marie to make up square number two. Everyone was in their barn dance finery, if there is such a thing. Clean, pressed jeans and country shirts. Kathleen wore a crisp, white blouse with an enlarged collar and a bolo string tie. She seemed taller in jeans and cowboy boots. She looked elegant. Ginnie and a few of the other ladies sported loud western shirts. Even Rayland had found a nice plaid shirt that he'd ironed himself. Everyone looked country.

"Okey dokey," Billy announced. "The first thing we're going to do is walk you through the basics. Go as slow as you'd like. Ready?"

Billy got things started. "Bow to your partner. Bow to your corner. Circle right, circle left. Do-si-do. Promenade. Sashay. Right hand star. Left hand star.

"You're doing good. Okay, I think we're ready for some dancin'."

"So far so good, Albert!" John chided.

"Here we go. Okey dokey. All join hands and circle to the left."

The fiddle and accordion kicked in.

Circle left, listen to the music of the carousel,
The ting a ling of the ice cream bell.
Allemande left your corner, partners do si do
Men star left once around you go
Do si do your partner, your corner allemande
Come back and promenade around the land
Here come summer sounds
Summer sounds I love.

And so it went. Everyone was smiling and enjoying their success with their square. Even Albert was doing well. That might change when the call changed to "Duck for the oyster. Dive for the clam." But everyone had the ability to screw that one up.

Apple Smashers music reverberated off the beams and walls of the barn. Squares changed. Couples switched partners. This was a good old fashion barn dance.

Rayland and Kathleen took a break after their third square.

"Phew. Long time since I've done that. I guess I don't get enough exercise," Rayland said.

Kate rolled her eyes and chided, “Right. You’ve got to stop just sitting around. Get out and get some exercise.”

Norman walked over. “Rayland, when the Smashers take a break, I’m giving anyone who would like a tour of the refrigeration room.” He was excited to show off his new operation. “Join us?”

“Sure will.”

At the break, several men headed off as Norman proudly led the way. Kate joined Rose Sherman and Freddie Lumfield, whom she knew from having their children in school. “Hello Rose. Hello again, Freddie. Good party, isn’t it?”

“I haven’t danced like this in years. You forget how much fun it is,” Freddie beamed.

“This is my first square dance. Ever.” Rose confessed, laughing. “It’s great fun. We didn’t square dance in Philadelphia. We were too snooty, I guess.” She paused, “Our loss. This is fun.”

“How are your kids doing in school?” Kate inquired.

“Well, you probably know better than we do, but mine are happy and seem to be learning.” The conversation continued about school and their kids’ progress. Soon the men started to return from their tour.

Rayland was talking with Edward Walker. “Ed, you know Kathleen, I think.”

“Sure do. Good to see you, Kate.”

“What did you think, Rayland?” Kate asked. “Edward, did you pick up some ideas for your operation?”

“Wow. Hard to say, Kate. I never saw so much stainless steel or such a clean operation. Pipes. Filters. The refrigeration control room. Sorry, I mean the milk cold storage room, of course. Looks more like a doctor’s office. But the actual cooling and storage tanks aren’t as big as I thought they'd be. They're about as tall as I am, and what would you say, Rayland, about eight feet long?"

"Sure was cleaner than my barn," Rayland added. "Norman has himself a first class operation. It's really something. He's in a different league now."

Edward was thinking out loud, "Once this highway thing is settled down and we know what's what, I've got to look into that financing plan the Wilcox Brothers are offering. Might be the way for me and the missus to go. Hauling those five gallon cans full of milk over to the creamery by myself might make me an old man earlier that I'd like."

They chatted a bit longer, then Ed asked, "Kate, you're not going to let Rayland hog all your time tonight, are you? I'd love to dance a square with you."

"Sure, Ed. Sure thing."

A new square was forming and they headed onto the floor. Billy Weststock was getting into the tougher stuff.

Head star through, pass through, circle round the back.

Pass through, wheel and deal, centers star through.

Pass through, cloverleaf, the new center two.

Square through, three quarter turn, turn the corner by left.

All the way round and promenade the set all the way home.

They returned at song's end. "She's a mighty good dancer, Rayland. Thank you, Kate. Good luck keeping up with her tonight," he teased.

Rayland and Kate headed back onto the floor.

Join hands, circle to the left, that riverboat is awaitin'.

All aboard, it's time to go.

Allemande left the corner girl, turn a right hand around your partner.

Men star left and turn it once around the town.

Midway through the square, Rayland could see couple number three out of the corner of his eye, and Albert was coming at him. With his good eyebrow raised, it was hard to tell if he was going to veer to the left or keep straight, but if he kept coming straight, Albert was going to be his new dance partner for sure.

"No, Albert. Other way. That way," he laughed and pointed. Albert laughed. Kate laughed. John and Ginnie laughed. Albert could sure get people laughing when you least expected it. It was a fun, happy evening.

After a frenzied version of Buffalo Gals, the Apple Smashers took another short break. Buffalo Gals was a gasser. Everyone needed to catch their breath. Most of the men headed to the lawn under the tree where there was the bucket with ice and beer and cold water. Norman, Rayland, Preston, Otto, Ron Davies, and John Hurley were cooling off and enjoying each other and the summer air. The ladies were refreshing the food table while Mazie Davies argued about changes to the school food program with anyone who would listen. No one seemed to be concerned.

"Good evening, sheriff," Norman welcomed Melvin Moore to the group.

"This s a heck of a party, Norman. Thanks for including Amylin and me. Your new barn and cooling room are magnificent. State of the art. I hope you're not making these boys jealous."

"Thank you, Mel. You boys help yourselves to the beer. There's a spread of food inside too."

Melvin was a big man who loved to eat. He was sure to help himself to the buffet.

"Did Aud make that salad with the flowers in it," Preston asked. "Never seen anything like that. Mighty pretty."

"It's tasty, too. Give it a try, Pres."

Preston helped himself to another beer instead. He leaned back, sort of puffed up and observed, "This is what a modern dairy is supposed to look like. This is what Vermont needs. Mark my words. The state, the highway department, everyone concerned wants to see operations like this. Up to date. Modern." He sipped heartily from the frosty can.

"I suspect those surveyors will pick off some small operations that probably wouldn't make it another ten years anyway. Like your place, Otto. Geez, you've been struggling forever. They'll give you a nice price, and you can go do something else with the rest of your life. Not be stuck pulling the same cow's teat day after day." He was on a roll. "Get out now while someone is offering good hard cash. Things going the way they are, if you wait too long, your place might not be worth a plug nickel in a few years. Hell, Rayland, yours might not be worth that much now."

Press belly-laughed at his own bad joke.

"That barn roof of yours looks like it might not be able to handle another heavy snow. Those college kids doing the surveying will probably shoot a line straight through that broken old cupola sitting on top. Take the money and run, Rayland. Take the money and run."

The others shifted about uncomfortably without making eye contact with each other.

"Why don't you stuff a sock in it, Preston," Rayland snapped. "The beers are getting the best of you."

"Whoa. Whoa, Rayland." Preston tried to explain. "I didn't mean anything more than to say, when the state offers good hard cash, take it. Go get a piece of land, one of those nice trailers and settle down." He looked at the farmers. "Stop clutching your pearls, ladies. Step up to the future. That's all I meant."

"Well, here's what I mean, Preston. I think you're full of it. The only thing you know how to do is show up in town and shoot off your big mouth. Once you've said enough stupid things, you go back to Boston."

"Come on, Rayland." Norman stepped in. "I don't think Pres knows the situation. All he's trying to do is help."

"Norman, I don't think Preston knows his ass from a hole in the ground."

Norman turned to Preston. "I don't think this is helping anything, Pres. Let's go in and get something to eat."

Rayland was fuming. Several of his friends tried to calm him down. He heard none of them. He walked away, further out into the yard, looking for the North Star.

After a few minutes, Norman came back out.

"Rayland, I'm sorry. You know how Preston is. He gets a few drinks in him and he tries to be a big shot. I don't think he was trying to hurt anyone." They stood there in silence.

"I know you better than he does, Rayland. I know what that farm means to you. Preston doesn't have a clue. I know what it means to you. You're my friend, Rayland. These people are your friends."

Silence.

"Please come back in when you're ready. Half the people inside are as mad at Preston as you are. Especially Aud."

Silence.

"Please come back in if you want to. We want you there."

After finally calming down, Rayland went back into the party, but he'd lost his appetite for partying. He spent a few minutes letting Aud and Norman know that he was okay and thanked them for such a wonderful party. He stayed long enough to be polite, but he wanted to go. He got Kathleen alone and quietly told her he'd like to head home if she could give him a ride.

"Actually," he whispered to her, "you know what I'd like to do with the rest of this evening? I'd like to take you up to my secret place in the upper meadow and show you some more stars."

"Rayland, I haven't been with a man since Vincent died in that automobile accident several years ago. I'm not sure."

"Kathleen. Kathleen, I'm not suggesting anything. Nothing at all. I'd just like to spend some quiet time with you. I guarantee you that I'll..."

She cut him off.

"Hush, Rayland. I'd like to spend some quiet time with you, too."

They returned to the farm, and thanks to the lighting installed by Norman, Rayland flipped a switch and lights went on. The cows were mostly bedded down, and those that were got up to see what was going on. "Back to sleep, girls. Too soon to milk."

He picked up two heavy horse blankets and a plastic jug for water. He filled the jug from the cow trough. Realizing what he was doing, he sheepishly told Kathleen, "It's from the same spring as the water in the house."

There was enough moonlight to show the tracks that the horses and wagon had rubbed raw over the years. They hiked up the shallow incline alongside the pond and into the upper meadow. It was a gorgeous summer evening. The air was mellow. It caressed your skin and made you happy to be outdoors.

“How do you mow all these fields?”

“Well, the best plan is to first be sure you have a good stretch of weather. Start at the crack of dawn. It’s a long day.” Breathing became a bit more labored as they climbed. “And keep your scythe sharp. You’d have to be a gorilla to cut hay with a dull scythe.”

“Seems to me you’d need to be a gorilla anyway.”

“It’s not as hard as it might appear. After fifty or so years you learn a few tricks. It isn’t a power move through the grass. It’s more of a swinging rhythm. Keep the rhythm and keep moving forward. After that, you rake. Turn the hay once or twice to keep it fluffy. Get done before dew sets in. Like I said, it’s a long day.”

He caught a firefly and gave it to her.

“But the best trick I learned, and I didn’t learn it until recently, is that once the hay is laid out in windrows, get a hold of Karl Zalewski. He bought a used baler, and he’ll come up and bale the hay for me. Otherwise I’d be stacking and loading by hand.”

They arrived at his favored spot.

“Good old Karl.”

Tossing the blankets onto the ground, he inhaled deeply. Yes, this was his favorite spot, at the top of the meadow, on his family farm. Standing there, he could see most of the farm, the church steeple in the village and the upper reach of the river with the moonlight reflecting off the moving water. “I love this spot. I don’t come up here as much as I used to.” He looked out onto the town lights in the distance. “I think the hill has gotten steeper.”

She helped him spread one of the blankets and rolled the other to use as a pillow. Soon they were lying side by side, quietly resting, looking into the summer sky.

"Watch the sky. Look deep into the sky and tell me if you see a shooting star."

They both concentrated on the night sky.

"There's one. There's another," he pointed.

"I didn't see anything. I've never seen a shooting star."

She wanted to see one badly.

"Bet it's because you've never looked. Sometimes you need to look long and hard before you see something right under your nose. I wish I could tell you that shooting stars are out every night, but that's not true. The end of summer is the best time to see them. But there are always plenty of other things to enjoy any time of year. You just need the time to look."

"Oh, there's one, I think. Yes, yes, there's another." She kept looking. "You should be the educator, Rayland. You'd be a heck of a teacher."

They looked up at the stars and enjoyed the wonderful night air.

"It's so quiet and peaceful. This is a wonderful place. Thank you for bringing me here."

"Peaceful it is, but just lay here a few minutes. Tell me what you hear."

After what seemed a long wait, she said, "I'm not a city girl by any means, but I think I'd rather hear what you hear, Rayland."

"I think it's kind of noisy tonight. Noisy in a pretty way. Sounds of summer. Hear the crickets? The chirping is their mating call. They rub their wings together. Listen."

They lay quietly.

"Do you hear a little squeak now and then? That's probably a mouse. Making a nest or gathering food. Bats squeak too, but not very loud and they won't hang around here. They're probably down by the barn or the pond eating insects."

Again they listened.

"I hear the chirp and trill of cicada in the tree tops."

He stopped.

"Hear that? That's probably a hermit thrush. They're a very shy bird that hangs out on the edge of the woods. You'll recognize their song when you hear it. It's beautiful. They love a summer evening as much as I do. Or maybe that's a grouse nesting."

He stopped again.

"What else is out there that we might hear?" Kate asked.

"Well, we've got skunks. They squeal and grumble and smack their lips. Really."

He listened.

"A fox will scream or bark. Owls hoot."

He paused.

"So do bears."

"They do not."

"Yeah. They do. It's hard to tell the difference. The owl hoot is consistent and a little forlorn. A bear will give two long hoots then two short hoots and one long one. But the easiest way to tell it's a bear is by waiting for an answer."

"An answer to what?"

"Bear can be heard over a long, long distance. That old bear you might hear is probably looking for a date. He calls out from this mountainside. Then listens. The female answers from her mountainside way over there. Hoot. Hoot. Let's get together tonight, honey, and see what's happening. Hoot. Hoot. Meet you over at the Jensen farm. But watch out for Rayland. He's an odd old duff."

"Odd old duff. You are not an odd old duff."

They lay silently for a moment.

"I think you're sweet. A little quirky perhaps ... but very sweet."

They laid there together for the longest time. Enjoying the soft summer air. Happy to be together. Rayland cupped his hands and did his best bear imitation. "Hoot. Hoot. Hoooot."

He looked at her and gave her a big grin. She playfully punched him in the ribs, and then nestled in close, resting her head on his shoulder.

Chapter 9

NO FISH FOR DINNER

Monday - September 16, 1963

Associated Press – *A time bomb exploded in the basement of the Sixteenth Street Baptist Church in Birmingham, Alabama, killing four Negro girls and injuring 22 other children who were attending a Sunday school class. The blast occurred at 10:22 a.m. in a room with 80 children. Coming only two and a half weeks after Martin Luther King's speech to the Million Man March in Washington, D.C. where King dreamed of equality for all, the bombing triggered another round of racial violence. The church was believed to have been targeted by the KKK because it was a central meeting place and staging ground for Civil Rights activities.*

Daggone it was a pretty day. Crisp. Fresh. A touch of fall in the air. Just enough chill to start the trees turning out their fall colors. Rayland was up in the woodlot splitting logs he'd previously cut. He liked splitting. He'd stand a sixteen-inch log on his twenty-inch splitting stump, and go to work. The logs were dry enough that most split with one whack of the axe. If he hit it just right, it would almost pop apart into two clean-cut pieces. But they needed to be split again into smaller pieces so that they'd fit into the cook stove. The second split was always easier than the first. The smaller logs gave little resistance.

Knots are difficult and there are always logs with knots. Those ornery knots made you pay the price. For starters, the axe would get stuck in the middle of the log. It never got through the knot cleanly. The axe didn't come back out any easier than it went in. After you finally got it out, you had to use the splitting mall and cut through that knot little by little. The damn thing took three or four times as much effort and time as a log without a knot. Once you'd split that gnarly bugger, after all that work, you probably wouldn't have a log that would fit into the stove. They were odd shaped, jagged and impossible to stack. Usually a heavy splinter stuck out, or a spur like a wild, bushy eye lash. It just wasn't going to stack. Half the time you ended up throwing it into a pile for outdoor use, like boiling sap for sugaring. Logs with knots were a waste of time, but trees have knots. What are you going to do?

He enjoyed the splitting, which was a good thing. From October to May, he burned lots of wood. It kept the ell cozy and warm. When he split wood, he liked to say that he got warm twice. Once while splitting and again when the wood was in the stove. He knew that to be true. Right now, he was warm. In fact, he was hot. He sat on the splitting stump and reached for his jar of switchel. As he caught his breath, he saw Norman's Ford pickup pull up to the barn. A good time to take a break and go down to see what was going on.

Rayland picked up his shirt, mopped his brow with it and headed toward the barn. Someone was coming out the side door walking toward the ell. It was a young man in jeans, T-shirt and ball cap. Obviously not Norman.

"Hey, Ralphie." He finally could see who it was. As he got closer he yelled, "What's up? Where's your father?"

"Hi, Rayland. Dad wanted me to stop by and see if you needed a ride over to Leo's."

"You're going to drive me to Leo's?"

"Yeah. I got my driver's license this morning," he announced with a broad smile. "Dad is letting me borrow the truck."

"Well, he took me to Leo's yesterday. I really don't need anything."

Rayland watched Ralphie's face drop and his enthusiasm wane. Maybe that wasn't the right answer, he thought.

"That doesn't mean an old recluse like me couldn't benefit from a good ride around town on such a nice day. I could use a break."

Rayland was covered with sweat. Small wood chips stuck to his chest and arms. It didn't seem genuine when he said, "You know, Ralphie, sometimes I just like to do nothing, and when I'm tired of that, I take a rest." Even 16-year-old Ralphie knew that was baloney. "How about we drive down to Baker's Four Corners and get a cold drink or something?"

Baker's was five miles or so away. "If you aren't too tired from driving, we could then head on down to the Black River and do some fishing. I haven't fished all summer. What do you say?"

Ralphie perked up immediately. "That's a great idea, Rayland," he said. "I'll run home and get my gear. Be right back."

"Don't speed, Ralphie, or your old man will yank you out of that truck as quick as he let you in. Take your time. I need a few minutes to clean up. And to find my fishing rod. No idea where I put it."

"Okay, Rayland. See you in a few minutes." Ralphie trotted off to the pickup.

Twenty minutes later the '58 Ford 100 drove slowly and very carefully up to the barn. Rayland was waiting, rod in hand. Actually, it wasn't a rod. It was a pole. A nine-foot bamboo pole with a line tied to the tip that ran down to the handle. No reel. He placed it in the bed of the pickup and off they went.

Rayland rolled down the window and enjoyed the fresh air.

"Ralphie, look at you, young man. Cool as a cucumber cruising down the road." They smiled at each other and laughed. "Cool as a cucumber."

"Do you drive, Rayland?"

"Drive what? I've got nothing to drive. Well, I drive my team of horses. When I was in the Army I drove a truck. I guess it just didn't take." They both watched as the fall foliage passed by. "What's happening in high school these days?"

"I'm a junior. One more year to go."

"Think you'll go to college?"

"Yeah. Dad would like me to go to the University of Vermont. Eben's giving me some ideas, too. Ricky thinks I should go to the University of New Hampshire. Liz thinks I'd like Middlebury. I don't know. It's kind of confusing, but I've got time to figure it out."

"Do you get good grades?"

Ralphie muttered "U-huh."

"That's the important thing. If you get good grades you can go any place." They drove on, windows down, air streaming in.

"Heard anything from Ricky? He goes into the Navy soon, doesn't he?"

"He's in. Started about three weeks ago. We haven't heard much from him yet." He glanced at Rayland. "Eben got a letter. About all he says in his letters is 'This is different.'" Ralphie looked straight ahead. "Can't tell much from that."

"Remember Hannah?" he continued. "Liz is in touch with her. She's really something. Now she's getting involved with voter registration down south. Liz says she's taking off this fall semester to go to Alabama and register black voters. Liz thinks that's nuts."

He lowered his sun visor.

"You may have read that all-you-know-what is breaking loose down there. Just yesterday, the KKK killed four little girls in a church bombing. A church bombing! That's the worst thing I've ever heard of." He wrinkled his brow in thought. "I think that's the town where she's headed. Birmingham."

Rayland shook his head. "I heard it on the news, but I don't understand that stuff. I don't understand why. Why all the hate?"

"Not sure I do either," Ricky delayed. "What I know I get from Liz and Eben. It's crazy. The black people march, and the cops come out and beat them up. The white people from the North go down and march, and the cops come out and beat them up."

He readjusted the visor.

"Hannah is trying to organize a big march for next year. Her group wants to march in Selma, Alabama. Want to know why they picked Selma?"

He looked at Rayland. Rayland looked back and shook his head.

"Because they have this really nasty sheriff who attacks civil rights marchers. He and his police officers and buddies come out and squirt marchers with high-pressure fire hoses. A hose that will knock you off your feet and slide you across the pavement. Then they beat them with clubs. That's part of what she's going down there for."

He shook his head looking as confused as Rayland.

"She wants to line up support and get more marchers involved. Is that the dumbest thing you've ever heard? She wants Liz to join her. Mom says she'll squirt Liz with a hose herself if she even thinks about it."

He looked a Rayland.

"Squirting and beating people who march? Wow. Are they making trouble while they march? Are they trouble makers?" Rayland asked. "Wow. That's a new one for me."

The conversation was tabled for the moment as they pulled in to Baker's. Ralphie parked carefully. They got out and entered the little general store. "My treat, Ralphie. Load up." He picked up a bottle of Coke and a slice of apple pie. Rayland settled for a Dad's root beer, two Sky Bars and a carton of worms. The bill came to a $1.10.

"A dollar ten cents. Old man Baker charges way too much for his worms," Rayland muttered. "They'd better be good ones." They headed to the truck, snacks in hand.

The Black River was another four or five miles' drive. The dirt road followed the river through a narrow valley. The place to catch fish was down by the old covered bridge another three miles or so.

It was a beautiful autumn day with full sunshine. Along the river, the sun came through the trees in a dappled splash of light. It highlighted the foliage like a spotlight. It accentuated this, but not that. The ripples in the shallows sparkled silver where the sun shone through. The riffles around the rocks danced up and down in tiny patterns as the water raced along. The sun highlighted the red of the maple leaves along the water's edge and gave the yellow maples a golden glow. The colors were framed by pines that hung over the river's edge. Greens and reds and yellows. Dancing water splashed blue and silver and black against the greyish rocks and boulders. It was an amazing display of autumn's best.

"This might be the prettiest road in the world. What do you think, Ralphie?"

"Well, I haven't been to many places outside of Vermont yet, but this sure is pretty."

"You should be keeping your eye on the road anyway. Don't drive us into the river. Don't look."

"I'm watching the road, but you can't miss how pretty this is. I should bring Mom down here. She'd love it."

"Yeah. Good idea." He opened his Sky Bar, and handed the other to Ralphie. "How is your mother? She's about the nicest lady in Vermont."

"Yeah. I think so. too." He looked as Rayland approached his Sky Bar with obvious high anticipation. "Is Sky Bar your favorite?"

"Yeah. The cows like them. too. What's your favorite?"

"The cows? Now you're pulling my leg."

"Nope. On occasion, not all the time, but on occasion. Christmas and maybe Fourth of July, I get some Sky Bars. They break into four nice pieces. Each cow gets one. I get what's left. Seems to work for all of us. Yep. They love 'em."

He bit off half of the first section and looked at it.

"I can never tell where to start. I want the vanilla first but I can never remember which end it's on." He looked. "Hmm. I got caramel. Still pretty good. What's your favorite?"

"Well." Ralphie pondered. He definitely pondered. "Well, I like Bonomo's Turkish Taffy a lot, but I really like Snickers, too." There was a thoughtful pause.

"Baby Ruth is okay and, oh yeah, Pay Day. I like Pay Day now and then." Damned if he wasn't still pondering. "I'm not too crazy about Three Musketeers bars. It's filled with all that white stuff. Nougat, I think it is. Charleston Chew, they're good. Yeah, they're really good." Another pause. "My friend Jeanna likes Reese's Peanut Butter Cups. They're okay once and a while, but not too often, if you know what I mean."

"Damn it, Ralphie. All I meant was what's your favorite section of a Sky Bar. You eat all those candy bars you're talking about and you're going to end up with a pimple on your nose the size of an acorn."

Ralphie laughed at himself. "Okay. I got ya." He pondered again. "Vanilla, I guess." A thoughtful pause. "Maybe the peanut butter."

The covered bridge was coming into sight. Rayland thought, thank goodness.

Ralphie looked good with his fiberglass rod and spinning reel, but Rayland's homemade rod proved every bit as effective. He gathered his pole and extra hooks along with the worms and inched down the steep bank toward the river. Ralphie wasted no time wading into knee-deep current in his jeans and sneakers. Sixteen and fearless. Wearing his overalls, felt hat and barn boots, Rayland slid himself down the slippery bank to the water's edge. He didn't look much like a fisherman, but he was happy to be out on the river.

Forever, he had fished his 'secret' pool. An old dead tree hung over and into a large pool, giving the trout extra protection from predators and fishermen. Just above the pool was a flat rock right on the edge of the stream. He placed his hooks and worms on the back edge and then picked up a good-looking worm and baited his hook. Ready to fish, he held the string just above the worm and hook and gently pulled the rod into a slight bow. Upon release ... boing. The worm floated in a high arc and landed gently where he had aimed.

Rayland watched Ralphie for a minute to be sure he'd be okay. He thought, he doesn't look much like a fisherman in his ball cap and Bo Diddley T-shirt, but he seemed comfortable in the water. Why does he cast out so far? He seems to cast for distance. Not accuracy. Those casts are as far as he can cast it. He watched as Ralphie tossed one into a pool, the next into the riffles, and then he'd bounce one off a boulder. It eventually fell into the stream. He's enjoying himself. That's all that counts. The little silver spoon moved through the water like a minnow as he reeled it back in. That was followed by another long cast.

The favorite part of fishing for Rayland was releasing the trout he'd caught. He'd keep a few of the small ones for dinner, but after removing the hook from an exhausted rainbow, brown or brookie, he'd hold the fish gently in his palm and lower his hand into the water. Gently, gently he'd rock the fish back and forth to get water moving over its gills. Soon enough, the fish flicked its tail slightly and moved. A few inches at first. Then another slight swish and it was a foot or so away. Then, recovering, a quick swish and it was gone.

"Rayland. Rayland. Look at this one. Rayland." Ralphie had a nice rainbow on the line. You could see the bright raspberry markings each time it jumped and tried to spit his hook.

"Nice one, Ralphie. Take it easy," he coached. "Don't pull him in too quick. Take it easy. Take it easy. Play him." Rayland took his line out of the water and watched.

"Keep the tip up. When he jumps, keep that tip up. Don't let him spit your hook out." Rayland reached into his pocket and pulled out an old biscuit. "Take it easy. Take it easy. That's a big fish." He dusted the pocket lint and old straw off the biscuit before taking a small bite. "I think you've got him, Ralphie. Let him play himself out. You've got him."

Ralphie was still in knee-deep water. He slowly brought the trout in, letting the fish tire himself from the fight. He pinned his rod between arm and body so that he could bend down and cup the exhausted fish in his palm. With the fish on the surface, he reached down with his other hand to remove the hook. Carefully, he lifted it out of the water. He'd caught a beautiful eighteen incher. He stood to show off the fish to his fishing partner, but as he stood, the slippery rainbow twitched slightly in Ralphie's slippery hand. It popped up in the air before doing a perfect nosedive back into the river.

"Oh no." Hard to know what to say. "I saw it, Ralphie. I saw it. Prettiest rainbow I think I've ever seen. I saw it." Rayland tried to help the situation. "Damn nice fish. Damn nice fish."

Ralphie was crest-fallen.

They drove back to the farm relaxed, happy, and a little sunburned. After a wonderful afternoon with young Ralphie Cairnes, Rayland thanked him for the ride and the afternoon of fishing. He kept three trout for his dinner, congratulated Ralphie again on the one that got away, and headed to the ell. Star and Champ were waiting to welcome him home. He placed his trout on the counter next to the sink, and went to get a knife to clean them with. The mail was on the table. Right where Jeep always put it. On top was a letter from the State Highway Commission. A large red notice was printed near the bottom. "Important: Open Immediately."

Chapter 10

A BETRUF PRAYER

Wednesday - September 18, 1963

Chualar, CA – *A truck carrying 56 migrant farm workers, mostly from Mexico, was struck by a train as it was returning from a celery field at the end of the day. Twenty-two of the men died at the scene, and another ten died of their injuries later. Local authorities have asked for a formal inquiry.*

It was a gorgeous autumn morning. Norman looked out from the sunny alcove of his house, and he was pleased. He had built and improved a successful dairy business in rural Vermont. Aud had helped tremendously. She took care of the books, managed the household and farm budgets, dealt with the co-op, and ran a wonderful household. They both knew that they had just dodged a bullet.

Their notice from the highway commission told them they were going to lose their wood lot to the east, the lot they sugared with Rayland. Forty acres. The commission was prepared to give them what Norman thought was a fair price. It was almost enough to pay off the milk storage equipment loan with the Wilcox Brothers. They would soon be debt free.

Jeep not only delivered the mail, he also delivered the news. Rayland had been told he would lose everything. The entire farm was to be confiscated. The same for Otto, Garfield Pauly, Ed Foreman, Ron Davies and others. They were going to lose it all. It was a real gut punch for proud, independent men like these rugged, old farmers.

Norman and Aud were filled with a mix of relief and happiness with their situation, and sadness and pained empathy for their friends and neighbors. They promised themselves to be the best neighbors and friend they could possibly be. Where do you start? What can you do?

"Knock me in the head with a shovel if you ever find me gloating," Norman had told Aud. They agreed to be happy with their present situation, but to never let their good luck be reflected as something they had earned or accomplished. They realized and appreciated their good fortune.

"Let's go over and see how Rayland is doing." Norman suggested. "I can't imagine where his head is after reading that letter."

Aud agreed and added. "I'll take him some things from our garden. Goodness knows we've got enough."

Norman changed into a clean shirt and jeans. Aud donned one of her pretty aprons. She knew Rayland liked her dirndl and aprons. They decided to take Aud's Chevy in case the three of them decided to go somewhere. Maybe a Sunday drive.

Rayland was sitting in the kitchen, petting Star when they arrived. Just sitting and petting Star.

"Morning, Rayland. Can we come in?"

"Norman, you know you don't ever need to ask that question." He saw Aud behind him. "Hi Aud. Please come in." He took his hat off. "Excuse me if I don't get up. I'm not feeling right."

He looked unkempt and exhausted. "I didn't get much sleep last night."

He tried to fix his hair with his hand.

"Since Friday, actually. Nightmares. I wake up and I don't know where I am. I wake up scared."

He pointed to the letter still on the table.

"This damn letter's making me all messed up."

He looked up at Norman.

"I'm not a worrying man, Norman. I'm not, but..." His voice trailed off.

Aud placed the sack full of garden vegetables on the counter.

"Are these the fish you caught with Ralphie? Can I cook them up for you, Rayland?"

Aud picked up one of the trout, but put it right back down.

"Phew. These have gone by. You can't eat them now."

She picked the fish up by their tails and took them outside. As she hurried past, Norman got a whiff. He raised his eyebrows in agreement. She went out and tossed them in the compost. When she came back there wasn't much conversation going on.

"Can I make you something to eat, Rayland?"

She looked in the icebox. Empty.

"Have you been eating?" she scolded. "Have you been eating, Rayland?"

"I don't know. Seems all I do is worry." His anxiety was palpable.

"How about I go over to Leo's and get some hamburger?" Norman asked. "We can cook up some burgers and sit in the sun and eat them. How's that sound?" There was no response. "Aud?"

"Good idea, honey. Get potato chips, too, and some of Leo's coleslaw. And get extra so Rayland has something to eat with these vegetables."

"You two take care of each other. I'll be right back. Don't go anywhere."

He left in a hurry.

Once Norman had pulled away, Aud turned to Rayland and asked, "Do you worry about yourself, Rayland?"

"I don't think so."

He looked up at her.

"I worry about the farm and the animals. Oh, Aud. I'm a mess. This whole thing is a mess."

His breathing was erratic.

"How do I tell Em that I lost the farm? How do I tell Rho or Ella or Roslyn? How do I tell anybody?"

She pulled a chair directly in front of him. She sat, reached out and took his hands into hers. She looked into his bleary eyes. I've seen those eyes sparkle so many times, she thought. So many times.

"Rayland, take a slow, deep breath. Try to relax."

He did as asked.

"Do it again."

He complied.

"Again."

His respiration rate slowed.

"When you get anxious, I want you to sit right here and breathe like this. Slowly. Deep. Slow exhale. It will help you lose some of that anxiety."

He sat, breathing slowly as she had instructed.

"How do you know these things, Aud?"

"I don't know. I had a big family in Switzerland. You just learn some things." She put his hands into his lap. "You know that. You had a big family. You learn some things."

They sat quietly. looking at each other. She noticed the bags under his eyes. She thought, he hasn't slept since

Thursday night. He hasn't eaten since who knows when. I'll bet the dogs haven't been fed either. She got up to search for the dog food.

"Where do you keep the dog food? I'll feed them."

"Don't have any. Give them some of my biscuits. They like my biscuits." He pointed. "In the drawer. There."

She gave Star two biscuits and went outside and gave a couple to Champ. The dogs didn't seem hungry, she thought. I'll bet he feeds them before he feeds himself. I'd better have Norman check on the cows and horses when he gets back.

"Rayland, have you thought about a plan for what you might do?"

There was no reply. "

You know the government is going to give you a nice check for your property."

"I don't care about the government's check." She'd hit a nerve. "You know what they can do with their check." He was breathing more rapidly again. "I won't tell you Aud, because you're a lady. Besides...besides," he slowed, "once I divide that check among my brothers and sisters, there's nothing's left anyway."

"Why must you divide it, Rayland?"

He raised his voice, "Because it's their farm, too."

He took a deep breath and exhaled slowing.

"It isn't my farm. Ma left it to all of us. It's our farm."

"How many brothers and sisters do you have?"

"Eight."

"They won't be expecting money after all these years. You've worked the farm. You've keep it going. Without you there is no farm. They won't be expecting money." She looked at him and questioned. "Will they?"

"It belongs to us, Aud. Not me. Us.

"But, if you ask them."

"I'm not asking them anything. I don't even know how I'm going to tell them." He shook his head. "Rayland lost the farm! Rayland lost the farm!" His eyes saddened as he looked at her. "How am I supposed to live with that, Aud?"

He held to her eyes.

She remained calm. She looked him in the eye again. "I'm sorry you have to go through this." She searched for what to say next. "Maybe we can help you build a plan. You have time. You have time to plan. You don't need to do it all today. You can't do it all today. We have time to plan."

"We? What's that mean? We?"

She let that go, but she thought, oh, please step on it, Norman. I need your help, honey. The one-way conversations continued. She offered ideas. Rayland grumped at all of them. Finally, Norman returned with the lunch.

"How are you two doing? No coleslaw, so I bought an apple pie instead."

She took the pie and set it on the counter. "Apple pie. That's an interesting substitute."

Norman put the groceries on the table. She checked the fire in the stove to see what she had to work with.

"Norman, will you get this fire going again for me, please?"

Old wood stoves are efficient. A few sticks of kindling and the heat starts to rise. "How many hamburgers, Rayland? Can you eat two?"

"Actually, honey, I didn't get hamburger either."

She looked at him quizzically but said nothing. "I got chop suey."

"Chop suey?" Somewhat at a loss for words, she asked again, "You bought chop suey?"

"Well, Leo calls it American chop suey. He always has it in his deli and it always smells really good. You ever had it, Rayland?"

"No. But I've seen it." As an afterthought, he added, "You're right, Norman. It always smells really good."

"Okay then," Aud conceded. "Chop suey it is."

She opened the container to see what she had to deal with. Upon inspection, she asked, "What is it?"

"I think it's hamburger, tomatoes, macaroni and onion. It might be something from the old country."

"American chop suey." She scooped some into a pan. "Doesn't sound very 'old country' to me."

"Yeah. Maybe you're right. Let's heat it up and give it a try."

Aud put the pan over the fire and looked in the icebox again for ketchup or whatever else she might find. Nothing. Milk and homemade butter. Maybe it's in the cupboard. Then she realized, what are you doing, Aud? There is no ketchup. This is Rayland's house. Stick with the basics. If I'm lucky, I'll find a couple of plates. Keep it simple.

Leo's chop suey did smell great as it warmed on the stovetop. Norman and Rayland moved outside and sat on the porch while Aud fixed the plates. The warm sun felt good. Aud joined them and handed each a plate of Leo's concoction.

Rayland picked at the chips, but avoided the chop suey. Tussle jumped up into his lap. That seemed to liven him a bit.

"Where you been, old boy?" He scratched the cat behind his ear. "You haven't brought me a mouse in days." He gave the cat a small piece of the hamburger.

Aud watched him relax with the cat. Finally, he picked up his fork and tasted his lunch. That seemed to go well. I hope he eats, she thought. He took another bite. Then another. Good, good, good. Maybe we can sneak in a piece of pie too.

Rayland finished his plate of chop suey and ate a piece of pie but didn't seem ready to return to his normal routine.

"Norman, I fed the dogs," Aud said. "Will you check to see if the cows have been fed, please?"

She got up and collected the plates. "Horses too." Rayland followed her inside.

As she cleaned up, Norman went off to the barn.

"Rayland, why don't you go back outside and sit in the sun? I'll be out in a few minutes."

He went out and sat in his favorite chair. The lunch was good and the sun was comforting. By the time Norman returned, Rayland was asleep in his chair. Norm walked past and went into the kitchen, closing the screen door quietly.

"He's asleep. It appears the horse and cows are being fed. The cows are milked out." He picked up a taste of piecrust. "What did you two talk about?"

"Leave that pie alone. That's for Rayland."

Her husband looked disappointed.

"At least we got him eating." She washed the dishes. "He's a mess, Norman. He's taking it hard. I think the hardest part is he's afraid of being judged by his brothers and sisters. He's afraid they'll think of him as not working hard enough to keep the farm or not being a good enough farmer to survive."

She looked for a dish towel.

"He seems worried about too many things all at once. He never was one to look to the future, but now he's frozen by the thought of it."

Finding no dish towel, she dried her hands on her apron.

"He was hyperventilating when you left. He doesn't have any plan on where to go. He wants to split his eminent domain money with eight brothers and sisters. That leaves him with almost no money. And he doesn't want to face them and tell them what has happened."

She finished with the dishes.

"Ai-yay-yi. This is what we called a 'grand desordre' back in the old country. A big mess."

He took her in his arms and gave her a comforting hug. They stood holding each other for several moments.

"Let's go out and sit with him until he wakes up," he whispered.

The porch was filled with soft afternoon sunshine. They sat. And they sat. Eventually, Norman looked at Aud, laughed quietly, and whispered, "He's sound asleep. Gone."

She hunched her shoulders at him as if to say what are we going to do?

"He'll be okay, and I don't want to wake him. He obviously needs some sleep."

"I'll get a blanket."

She got up and quietly went into the house. Minutes later, she returned empty-handed.

"Well, the sunshine is warm, and when it cools, he'll wake up. Can't sleep out here all night anyway." She looked at Norm. "That lunch was pretty good. Wonder how Leo came up with the dish. Pretty good."

"And there is plenty left for Rayland to eat later," Norm added.

Aud looked at Rayland sleeping. Then she looked at her husband. "He's dead to the world. I think we can go."

They quietly departed.

Aud got behind the wheel and slid the front seat forward. Norman got in and they pulled out slowly.

Sunday afternoon and the road was empty. The car windows were open and her blond hair fluttered in the wind. She no longer wore ponytails. Her hair now parted in the middle hung down to just above her shoulders. She drove straight past their farm. He knew she had something in mind.

"Where we going?"

"We're going to go make a Betruf prayer."

"Yes. Of course we are." He looked at her. "Exactly what I wanted to do this afternoon." Still looking at her, no explanation followed, so he said, "By the way, what is a Betruf prayer?"

"Well, in the mountains around central Switzerland, in the summer, when the cattle are in the high meadow, the shepherds and herders end the day with a prayer. They climb to a high elevation and give thanks. They thank the Lord for healthy cows and a day free from mishap. Thanks for protection for all the animals and people in the valley below."

She looked back at him. "As a girl, I heard their chant many times. It's lovely."

Another quick look to see if he was interested. He was.

"They use wooden milk funnels. They use them like a megaphone so that the sounds echo around the mountains. It's really pretty." They drove in quiet.

"I imagine it is."

Turning toward her. he added, "If that's what we're doing this afternoon, I hate to tell you, but I didn't bring my wooden milk funnel."

She smiled. There was a slight gap between her front teeth, which made her look a bit impish when she smiled.

It was a beautiful smile, with bright, shining eyes. "That's okay. I know a trick."

She pulled into a small dirt parking lot, and parked next to an old hand water pump.

"Where we going?"

"Up." She nodded toward the trailhead. "Brownsville Rock trail."

They continued their conversation as they hiked. "I thought you were Catholic. Was this a Catholic thing?"

"No. No. it's a Swiss farmer thing. Nothing to do with being Catholic."

Conversation slowed as their respiration rate increased. They started out on a wagon trail but it grew steeper as they climbed. The wagon trail led to an old stone quarry where they stopped to rest.

After they caught their breath, she said, "We're almost there. Come on. Let's go."

"How do you know we're almost there?"

"Ginnie and Anna and I hike this trail now and then."

He looked surprised.

"Yeah. We do. While you're playing in the barn. Come on."

She held out her hand to help him up. He jumped to his feet on his own and was going to chase her, but he wouldn't have a chance. The trail ended at an old stone foundation next to a large rock outcropping. Brownsville Rock.

"Wow. Wouldn't you like to know about this house?" He examined the foundation. She went out on the rock to enjoy the vista. He eventually joined her.

"Some view, isn't it?"

He agreed.

"That's Brownsville down there."

They sat and took in the mountain panorama for some time.

"Okay. You ready to do this?"

"Do what?"

"The Betruf prayer thing."

He looked at her and said, "You go first. You're my leader."

She walked out onto the outcropping as far as she could safely go, looked back to him and smiled. Turning back she looked down the valley, cupped her hands and yelled, "Our Father who art in heaven, please be with our friends and neighbors who are being forced off their land. Keep them safe and well and help them through this very trying time in their lives. Be with them and bless them. In Jesus name, Amen."

It was more a singsong shout than a chant, but he was impressed with how lovely it was. She watched as the words floated out to the valley, then she looked back.

"Your turn."

He was nervous. She could tell he had no idea what to say.

"The words will come. Go for it."

At the edge of the outcropping he paused to think. He cupped his hands, but then looked back at her. Aud just nodded her head. He turned back towards the valley below.

"Lord, I agree with Aud. Please help those losing their homes and their farms. God bless them. Amen."

He walked back. "I wasn't very good. I've never done this before."

She took his arm. "Me neither. You were great."

"What do you mean you've never done this before? I thought you did it as a kid in Switzerland all the time."

'No. No. I heard it all the time when we were hiking in the mountains. I never did it, really."

They started back towards the trail.

"Sometimes you'd hear the herders yodel. You can really hear the yodel bounce around the mountains. That was amazing."

"Can you yodel?"

"Sort of. Everyone who is Swiss thinks they can yodel, but it's not easy."

"Yodel for me."

"No. You yodel for me."

"Not allowed." He was following her down the trail. "I'm Methodist. Methodists aren't allowed to yodel."

She looked at him with a big grin.

"It's a rule." They continued downhill. "But you're Swiss. Come on. Let me hear you yodel."

She walked ahead of him, obviously thinking about it. "Okay. Okay. But if you laugh at me, I'll come back there and punch you." She regrouped. "Yodel oh ee dee. Diddly odel oh ee dee." She did a second verse, same as the first. "Yodel lay ee dee. Diddy odel oh se dee."

"Bravo, frau Cairns. Bravo." He applauded. She turned and smiled. "I love you, my little fraulein."

"I love you too, Norman. Even if you are Methodist."

She hiked on.

"That's good. You are the mother of my children, you know."

He followed behind. "I sure hope that water pump by the car works."

Chapter 11

CHANGED FOREVER

Thursday, November 21, 1963

Washington D.C. – *President Kennedy and his wife Jacqueline Kennedy departed the White House on the Marine One helicopter, and then flew to San Antonio, Texas on Air Force One to begin a three-day speaking and fund raising tour. The Kennedys then traveled by motorcade through San Antonio where he dedicated the USAF School of Aerospace Medicine at Brooks Air Force Base. Speeches are set for tomorrow in Fort Worth, Dallas and Austin.*

The November days were getting shorter and there was a chill in the air. The cold, dark reality of eminent domain and its consequences was setting into the community. Norman was concerned about his friends who were facing eviction. He was especially concerned about Rayland. He had not found his footing yet. No path forward. The morning chores were done. He and Aud were relaxing and having a late morning coffee together. She's as pretty as the day I met her, he thought.

She looked at him and smiled. "Are you thinking naughty thoughts, Norman?

"Aud. You should be embarrassed. Never." He sipped his coffee. "Not at the moment is what I meant."

She smiled again.

"I'm going to do some sewing. If you need anything repaired, go get it for me."

"I'm good. I'll be out in the barn. Lunch at one?"

He finished his coffee, gave her a kiss on the cheek, and headed out the door.

The morning milking operation was over. Norman was overseeing the cleanup. Jeep drove into the long driveway like he did almost every day, but today he was late, and he was troubled.

"Norman, I hope you've got a minute. I'm really concerned about Rayland."

Jeep was nervously punching his right fist into his left palm like a ball player might do with a ball and glove.

"I spent a bunch of time with him this morning. I felt like I was trying to talk him in off the edge of a cliff, if you know what I mean."

"No, Jeep. I don't think I do know what you mean."

"Ever since that eviction notice, he's been different. I show up with the mail, and I can tell he isn't like his old self. Sometimes I don't know where he is. Can't find him. That's not like him. Usually he's in that barn holding court."

He put Norm's mail on the workbench.

"I'm not a farmer, but I can tell those cows are in a pissy mood. Mooing and butting each other. That's not like them either. Can't tell if they aren't getting fed or not getting milked regularly. Just can't tell, not knowing."

He banged his fist into his palm again.

"Most days I don't know where he is. In bed? Hiding? I don't know."

He lit a cigarette and offered one to Norm who declined.

"When I do catch up with him, he's so flummoxed he doesn't know whether to check his ass or scratch his watch. He just can't seem to function. Today I did find him in the barn, and I tried to talk to him. Put a good face on things, you know? But he's not talking much. I hope he's listening. He's sure not talking. It's hard to say what's going on. Know what I mean?"

"I think so. Aud and I were over to his place the other day. Thought we could cheer him up some. Humph. That was wishful thinking." He looked at Jeep. "Damn. I just don't know what to do, Jeep."

Norman picked a used rag up off the floor.

"If we can help him focus on going forward, maybe we can get him thinking about the future rather than the past. He'll be all right, but we need a plan. We tried to get him thinking about the future. Get him to realize there are other options in life. We need a plan. Something."

"Yeah. I think so. I think so, too. I think you're right."

Jeep's lips tightened across his front teeth. He was anxious. Rayland was not a complex man and Jeep knew it. He and that farm were one and the same. Jeep started to elaborate his concern when the house screen door slammed and they looked up.

Aud called out in a very distressed voice, "Norman, Norman." She ran to the barn. "Come quickly. President Kennedy has been shot. Oh God. It's awful. He was driving in some motorcade when somebody shot him. I don't know if he's dead or not. There was just pandemonium."

Grabbing Norman by the arm, she repeated, "Come. Come. This is terrible."

They all took off toward the house. The TV was on and playing for no one. *As The World Turns* had been interrupted for the emergency broadcast. They stood in front of the set and could see the confusion and emergency playing out on the little screen. Spectators, who had waited to see the president were running. People were crying. Some were hugging one another. Replays of the parade and the shots fired were being shown again and again so people could see first-hand what they had missed.

"This is Walter Cronkite in our newsroom, and there has been an attempt, as perhaps you know, on the life of President Kennedy. He was wounded in an automobile driving from the Dallas Airport to downtown Dallas, along with Gov. Connally of Texas and the First Lady. They've been taken to Parkland Hospital where their condition is yet unknown."

"Oh my God. Oh my God. This is terrible," Aud cried out.

"We can report that President Kennedy has been taken into surgery. Kennedy was apparently shot in the head. He fell face down in the back seat of his car. Blood was seen on his head. Mrs. Kennedy cried, 'Oh no!' and tried to hold his head. Governor Connally remained half-seated, slumping to the left. There was blood on his face and forehead. We have nothing further now, but we will pass on information as it is received."

The three watched together for a long time, until Walter Cronkite, his emotions apparent, announced, "The president was pronounced dead at 2 p.m. Eastern Time."

"Oh my God," Aud sobbed. "Oh my God."

"Vice President Johnson has left the hospital and has gone to an unknown location, where it is assumed he will shortly take the oath of office as the president of the United States."

"Come on," Norman commanded. "Come on. We have to go to town and see what's going on. We need to check with the others and see how they're doing. This just doesn't seem to be a time to be alone. Let's see what we can find out. Jeep, we'll meet you at the post office. I'll swing by and pick up Rayland. I imagine he doesn't know what's going on at all. He turned and asked, 'Ready, Aud?'"

"No. Let me change this dirty apron. I'll hurry. I promise."

He pulled the truck up to the front of the house and Aud jumped in.

Ten minutes later they were hurrying into town. In the frenzy of the moment, they forgot Rayland. They also forgot Jeep. Tanner's general store seemed to be where the people were gathering. At least eight trucks were in the parking lot along with several cars. Jeep had figured things out on his own. He had a front row standing spot by Tanner's tiny TV set near the coffee and donuts in the rear of the store. A group was gathered around the TV as best they could. Walter Cronkite continued. His voice was soothing, but it was not a soothing broadcast.

"We just got word that Lyndon B. Johnson has been sworn in as the president of the United States. He was sworn in a 2:38 Eastern Standard Time. The oath was administered to him by U.S. District Judge Sarah T. Hughes."

Totally absorbed in the broadcast, Norman finally remembered that he'd forgotten Rayland.

"Aud, we forgot to pick up Rayland."

Anna Jaffe overheard the conversation that followed and offered, "Norman, I need to get out of here. I need some fresh air. It's a good day for a drive with a prayer thrown in for good measure along the way. I'll go get Rayland. Does he know you're coming?"

"Rayland never knows you're coming until you get there. But he should be there. Thanks, Anna." Off she went.

"President Johnson has sent a message to the country. I quote 'We have suffered a loss that cannot be weighed. I know the world shares the sorrows that Mrs. Kennedy and her family bear.'"

Anna tried to organize her curly ringlets under a bandana as she hurried from the car, through the barn and to the house. When she arrived at the door, she simultaneously knocked and entered. Rayland was seated with Star at his feet. He looked up from staring at the stove.

"Hi Rayland. What ya doing?"

"Not doing much, Anna. What brings you by?"

"Rayland, this is kind of hard to explain quickly, but President Kennedy has been assassinated."

She had no idea what kind of a reaction to expect, but she sure didn't expect the one she got. Nothing. She repeated the sad news: "President Kennedy was killed today while driving in a motorcade."

He looked confused. "Who did it?"

"We don't know yet. Everyone in town is very upset. They're hanging out at the General watching Tanner's TV. We thought you'd like to be there. They sent me to pick you up."

"I was down at the store getting supplies yesterday. I really don't need anything." He shifted forward and put another stick of hard wood in the firebox.

"No. No Rayland." She smiled. "No. You're missing something." She stepped in front of him. "Look at me. Look at me, Rayland. We want you to come to the store to be with us. You." She pointed. "Us." She pointed to herself with both thumbs. "We want you to come along and be with us. Misery loves company. We want to all be together. We need to cheer each other up and hold on to each other. Especially during tough times. People are really upset."

She zipped her jacket.

"Come on, Rayland. We want you there. You're part of us, too."

"I'm pretty busy, Anna. Afraid I can't join you."

"Damn it, Rayland, get in the truck. We're going to town."

He shifted in his chair.

"I haven't finished milking yet. I've got to take care of my cows."

"Rayland, for crying out loud, it's after 2 o'clock. You haven't finished milking yet?"

"Actually," he paused, "I haven't started."

"Damn it, Rayland. You know what happens to cows if they don't get milked regularly. Come on. Grab your jacket. Let's do it."

She picked up his barn jacket and tossed it into his lap.

"I can milk too you know. Come on."

Rayland stood and slowly put the coat on. As they entered the barn, the cows all looked up as if to ask Rayland where the heck he'd been.

Anna threw her coat over a half door to the bedding area. "I've got to have a stool, Rayland. I'm good, but I can't do this standing up." He got the other milking stool for her. Being as familiar as Rayland with the underside of a cow, they were milking within minutes.

Shinggg Shinggg Shinggg Shinggg

He couldn't help but notice the skill and experience with which she approached the job. Rayland had a flashback to when his brothers were still on the farm. Before Pa died, he and Greg and Jeremy used to hold the Milking Olympics. Who's the fastest? Who's the best with just one hand? Who could knock over a tin can and squirt it across the barn floor to the wall the quickest? He recalled that he was pretty good at that. He also recalled that Pa didn't take to the messing around so much. He'd usually just go find something else to do. After he died, we all grew up a bit, he thought. The Milking Olympics kind of died out. Rayland looked across at Anna and came back to the present.

"You're pretty good at this, Anna."

"Pinch and squeeze, Rayland. Pinch and squeeze. Just like getting tooth paste out of a tube." She had a nice milking rhythm. "How many of these cows did I help bring into the world?"

"Don't know for sure. Quite a few, I guess."

"Which one is the one who wanted to come out upside down and backwards?"

"That's Ida Mae. Two down the line. Big white marking on her flank."

"Hello, Ida Mae." She smiled and waved to the cow. "Damn, Rayland. That calf was a tough one." She looked down the line again. "We used so much petroleum jelly, we could have both gone up in there and gotten her. I had that stuff on my clothes, in my hair, in my ears, everywhere."

Shinggg   Shinggg   Shinggg   Shinggg

"What happened to the milking machine Norman gave you?"

"It's over there. In those boxes."

"Oh, that will help you a lot. Are you waiting for the boxes to rush over here and hook the cows up?"

The milking continued until Rayland said, "You mad at me, Anna?"

"Rayland, why in the world would I be mad at you?"

"Cause of what I told Preston at the party this summer."

"Ah hell, Rayland. Preston just likes to blat off a bit. That's all that was. He's not mad at you or anybody else."

"He told me and Otto that we were like old ladies clutching our pearls."

"He said that?" She shook her head and laughed. "That's a good one. Dag gone, that's a good one." She chuckled. "He throws out his old school bromides all the time. He thinks they're funny." She continued milking. "Dag gone. That's a good one, though."

Shinggg Shinggg Shinggg Shinggg

"He doesn't mean any harm. He just sees everything as progress and progress, to him, is all good. He has no clue that some of us like things a little more simple than folks in Boston." She pinched and squeezed. "He's pretty lovable once you get to know him."

"Hmm."

Shinggg Shinggg Shinggg Shinggg

The milking went quickly with four experienced hands working. Soon they were wrapping things up for the afternoon. Rayland headed back to the house.

"Come on. Let's go down to the General. Come on, Rayland. They sent me to get you. I'm not going back empty-handed." She shook her head in desperation. "Hell, Rayland. All we're trying to do is get you off the dime. Get you back into things."

She put her jacket back on.

"We know you were dealt a bad hand, but damn it, you still have to play it. You can't just sit here and mope."

Try as she may, she could not get Rayland into the truck. He didn't seem to care about President Kennedy. He didn't seem to care about his friends. He didn't seem to care about his cows. Well, maybe the cows. But not like normal.

Anna headed back to the store sad about too many things. The crowd had thinned by the time she got there.

"Where's Rayland?" Norm asked.

"Ah hell, Norman. He's lost in the weeds."

She opened Tanner's cooler and pulled out a Schlitz.

"He's irritable, and remote, and not at all like the Rayland Jensen I know."

She opened the can and took a healthy sip.

"He said to me 'The days go by, I get nothing done, and I don't know where the day went.' You tell me, is that like Rayland?"

She took another sip.

"He looks like he could use a bath and a good meal. He's just sitting there with his cows. This isn't right. This isn't healthy."

Anna took a big gulp of her beer, looked up and belched. That was followed by a rosy-cheeked grin.

"Sorry, Norman." She wiped her lips. "I've had a bad day."

"Yeah. We all have."

He gathered his thoughts.

"The assassination of our president. The mess our neighbors are facing. They're worlds apart. Worlds apart, but they both..." He struggled to come up with the right words. "They both tear me up. They both hurt something awful."

Chapter 12

DARK DAYS OF FEBUARY

Monday – February 10, 1964

New York City – *The Beatles appeared on the Ed Sullivan Show at 9 p.m. in New York City last night, marking their first live performance on American television. According to an AP report, "The 721 members of the audience, mostly young girls, kept up a steady stream of squeals, sighs and yells." The show also featured Welsh stage actress Two Ton Tessie O'Shea in between The Beatles' two performances. A.C. Nielsen Company reported that the show was seen by over 70 million people.*

It had become Jeep's habit to check Rayland's barn first to be sure that the cows were being attended to. He was the information officer for the town folk on how Rayland was doing. He passed through the barn and took the mail into the ell.

"Hello fellas." The door banged behind him as he acknowledged the dogs. "Where's Rayland?"

"I'm here, Jeep." The voice came from the stairwell.

Jeep crossed the small kitchen and looked up the stairway. "Holy cow, Rayland. What are you doing up there?"

Rayland sat three quarters of the way up the stairway that lead to his bedroom. It was narrow and steep. Narrow enough that his shoulders almost touched both walls. His feet rested two steps below where he sat. It looked to Jeep as if he had just taken his head out of his hands.

"I don't know, Jeep. I like the darkness, I guess. I'm not scared when I sit here." Rayland took a deep breath and exhaled slowly. "Aud taught me that. It calms me down some." He did it again. "It's easier up here."

"Rayland. Rayland, we've got to get you some help. Someone to talk to."

"I talk to you, Jeep. Just about every day."

"I know. I know, but I'm not a shrink. I don't know how to help you. I don't even know what to talk to you about." He extended a hand to help Rayland get up and come down the stairs. "Rayland, you worry me, my friend."

He stayed for a while and talked to Rayland. It was a one-way conversation. He talked; Rayland listened. Maybe. He couldn't tell.

"Rayland, I've got to get this mail delivered, but if I see Kate, I'm going to tell her to come by to see how you're doing. You need someone to talk to, and she's pretty smart. I don't know if she can help or not, but it sure won't hurt."

"Yeah." he mumbled. "I'm always sad, Jeep. I'm sad about losing the farm. Other than the Army, I've never slept any place else in my entire life." He shook his head. "I've got to figure out something. But what?"

Jeep tried to console him. "You've got a hard row to hoe, Rayland. Sorry I don't have more time, but I've got to skedaddle. Got to finish my rounds." He put his toque back on against the cold. "But if I see Kate ... Okay? Okay, Rayland?"

He nodded. Rayland nodded back.

Rayland watched Jeep leave then turned to the dogs lying on the floor. "Star, I don't want to see Kate right now. I don't want her to see me like this. She already thinks I'm, what did she call it? Quirky. Yeah, quirky. She sees me like this and she'll think I'm a full blown nut job."

He looked in the icebox for something to eat. Nothing. He settled for two old biscuits. "I'm not a nut job, Star."

He looked at the dog as if waiting for an answer.

"Am I?"

He gave Star half a biscuit and Champ got a half. He ate the other.

"I'm just worried sick about our farm. About you guys. And the cows and the horses. Worried sick."

A bit foggy and not paying attention, he stood and almost tripped over the dogs. A quick side step left him standing in front of the door to the main house. He looked at it as if he'd never seen it before. Since his mother died six years previously, he hadn't been through that door more than a dozen times. His nieces and nephews would sneak into the parlor on occasion, but he always thought of it as Ma's room. For some reason, this time he slowly reached for the doorknob.

He opened the door, and he stood and looked in. It was just like always, a good-sized room, once well appointed. Now most of the furniture was covered with bed sheets. It was practical furniture, basic side tables with skinny legs, and a few straight-back chairs. There was a small china hutch in the corner with a blue water pitcher and a few plates. The armchair and the sofa were covered, but he knew what they looked like. Under the window, a window seat with cushions presented itself in the sun. Next to it stood a high backed secretary desk with a dropdown writing leaf. That's where he had learned to read. There were a few kerosene lamps, knick-knacks scattered about, and an ornate mirror on the wall. Other than being dusty, everything was in order.

It was surprisingly easy to step inside. He stood and took in the entirety of this old family room. He walked to the couch, and looked carefully at it. Slowly, he reached down and picked up the edge of the sheet. After pausing, pausing as if he might find something haunting, he pulled the sheet off the couch and let it drop to the floor.

He stood and looked at it for the longest time. Then he said, "Hello, Ma."

He tried to swallow but his mouth was dry.

"It's me, Rayland. Your couch is still as pretty as ever."

He touched the couch and ran his fingers along the flowered fabric.

"I remember as kids, you wouldn't let us sit on it unless we were wearing our Sunday best. 'Don't you get my couch dirty. No cow poop pants on my couch.' The couch looks good. I guess your plan paid off."

It was truly her couch. When she was sick and dying, she wanted to be on the couch. Her blankets were still neatly stacked on the backrest. Being on the couch, she could avoid the stairs and be with the family during meals, even if she couldn't eat. The family could hear when her coughing got loud and uncontrollable, and they could do their best to comfort her.

After she died, her daughters dressed her and laid her out on that same couch. She laid there until the undertaker picked her up to get her ready for burial.

"I remember that, Ma. You looked beautiful. The girls really fussed. They put your finest dress on you, and they fixed your hair. You looked beautiful, Ma."

He started to move on, but stopped.

"You *were* beautiful, Ma. In so many ways. The way you took care of all of us. Fed us. Taught us. Loved us. Taught us to love each other. You were beautiful, Ma."

He again started to walk away, but returned.

"I'm having such a hard time of things right now, Ma. I wish you were here to talk to."

He sat in a chair across from the couch.

"I'm in a mess. I don't know how I got in such a mess."

He took off his hat as if he might have been disrespectful in wearing it.

"They tell me I'm going to lose the farm. They're going to knock it down and put a highway right through our property."

He hung his head.

"Oh, Ma, I'm so sorry."

He sat for a long moment.

"I remember Pa telling me he walked here all the way from New York. He had a mule, a horse, and a new wife. That was you, Ma. And he had a dream. Clear these fields, divert the streams, and build a home. I don't know what I did to deserve this."

He buried his face in his hat and cried. He cried for some time.

"The state is going to take everything away from me. Everything. They're going to give me $10,400 for the whole farm." He shook his head. "They tell me that's a fair price. I don't know. I don't know."

He sat and thought about what to say next.

"Even if it is a fair price, it isn't much to spread among us who built this place. Divide that by the nine of us, and what do we get? Not much. Hard to find another farm on what's left. After you died and Gregory moved on, I guess I couldn't do enough with the farm, working all alone and all, to make it worth saving. Working alone didn't matter to me. In fact, I liked it. I like the solitude. I could set my own routine and not worry about things. I never was much for planning about the future. Just take it as it comes. But now, I feel like the future is coming after me. Chasing me. It won't leave me alone.

"This old farm was always worth saving to me. Always. I love every inch of it. But it isn't worth saving to the state. Not enough value in the eyes of the big shots who decide these things."

He swallowed hard.

"I'm sorry, Ma. I'm so sorry."

After a long pause, he regained some composure. "You remember Norman, Ma? He built-up his farm really nice. Nice enough that the state swerved the road around most of his place. Maybe they thought I was just lollygagging in the barn, but they don't plan to swerve around us. No sir. No swerving around the Jensen farm. They're planning to plow it under. Plow it back to dirt so they can build a road." He sighed. "I'm sorry, Ma."

Rayland gathered himself and walked around the room looking closely at everything. It brought back so many memories. This was the family room. If they were in this room they were together. Sometimes learning. Sometimes playing card games or working on a puzzle. Sometimes reading. Meals, especially the dinner meals, were where the family did their talking and solved their problems. The family room was where they took a rare break from the daily chores and enjoyed each other.

When he got to the desk, he stopped again and looked. The old drop leaf was raised and locked. The skeleton key was always in the keyhole at the top. If it was Ma's couch, it was even more Ma's desk. When she had a few free minutes, which wasn't often, this is where she sat and did her Ma chores, she called them. He wanted to open the desk, but couldn't muster up the courage. Maybe he was afraid of the memories he'd find once the desk chamber opened.

Walking back to the couch he asked, "Ma, can I open your desk?"

With no answer forthcoming, he took it as a sign that it was okay to open it. Rayland walked back to the desk and sat.

In front of him was a smooth panel of maple that he knew would fold out to become the writing surface. Next to the desk was a straight back cushioned chair where he'd sat many times during lessons. He couldn't bring himself to reach for the key. He looked back toward the couch hoping Ma would say to go on and open it. But she didn't. He knew he should forge ahead.

Finally he reached for the key. Reached as if it might blow-up in his hand. When he turned the key to open the desk, the key simply spun in its hole. At first confused, he quickly realized the lock was broken and the desk was not locked at all. It had probably never been locked.

Ma always told us not to open the lock on her desk. It was never locked. He laughed at himself. He laughed with his mother. He laughed at his brothers and sisters. He hadn't laughed in months. He laughed himself from happy back to remembering how much he loved his family. Then he sat there saddened again with a deep melancholy eating at him from the insides.

"Oh, Ma, we were lucky to have you and to have each other. I've been a lucky man, Ma. Thanks to you."

He pulled gently on the key using it like a small handle. It was as if he were opening a vault. Slowly the desk opened. He peered over the top to see what lay inside. When it appeared that it was indeed okay to proceed, he lowered the writing platform to parallel. There before him, on the right, were pigeonholes. They held notes and letters. Three small drawers on the left. In the center, there was room for a few books. *The Tale of Peter Rabbit, King Arthur and His Knights of the Round Table*, a family Bible along with loose photographs and odds and ends. He ran his finger along the spine of each book.

"This is where I learned to read, Ma. You taught us all."

He ran his fingers over the book. “School was okay, but I learned more here with you and the others. The funniest part of school was walking there with everyone. You wouldn’t believe the trouble we could get into.” He picked up a book and looked at it. “I didn’t like taking that bus later on. When Pa died, I quit. I remember that day. I walked into the icehouse and saw him laid out on the ice all blue and stiff. That was awful. Blue and stiff. I never forgot. I was twelve. That’s the day I really became a farmer.”

He sat remembering Pa. Then he smile and almost chuckled.

“Gregory and I always wanted Pa to take us to deer camp. Remember that, Ma? Go hunting like the other kids did with their Pa. Well, you know, we knew that Pa didn’t have a deer camp. Heck. Pa didn’t even hunt. Finally, after we pestered him enough, he promised to take us to his special deer camp. Remember? One afternoon, probably in November, the three of us went out to the barn around dusk. Rifles loaded, we sat there.”

He smiled at the memory.

“As it got darker, just like Pa knew they’d do, the deer came down to dig for apples under the snow. Pa says to Greg, ‘Okay. See that buck out on the edge? That’s the one you want.’ Pa could see that Greg was eyeing the buck. ‘Your shot. I think you’re only going to get one.’ Greg was nervous. I watched him. I could tell. He was nervous.”

Rayland could not help but smile at the memory.

“Bang! That deer went down hard. We hooted and yelled and banged each other on the back. ‘He got him, Pa. He got him. Great shot, Greg.’” He stopped to enjoy the happy memory. “We gutted that ole deer and hung him from the maple tree out front so he could bleed out. Really, it was so our friends could see that Greg and me had indeed been to deer comp."

He thumbed through the old photos squeezed between the books. Everyone was so young; it was hard to tell who was who. He picked up the Peter Rabbit book. "When we were little, this was the book you'd read to us. When we were old enough, we'd read to you."

He put the book back, and pulled out *Knights of the Round Table.*

"This was my favorite. King Arthur and all those adventures. All those knights. My favorite was Galahad. The chosen one. I loved that story. Even more, I loved sitting with you and reading together. Emory liked it too."

He opened the book.

"I see Emory a lot, Ma. He's well. His kids are nice young folks, too. I'll show him the book."

He turned the pages as if looking for a familiar tale.

"Actually, I haven't seen Em much at all since they told me I've got to vacate the farm. Embarrassed, I guess. I can't even look him in the eye. He and Alina said they'd take me in, but I slept with his feet in my face for too long when we were kids. I'm not going to put my burden on them. It wouldn't be fair to him and Alina."

He slid the book back into its space and sat quietly.

"I thought about really changing things, Ma. I thought I might ask Kathleen to marry me."

He lightly scratched his brow.

"But, that wouldn't be fair to her. I'm an old Yankee farmer set in my ways. I've done things my own way for a long time. A long time. It wouldn't be fair to her."

Turning toward the couch, he said, "Heck, Ma. It wouldn't be fair to me. I'm not much for conforming to rules or routines. I love being with her, but I also love being able to walk off and do my own thing. I'd drive her nuts. As lovely as she is, I want my freedom. Besides, Ma, I'm not leaving."

A familiar little music box sat in the corner of the old desk. He slid it toward himself.

"I remember this, too. I think you told me Pa gave it to you when you were married. I know you loved to play it, but I never saw you play it just once. You'd sit alone and play it two or three times. It was a beautiful tune. Soft, slow, soothing and relaxing."

He picked it up and looked at the name on the side.

"Claire de Lune. I'm glad they wrote that on the side here. I don't think I'd have remembered. Can I play it, Ma?"

Slowly he cranked the little, delicate handle. The notes still rang true. Soft and pretty. Just like he remembered. The melancholy he felt was painful.

"What am I going to do, Ma? Where am I going to go?"

He sat staring at the little music box.

"Everyone I love was born on this farm. Now, I'm the only one left and they want to throw me off. It's like somebody wants to put me in a box and take me away. They want to get rid of me. So much is gone. So much is gone. It seems everywhere I turn, I end up in that box. I don't belong in a box. I'd die in a box."

He slowly cranked the little handle again and listened.

"Emory will take me in. I can't live in the city. I'd die." He slid the music box back into the corner. "Preston keeps telling me to buy a trailer and retire. I'd die in a trailer. A trailer is a box, for sure. I could work and live with Norman, but, Ma, I've never worked for anyone. Except maybe the cows. Where do I fit in on a modern farm? Reading temperature gauges and operating chilling tanks? That's not me."

The staring continued.

"Everywhere I turn, I'm in a box. I die in a box."

Rayland put his face in his hands and sat still while a great despair set in. He had no idea how long he sat at the desk when he heard shuffling from back in the ell. He looked up to see Kathleen and Star standing in the doorway.

She asked from outside the doorway, “Are you alright, Rayland?”

“I don’t know, Kathleen. Yeah. I think I’m okay.” He started to close the desk. “Come in. It’s okay. Come in.”

“I don’t think so. Not yet. This is a special place. I can tell.”

Standing at the threshold wagging his tail, Star seemed to know the limitations too. “I’ll get Star something to eat. Join us when you’re ready.”

Rayland entered the ell and closed the door behind him. Star realized that regular routines were no longer regular. “How long have I been in there?” he asked as Star approached Rayland for a long overdue scratch.

“I have no idea,” Kate answered, knowing the question was not for her. She added, “But your fire is almost out. It must have been a long time.” She put wood chips on the embers to get it started again. She zipped up her cardigan and hugged her shoulders against the chill. “Brr. I’ll get some wood.” She stepped out to the wood box on the porch and came right back.

“I remember I was talking to Jeep. Then, I went in.”

“You’ve been in there a long time, I’d guess.” She put a small log on the fire. “That room’s a special place, isn’t it?”

“Yeah.” He gave a thoughtful pause. “Lots of memories.”

“Why don’t you use it more often?”

“I don’t know. Seems like the only time I go in there is to chase nieces and nephews out.”

“Memories don’t need to be locked up. Memories are things that make our lives rich.”

Rayland sat at the table. "I'm not doing so good, Kathleen. I've never been in this place before." He sat and looked at her. "I like every bit of the past. The memories and things. I like the past, but I was never one to cling to it. I always looked forward to today. The chores. The animals. The natural order of things. Now I cling to the past. Today and the next today only make me sad. And afraid."

She noticed that he seemed to be without energy. Without vigor.. There was a sadness where before there had been so much more. He still had his gentle way, but his eyes were sad. The drip of water in the sink and the flicking of the fire were the only sounds to be heard.

"I have a colleague, Rayland; she serves on a board that directs health care. I'd like you to talk to her." She watched him recoil. She could tell her offer didn't set well. "Just talk to her." Kathleen scratched her forehead with her pointer finger as she had a habit of doing when she was concerned.

"She might be able to give you some ideas on how to cope with what you're going through. She works with others who are going through the same thing. The same kind of loss."

"I don't need another shrink?"

"Another?"

"Jeep is my shrink."

They both smiled. Then laughed.

"I know that Jeep means well, and Norman means well, and everybody means well, but maybe someone who has dealt with this situation before could be of more help. You aren't the only one going through this, you know. We can name seven or eight others right here in town. It's a shared difficulty. My friend understands the situation better than most."

Kathleen was starting to sound like the school principle that she was.

"Knows what situation? Eviction? Getting thrown off my family farm?"

"I know you don't trust anyone right now. I know that, and I understand, but maybe she can help you."

Silence.

"Will you do this for me Rayland?"

No answer.

"Okay, Rayland Jensen. Here's what I want you to do. Tomorrow, I want you to get up and show up. Get up and take care of your animals. Get up, and get up early. Wash your clothes. Wash your hair. Clean up this kitchen. Take care of your animals. Show up."

She looked at him.

"And, I want you to think about letting someone help you. That's all. Think about allowing someone to help you."

She crossed her arms.

"I'll tell you what. If you'll promise to do that, I'll come back tomorrow afternoon with supper, and we can talk. Talk about anything you'd like to talk about."

She let that sink in.

"Deal?"

He shrugged agreement.

Chapter 13

TOWN MEETING

Tuesday - March 3, 1964

New York City – *The Dow Jones Industrial Average passed the 800 mark on Friday for the first time. In the last hour of what had been hectic trading, the Dow hit and closed at 800.14 points.*

March is a month of change. Early March can drop three feet of heavy snow on you. Late March can find the kids running under the sprinkler in the back yard. Or, it can again drop three feet of snow on you. The days do get longer. March always shows off several stretches of high-pressure bluebird days. The landscape is spotted with snow here but grass there. Snow banks are rock hard and dirty. Drippings from the eaves add to the melt runoff that gurgles aloud by mid-afternoon. By the next morning, the runoff might be frozen solid again. Sap runs the same way. Sap buckets seem to sprout overnight. The wood lots fill with them. Sap buckets line the roads. The maple trees in the front of the houses have at least one. This is maple syrup country.

During springtime in Vermont, you can rely on snow melting, maple sap flowing and the convening of town meeting. Towns around the state gather on the first Tuesday of the month to honor the essence of democracy. They gather in churches, school gyms, community centers, theaters, grange halls, town offices, firehouses, or municipal buildings, if they have one. The citizens do the town business. They elect municipal officers, approve budgets, and conduct the business of the community. The town comes together to legislate and decide.

The first order of business is electing a moderator to a one-year term. The moderator will review the warrant, decide questions of order, make a public declaration of each vote passed and oversee the proceedings. The warrant is available to the community in advance. There is an element of social attached to anything that brings people together after a long winter, so people arrive early. The Ladies of the Green serve coffee and breakfast cake in the hall that leads to the gym. Voting for state or national primaries takes place in the hall as well.

Rayland entered the gym and noticed the American flag on the right, the state flag on the left, and Kathleen sitting on the far side of the room. She was talking with a well-dressed woman in a beige suit, hair in a bun and glasses. That's the consultant she wants me to meet, he thought, unsure of what was to happen next. Kathleen calls her a consultant, but she's a shrink, he thought. Probably not much different than Jeep.

Kathleen caught his eye and signaled for him to join her. He walked in her directions and thought I can blow off the shrink, but I can't blow off Kathleen. He went to say hello, stopping to chat with friends along the way.

She had on a Norwegian sweater with a snowflake pattern. The colors accentuated her auburn hair. "Hello, Kathleen," he said, keeping his voice even. "This must be the friend you want me to meet."

"Rayland, this is Dr. Doris Buckman. Doris, my friend Rayland Jensen."

"Hello, Rayland, so nice to meet you. Kate has told me about the unfortunate circumstances the state has put you in. I'm sorry."

"Me, too."

"Perhaps the three of us can have lunch together after the meeting and talk." The thought went through Rayland's head: That's a great idea. Lunch with the whole town listening in. Why don't we make an announcement? Rayland Jensen is losing his farm .... and his marbles ... and I'm here to help.

Kate, ever hopeful, asked "Want to sit with us, Rayland?"

"No. I want to say hello to my farmer friends. Didn't see much of them this winter." Turning to Dr. Buckman, he added, "Nice to meet you, doctor."

"And you, Rayland. I'll look forward to our conversation."

He joined his friends gathered in the back drinking coffee, eating cake and catching up on milk prices and other local news. No one was in a hurry for the meeting to begin.

A small podium was placed near the flag. Were it on the stage, the basketball backboard would block the view of some in the audience. The select board sat to the left at a table cluttered with papers, reports and coffee cups. At 9 sharp, Thomas Lumfield called the meeting to order.

Rules and procedures were reviewed. There were a few introductions. A moment of silence was held for those who had died the previous year. The meeting usually ground to a slow and boring start with various office slots being filled. Nominate. Second? All in favor, and so forth. Once that was out of the way, budgets took center stage.

"To see if the town will appropriate..." this much for road repair, so much for a new plough blade for the town truck, money for a necessary culvert near the school, and so forth. Article 18 appeared to be interesting. "To see if the Town will appropriate $5,000 to study adding a bathroom to the town library?"

Freddie Lumfield was called upon to explain #18. She was head of the library board. "Well," she cleared her throat and gave the gathering her biggest smile, "the town has owned, maintained and run the library since 1910. That's when the Crossfield house was given to us by the family. They specified that it be used as a library. It's been in operation ever since." She smiled again and made eye contact with her audience. "We operate five days a week using all volunteer librarians. The house, and now the library, has never had a bathroom."

"Point of order." Nothing was going to get past Everett Thompson. He stood and slowly took hold of his overall straps, puffing out his chest. "Are you saying it needs a room for bathing?"

"No Everett. It has never had a toilet." You could tell from the shifting in their seats that this was going to be more interesting than appropriations for a new culvert. "While we have gotten along for fifty years without a toilet, this has made it very difficult for the volunteers and some of the patrons."

"How do you plan to put a toilet into that old house?" Everett asked.

"The first step is to study our options. That's what Article 18 calls for. We want to allocate some money for the study."

"What do they do now?" he continued before sitting down.

Her smile faded as she was getting annoyed. "They run across the bridge and go in the town office." Ad libs and offhand comments were plentiful, most from the back of the room.

Everett got back on his feet. "Five thousand bucks to study if going next door works or not?" He raised his hands as if exasperated. "How many hours a day is the volunteer on duty?"

"Four. Four hours a day. Tuesday through Saturday."

"Well, there you go. Cut it to two hours a day." Everett suggested. "They can hold it for two hours."

From the other side of the room his wife Sara shouted, "Sit down, Everett! You sound like an idiot." Scattered laughter made its way around the gym.

"Order. Order," Tom gaveled. "Everyone has a right to speak, Sara." He raised his eyes as he spoke. "Please continue, Freddie. I can see where this could be an urgent matter." He raised his eyes again and mugged for his male counterparts.

"Well, I don't see any of you men showing up to volunteer." Freddie was frustrated.

"They'd probably just go outside and pee in the stream," someone from the back suggested.

Hoping to elevate the discussion, she said, "We have certainly brought this down to a new, low level. I want to point out that we have a very nice library. It gets good use by the adults and the students in our town. At some point, it should have a toilet. I suggest that we allocate the money requested to do a feasibility study to look into this further. Will someone so move?"

The motion was moved, seconded and defeated. Moving along quickly, Tom announced that a lunch would be served by the Ladies of the Green at the conclusion of the meeting. Everyone is invited, so please plan to stay.

"Our next item of business is of utmost importance." He shuffled his feet, and then came out from behind the podium to address the town in a more intimate way. He lowered his voice and raised his level of concern.

"This past year, we've lost friends and neighbors who were evicted from their homes and farms through eminent domain. Let's just say, eminent domain has inflicted a great pain and worry on our community. Especially on those directly affected. Seven families, our neighbors, were evicted."

"As we lose these properties from the tax roll, we must figure out how to replace the lost revenues. At the same time, the town is determined to do everything we can to help those who lost property. Aud Cairnes has been working with a committee to help folks relocate and get back on their feet. Aud, this is a good time to turn things over to you."

Aud, who'd been sitting with the other ladies, came forward. Special occasions always warranted a special dirndl. She started slowly.

"We have put together a business committee to help our neighbors who are facing eviction. We hope to help them relocate." She checked her notes. "Money has been set aside to help find jobs, or housing, or search for a new property. We can cover some expenses and some services. Tom Lumfield," she pointed, "our moderator, will do free legal work on any deeds or purchase agreements. Karl Zalewski will put in a foundation for you if you're building a new home or setting a trailer site. No charge. Thank you, Karl." She looked around, and saw only a smattering of interest.

"Kathleen Ellison has a colleague who is a grief counselor. She is with us this morning. Doris, would you stand, please?" She stood and acknowledged the gathering. "Dr. Doris Buckman is with the Department of Mental Health in Waterbury. She will make herself available for free consolations to anyone who would like to discuss the difficulties they currently face." Buckman sat back down.

"Thank you, Doctor," Aud continued. "John Hurley has been very helpful. You all know John. He will show you available land or trailer financing deals. He and Ginnie have also donated two acres for a public garden. We will plant it this spring. It's a community garden. It's your garden. It's for you. Volunteers will tend it. The produce will be free for the taking."

She sensed a bit of interest but not much enthusiasm. "I know we have a short growing season. We have a short summer in Switzerland, also, so we harvest and store lots of food for the winter. We can do that here as well. We're going to do everything we can to make this work."

The message came out kind of flat. Otto stood up and listened. He just stood there, felt Alpine hat in hand. He raised his hand. Aud, nearing the end of her presentation, stopped.

"Yes, Otto?"

"Thank you, Aud." He wrung his hat in his hands. "Thank you, everyone." His hat went from one hand to the other. He started awkwardly. "This is the best home Helma and me have ever been to. Ja, dis is the best." He was nervous. "Ven I am sixteen, they take me out of school and have me go into da war. I am soon going to Italy." He was speaking slowly. Deliberately. "Before we even get with my division, my friend Heinz and me try to steal eggs from a farm. We are so hungry. The farm is an outpost house for da Allies." He swallowed. "We are now arrested. I never steal an egg. I never fire a shot." The hat was balled up in his hands.

"I am to go to a prisoner of war camp in Idaho." He shifted from one foot to the other. "I like Idaho. Ja. I like America. I want to stay, but no. After the war, they send me back to Austria." He swallowed hard. "My town is bombed. It is burned. It is ruined. Much of Austria is like dat. Ruined." He had everyone's full attention. "I meet Helma." He looked up and smiled at her. "We work. We save our money. Finally, we have money to marry and to go back to American." He wiped his eyes with his hand. "When I arrive in New York City, they ask, 'Where are you going to live, Otto?' I don't know, so I say Idaho. My English is not so good den. They put me on a train. Helma and me get off da train in Windsor, Vermont." He smiled at his audience. "I tell Helma, dis must be Idaho." He smiled again, but the tears on his cheek were apparent. "Ve got so lucky to end up here. You become my neighbors. We are so happy here." Balling up the hat again, "But now, dis is killing us." He wiped his nose on his hat. "Dis is tearing us up. We appreciate what you are doing, but dis is killing us."

Otto stood there wringing his hat. Again, wiping his nose. His eyes were red and sad. There was silence, the kind of silence that can fill an empty school gym.

"Helma and me are going to sell our cows and return to da old country. I can work on her father's farm." He wiped his eyes. "I see my friends here who are in the same very bad situation. Trevor and Debora, Rayland, Steven and Julie, Dennis and Betty, Wayne and Paula, I know dis tears at your heart, too." He sobbed. "I'm so sorry. I'm not mad. I'm sad. I'm sorry to be leaving all this behind." His sobbing became apparent. He was losing his composure. Again, he wiped his nose on his hat. Someone handed him a handkerchief. He blew his nose.

"I'm so sorry. We must be going by June." He again shifted from one foot to another, not knowing how to continue. "Thank you for letting me and Helma be your friends. I don't want your money or your food. I just want you to be there if me or Helma want to cry or if we need a friendly hug." Another long pause. "Thank you for being my happy town."

The citizens sat in dismayed quiet. Someone started to slowly clap. Others joined in. Someone stood. They all stood and they clapped, some with tears in their eyes. It became a prolonged applause. Rayland gathered his friend and helped him back to his seat. Otto slumped forward with his face in his hands. His friends reached in to touch him, to pat his shoulder, to slap his knee, to physically extend their friendship. The room slowly returned to order.

Speaking softly, Tom came forward again. "Thank you, Otto. You and Helma will be in our thoughts and prayers. We all wish you Godspeed." He paused, took a sip of water, and checked his agenda.

"Our last item of business is to recognize and honor this year's graduating eight graders." He looked to the selectmen and shrugged his shoulders as if to say, what awful timing. "Kathleen, let's just say I'm sorry I gave you such a tough and touching story to follow." He motioned for her to come forward. "Three young eight graders have been with us this morning observing how democracy works. I'm sorry they got such a hard look at eminent domain and how it affects a community."

He shook his head, and said quietly, "If the students will please come forward."

The youngsters quietly made their way to the front and flanked Kate standing by the American flag. She announced that the town would present each student with Webster's *Third New International Dictionary.* After awarding the dictionaries, and shaking hands with the students, she wished them well in high school and told them, "Democracy can be a messy proposition at times. Your first assignment is to look up the definition of democracy in your new dictionary."

Sitting at the select board table, Norman removed his glasses and turned to Fred Schmidt. He whispered, "This experience could turn them off community service for years." The meeting was adjourned, and the ladies started setting up for lunch. The men moved outside to get some fresh air and have a smoke. Rayland joined them for a few minutes, thought about his lunch date, but then kept on going.

Chapter 14

HARD HAT – HARD HEAD

Tuesday – March 17, 1964

Reuters – *What would become known as the "domino theory" became the basis for American policy after President Johnson approved the recommendations of Secretary of Defense Robert S. McNamara. "We seek an independent non-Communist South Vietnam. Unless we can achieve this objective, almost all of Southeast Asia will probably fall under Communist dominance. It will start with South Vietnam, Laos, and Cambodia, followed by Burma and Malaysia. Thailand might hold out for a period of time. Even the Philippines would become shaky.*

"Tom-John, make sure that charge is packed in. Four feet. More if you can get it." The order came from the boss man standing near the excavator. Tom-John, a broad shouldered, slim-waisted, twenty year old, handled the long drill like it was a lightweight pole. "Tuck 'em in there all along that western face. About four feet apart."

Heavy equipment was being moved in with the precision of a military field operation. The boss man walked over to a plastic water cooler, wiped his brow, and poured himself a drink of water. Tom-John was packing the drill holes with dynamite. After several gulps, the boss looked across the dirt flats and saw the old guy standing on the edge of the rough-cut road. He was standing there watching.

When he was done packing dynamite, Tom-John came over to get a drink. The boss flicked his eyes in the direction of the stranger. "He's here again."

Tom-John looked up. "Yeah. I saw him before." He poured himself a cup of water. "Actually, he waved to me." He gulped the water, had another cupful and splashed what was left on his face to cool off. "Seems friendly enough."

"Probably one of those unlucky sons-a-bitches that's losing his land." He looked over again. "I'm going to move him back some before we blast. Be right back. Then we'll let her blow."

The boss man walked away from the excavator and toward the spectator. Tom-John stood in the shade of the big machine and watched.

"Howdy." He got a hello in return. "I'm Marty Jackson, the foreman of this section of highway." Marty extended his hand. Rayland shook his hand and offered a pleasant smile.

"Look, you can come up here and watch anytime you want, but me and the boys have one request." He looked at Rayland who seemed willing to comply. "When we blast, you've got to stand back farther. Rock flies. Man, rock flies. It's a little like a war zone for a few moments."

Rayland nodded his understanding.

"That's Tom-John." He pointed. "Keep your eye on me and Tom-John. When one of us yells 'Fire in the Hole' and the siren sounds, we're about to blow out one of these rock faces. We don't want you ending up underneath. Know what I mean?"

"Where would you like me to stand, Mr. Johnson?"

"Marty. Call me Marty." He surveyed the area for a good 'spectator' spot. Rayland noticed that Marty was almost as tall as he was. And built like him, too. Strong arms. Big hands. Might have made a good farmer, he thought.

"How about over there?" Marty pointed. "Far enough behind the tree line that those pines block any small fliers. Okay?"

"Okay." Rayland said. "Will do."

"After the all clear siren, one long blast, you can come back out and get closer if you'd like. What's your name?"

"Rayland."

"Are you a local farmer, Mr. Rayland?" The overalls and barn boots had farmer written all over them.

"Rayland. Rayland Jensen. Yes. I own one of those farms you're headed toward. I'm about three miles down the way." He scratched his beard. "At least, I used to own it." Turning to Marty, he said, "Not sure what I own anymore."

It was an awkward moment.

"I'm sorry, Rayland. It kills me and the boys to plow through these properties." When we started, all we saw were trees and rocks and dirt. It wasn't so hard then."

He kicked at some dirt, surveyed the land before them.

"Been doing it long enough now that we actually see the people, too. Like yourself. The guy who lives on that property. It hurts each one of us to see what's happening to you and these other farmers."

He shook his head. "Sorry, Rayland. If I could change things, I would."

"You're not the decider, Marty. I know that. Probably the politicians. Maybe state officials. Me and the others who are losing out, we don't get to meet the deciders. They don't show their faces. Not sure the deciders give a damn, Marty. That's the hardest part. As long as they get what they want, I'm not sure they give a damn."

Marty gave Rayland a sympathetic smile. “Yeah,” he nodded. After a few seconds he pointed toward a large rock wall. “We’re going to blow that big one now. You’ll go back by those trees, right?”

Rayland nodded again and Marty headed back to the excavator.

After moving to his new position, Rayland watched Marty talking to Tom-John. Giving instruction, he assumed. It was clear who was the boss and who was the assistant. Tom-John opened the door and got in the excavator. Marty got in too, but didn’t stay. He came back onto the roadway, then walked across the rough roadbed toward Rayland with something in his hand. Rayland waited at his assigned spot as Marty approached.

“Here. Wear this when we blow,” Marty said, handing Rayland a hard hat. Bright yellow. Just like the one Marty was wearing.

“Thank you, Marty.” Rayland tried it on. Too tight. Marty helped him adjust the inside strap.

“It’s not a loan, Rayland. It’s yours. Maybe we can make you an honorary crew member.”

Rayland’s eyes smiled.

“Okay. We’re going to blow her now. Heads up.”

The boss man walked back to the excavator, got in and slowly backed the rugged piece of equipment away from the wall. At least 100 yards back. Marty and Tom-John got out. Tom-John prepared to man the detonation device. It was on the ground behind the massive piece of equipment. He seemed to be connecting wires. He knelt and looked to Marty for a signal. Marty surveyed the scene, looking every bit the boss in his heavy overalls and yellow hard hat.

Rayland thought it unusual that Tom-John didn't have a hard hat. But, they must know what they're doing.

"Fire in the hole," Marty shouted. And again, "Fire in the Hole." A siren sounded three times, followed by a loud boom. Three seconds passed. Boom again. Three more. And a final loud boom.

First Rayland felt the air compress. That was immediately followed by a shock wave. Dirt flew in all directions followed by rock. As the dust continued to rise, the wall of rock dropped to a pile of rubble. Rayland thought, Wow. I need a foxhole, not a tree.

After things settled, the excavator crept toward the pile with Marty behind the wheel and Tom-John on shotgun. Marty looked over in Rayland's direction and tipped his hat. Rayland tipped his hat in return.

The heavy equipment typically ran until dusk. That's when they called it a day. Rayland called it a day long before that and headed home.

From a distance he could see two cars and a couple of trucks parked outside the barn. Star spotted him coming and ran to be at his side. They greeted each other. Rayland knelt, rested on one knee and gave Star a good scratch.

"What's going on, Star? You having a party?" Star rolled onto his back for more scratching, but Rayland was curious about the vehicles parked in his yard. "Come on, boy," he said. "Let's go see what's going on."

Norman and Anna's pickup trucks, and Kathleen's and Em's cars were parked along the dirt road. How does Em keep that Chevy so clean even on these dirt roads, Rayland wondered. He and Star arrived at the barn just as Jackson Sherman drove up.

"Hello pastor. What's going on? Someone die?"

The pastor was wearing a crew neck sweater, white shirt and a fashionable straw fedora. He tipped his hat. "Hello, Rayland. Are you working with the construction crew these days?"

Jackson eyed the hard hat, but then answered Rayland's question. "No. No one died. Kathleen asked us to join her here for a meeting. I'm guessing that you're supposed to be there, too. Let's go in."

They entered the ell, the pastor leading the way. Rayland had no idea what was going on. Crowded in the small room, the others seemed confused as well. Kate, Anna, Norm and Aud were packed into the little kitchen. He noticed his brother and Alina by the back wall. They all looked at him.

He looked around, took off his hard hat and put it on the counter next to the sink, then asked the obvious question: "What's going on?"

Kathleen scratched her forehead with her forefinger and looked up at him nervously, then, haltingly, said, "Rayland, I asked our friends to join me today, and we're all here. We're all here because we love you."

He nodded as if to say okay then waited for more. Kate shifted her weight as if searching for where to go next.

"When I was young, my Uncle Edward was an alcoholic." She paused. "He drank himself to a point of sickness."

Rayland looked at his friends, moving from face to face, more confused than when he'd entered.

"It was obvious that he couldn't end his drunkenness without help," Kate continued, again trying to gather her thoughts.

"And?"

"And, we called our family together to help him."

She was addressing him directly and only him. "With alcoholics they call it an intervention. We're here to do the same. We're here to tell you that we're concerned about your health and your wellbeing. We care about you. A great deal."

Her words hung in the air.

"I hardly even drink."

"We aren't worried about drinking, Rayland," Pastor Sherman said, trying to help. "We know you're under a lot of stress, and maybe our community, these folks around you, can help you." He stopped for a moment and then continued. "We want you to know you're not alone in this. If we can get a dialogue going about the problem, maybe we can find a solution. Or at least a better path forward."

Rayland looked at Kate with suspicious eyes. "Is this because I cut out of the town meeting without talking to Doctor Butt-in-ski?"

"No." She stopped herself. "Well, yes. Somewhat." She stumbled along. "She is a professional. She knows what she's doing. We're just here as friends trying to help the best we can. We could use her help." She was exasperated. "You could use her help."

"Help with what?"

Em spoke up. "Rayland, it's not like we don't know what the problem is. We want to help find a solution. Me and Alina will do anything to help. You know that."

Rayland thought, come on, Em. You don't know what the problem is. The problem is I'm embarrassed. I lost the farm. I get so filled with emotions, I can't talk about it. Not to you. Not to anybody. I don't think you see it. I'm embarrassed and I'm ashamed that I lost the family farm. He paused, his thought changing a bit as it occurred to him that Em did see how confused the sudden loss of the farm had him. Maybe Em was ashamed of him.

He looked at his brother. “I guess I know that, Em. So what?”

“Norman and I want to help you, too, Rayland,” Aud pitched in.

They all looked at each other hoping someone else would go next, that the conversation would move from all these awkward statements of support to something resembling a plan for the future.

Anna tried, saying what some were already thinking. “Looks to me like you’ve got plenty of help if you want it. Doesn’t it, Rayland?” She fiddled with her red curls. “Somebody famous once said, ‘When you’re going through hell, keep going. Preston likes to throw around crap like that. Says he learned it at Harvard. That’s one of his favorites.”

She stopped to think. “You’re going through it right now, and we’re going to help you keep going.”

She looked at him with a tight smile and big eyes. “How many times have you helped me, Rayland? You fix my wagon when it breaks down. You introduce my business to your farmer friends. Heck, you saved my horse just this last fall. When you’re going through hell, keep going. We’re the committee to help you keep going.”

“Well said, Anna. Thank you,” Kate said, relieved with the potential Anna’s words had created for the group to come to some resolution to Rayland’s dilemma.

“Churchill.” Pastor Sherman muttered barely loud enough to be heard. Everyone looked at him, wondering what he meant. He looked up, smiled and softly repeated, “Churchill.”

“I appreciate that, Anna, but I’m not looking for help,” Rayland said bluntly. “I know what I’m going to do. And it’s not ‘keep on going.’ I was born here and, I’ll ...” He stopped short and turned away. Perhaps he realized the impact of what he was about to say. He shook his head, "I'll know what to do. I'll know what to do."

Everything felt awkward.

"Can we go into the parlor and sit?" Em asked. "It's a little crowded in here. We can't just stand here jawing at each other. Just, please, hear us out. Maybe we could move in there if you don't mind."

"Sure, Em."

Once inside the parlor, Rayland walked to the corner and sat at the desk. Others sat on the couch or in the straight-back chairs. No one relaxed. He picked up Ma's small music box and toyed with it.

"Okay. So, what?" he challenged them without looking up.

Kate's mind was spinning. Come on, Norman. Come on Em, she thought as if they could hear her. She felt a kind of desperation as she realized her plan was not working. I probably should have brought Dr. Buckman, she thought, then maybe not. Rayland would just have run away. He was like a cornered animal. The silence was unsettling. Come on, folks, she silently beseeched. Help me out.

She nodded to Norman, hoping he'd catch on and say something useful.

Norman stepped to the center of the room. No one was used to seeing Norman out of uniform. He looked funny. His muddy boots were in the kitchen. He stood there in his stocking feet with a hole in each sock and a big toe sticking out of both. Aud probably wanted to kill him, but Norman had more important things on his mind.

"We want what you want, Rayland. Maybe, sometimes, you can't have exactly what you want. If that's the case, we need to find something else that's good for you." He looked at the others seated around the room. "None of us have ever done this before. And, it's hard. But, we're going to get this out because we care." He hesitated again. "I hope you're not going to be a jerk about it. The whole idea is to stand before you, tell you we love you, and ask you to let us help you find a solution to the mess you're in." He moved a few steps closer to the desk.

"I don't know anything about depression, but I do know that you've been out of sorts now for too long. Way too long. That's not like you. We've got to find you a place to live. A place to live like you want to live. I'm here to help you. Aud is here to help you. So is everyone else here to help you."

"What do you want me to do, Norman?"

"I don't know." Norman conceded. "Let's make a list of all the places you could live. Places you could move to. Places that would be good places to be."

Rayland sat silently.

Not knowing what to do next, Norman plowed forward. "Okay. One..." He paused to think. "One. You can move in with me and Aud. I can employ you on the farm. You'll have your own room. Aud's a good cook. All you'll have to do is take your boots off when you come in the house. If you don't take your boots off, she'll beat you with a broom."

"Norman! Don't tell him that. I won't beat you with a broom, Rayland." Aud said, her voice a little louder than intended. "And I will darn your socks if you give them to me. Clean. But, no barn boots in the house."

Rayland smiled but sat fiddling with the music box.

"Alina and I think you should, I mean could, auction off these antiques and your cows, and move in with *us*. Ricky is off on his own now. You can have his old room. Rock 'n roll records included."

Jackson had yet another suggestion. "Or ... John Hurley can help you find a couple of acres with a mountain view where you can set up a trailer. Sit on your porch and watch the sun come up and stay until it goes down." Jackson waited. "You do have choices, Rayland. It's not just you that's going through this very tough ordeal. Lots of folks are being forced to make new choices."

Silence. They sat uncomfortably for a long time. Anna fiddled with her hair. Norman sat with folded arms. Aud picked at her fingers.

Finally, Rayland spoke, his voice low and devoid of emotion. "I don't have any money. Ma left this farm to all of us. Not just to me. Everybody gets the same share."

"Rayland, you know that's not what Ma wanted," Em said, jumping to his feet in exasperation. "She left the farm for everyone. Left it so everyone could return and enjoy it. A place for the grandchildren to grow up. To learn about farming. Swim in the pond. Run through the meadows. Ride the horses. That's what Ma wanted. And you ran the farm. If it weren't for you, none of us would have had a farm to go to, a place to hang out and play and work together and be a family. That's what Ma wanted. She was never leaving the farm to us for money. None of us want money." Em seemed to have run out of momentum. "We want the farm just like you do, but it's not going to be that way. So it's our turn to help out. You've done a lot for the family just by keeping things going like you did."

Rayland sat quietly sliding the music box back and forth from one hand to the other. Then he stood and looked at his brother. Everyone was hoping to hear 'Thank you, Em.'

But they didn't. Instead he asked, "You done?"

Kate lowered her head and sighed. The collective body language in the room sagged and showed disappointment. Kate looked up.

"Rayland, do you ever really consider what it is you don't want to do?" Her voice was stern. "This is how it works, Rayland. At some point you've got to face your future. That's the way it works."

"No, that's not the way it works, Kate." He looked at her defiantly. "Not for me. You don't see my problem. You don't understand. I lost the farm. Em didn't lose it. I lost it because of something I did or, more likely, didn't do. I didn't modernize. Like Norman. I didn't step into the future. Yeah, I always kept one foot in the past. Yeah, I always embraced the old ways of doing things, and now, and now it has caught up with me, and I'm paying the price."

She waited, giving Rayland plenty of time to add something. Hopefully this gentle and caring man she'd known would find something more positive to say. When he did not, the pastor asked, "Do you believe in a higher power, Rayland?"

Rayland looked aside. He grappled with the question. "I don't know that I've ever been asked that one. I don't know what you'd called a higher power, Pastor." He sat and thought about it. "I don't go to church much, but I don't feel the need. When I look at the clouds racing by or see the night sky, I feel the presence of God. The land, the sky, the animals, that's my church, Pastor, and they're trying to take it away from me."

Kate smiled and looked around. She was proud of Rayland's answer.

"They can't take that feeling away from you, Rayland." Pastor Sherman answered. "That feeling is you. That is the Rayland we know best." He smiled. He put his head down momentarily to recall something. "Rayland, are you familiar with Saint Francis of Assisi? He is the patron saint of animals and nature. He received sainthood because he had a way of seeing God through all things God created."

He looked to Rayland, hoping he'd heard of him.

"Isn't he the one who persuaded the wolf to stop attacking people in the village and stop eating their livestock? But only if the townspeople agreed to feed the wolf? I love that story," Rayland said as he looked at Norman, raised his eyebrows and smiled.

"Reader's Digest?" Norman asked quietly. Rayland nodded.

The pastor's smile faded. "Yeah, I guess that could be him. I thought you'd like him."

"Pastor, sometimes it's just easier to talk to animals than it is your friends. Especially if your friends don't see the problem. The problem isn't where to move to. The problem is moving. I can't move off the farm and watch it get plowed under. I cannot."

There were a few more comments, but the meeting seemed to have run out of momentum. Feeling obliged or desperately hopeful, Kate asked if anyone had anything more to add. She looked from person to person. All heads quietly shook no.

Rayland moved toward the door. "I've got to feed my cows," he said and, not waiting for a response, got up and walked to the ell. The others got up to follow.

Kathleen came out last. She grasped Rayland's arm firmly as he stood there letting his neighbors go by without saying a word. She gave him a serious look and said, "I want to go thank your friends for coming. Your friends, Rayland," she emphasized. "You should thank them, too."

She headed toward the cars where they were mingling. Norman sat and put his boots on. He took his time fiddling with the laces. He wanted a moment alone with Rayland. Not knowing what to say, he reached for the hard hat and examined it.

"You get this up on the construction site?"

"I did."

"Who's TJ?" He pointed to the initials on the interior band. "TJ. See?"

Rayland looked. "Yeah. TJ." He smiled. "Maybe TJ stands for 'The Jerk.' That's me, Norman. The Jerk."

It was Norman's turn to sigh. "Rayland, you're not a jerk. I'm sorry I said that. But, good Lord, I do wish you'd stop acting like one."

Chapter 15

RIDING THE RIDGE

Dateline – Friday - April 17, 1964

Detroit – *The Ford Mustang was introduced and put on sale at Ford dealerships nationwide with a suggested retail price of $2,238. Purchases and purchase requests totaled more than 22,000 units on the first day.*

"Middle of April and the roads are already turning to mush." Jeep talked to himself as he lurched from one mud rut to another. "Come on, Jeep, my boy, ride the ridge. Ride the ridge the best you can." The trick was to keep both tires up on the ridge. Like walking on the side rails of a ladder that's laying on the ground. It was a game to Jeep, but he knew that every now and then the mud would win.

Jeep's mail car lurched hard to the left and bounced him into the side of the door. It bounced the mail onto the floor. He reflexively knew to strong-arm it in order to stay above the deep stuff. He gave her more gas. The wheels spun without much traction, throwing mud and not going anywhere quickly. He picked the side of the road in the shade where the mud was still frozen. He started to make better progress.

Like Rayland and others who spend a lot of time alone, Jeep often talked to himself, especially in his automobile. "No wonder it takes me forever to make my rounds on days like this," he half grumbled. "If we had a bigger post office, people could come to us."

He thought about that as he wrestled his way along the muddy lane, changing his mind as his thoughts continued. "All those folks driving to the post office? Nope. These roads would be really bad then. Hard to believe, but they'd be worse. At least I've got a four-wheel drive."

Up ahead he could see someone enjoying the mud even less than he. A big red Lincoln Continental sedan was stuck in the middle of the road. Stuck up to its frame on one side. Who the heck thought they could get that city-mobile through this mud, he wondered. That thing weighed as much as an Army tank. "Alright, Jeep. Let's go see who the lucky driver is," he said to himself.

As he stepped out of his car, his boots met the mud with a soft splat. He walked carefully. On foot he could avoid the ruts. Once he got his hand on the trunk of the Lincoln, he steadied himself and picked a solid path to the driver's side window.

"Hello, Jeep. Any mail for me today?" A loud Preston Jaffe belly laugh came as a surprise. A laugh like that could only make the other person laugh along.

"Preston, what in the Wide World of Sports are you doing out here in the mud? And why are you dressed like you're going to a wedding?" Preston had on a black pinstriped suit. "Hell, you could be the groom."

"Yeah. Well, you can be my bride. But first you've got to get me out of here. I had a meeting with a bank over in Albany, and I forgot that this state doesn't have any decent roads that go east and west. Just these damn dirt roads. Not much better than trails." He sat back and put both hands on the steering wheel. "The paved roads all go north and south. Why is that, Jeep?"

"Don't know, but sit tight. I always travel with a chain just for special occasions like this. Sit tight. This is going to take a minute or two. I'll get you out." Jeep backed his car away from the big Lincoln, carefully passed him on the other side of the road and then backed in so he could pull from the front. He was better dressed for the situation than Preston, but there was no way he could lend a hand without getting dirty. Kneeling in the mud, he attached his chain to the undercarriage of the Lincoln. Once hooked up, he stood, wiped his hands on his pants and walked back to Preston.

"How much do you like this car, Preston?" He gave Preston his tight-lipped smile.

"Hell, Jeep," Preston laughed. "I like it a lot. I like it a lot. Why?"

"When I start to pull, give it a steady amount of gas. Keep it coming toward me. Not too fast or you'll hit me. Not too slow or I'll pull your bumper off."

"For crying out loud, Jeep. Have you ever done this before?"

"About two times a week during the season. Mud. Snow. There's always somebody who needs to be hauled out."

Jeep got into his four-wheel drive vehicle, and inched forward until the chain became taut. Okay, big boy. Here we go, he thought as he applied the gas. The four-wheel drive Jeep strained and bucked in the mud. He tried again. And then a third time, but he could not move the big car enough to get it out.

"We've got to get more help, Preston." He took off his toque and looked around, taking note of where they were. "Seems we've got two choices. Kurt Zalewski has a tractor. He's not too far from here, but he's never home.

We'd be taking a chance. Or Rayland Jensen has a team of draft horses. He lives right up the road. With the draft horses and this Jeep, we can get you out."

"Rayland might not be too keen on helping me out."

"To my way of thinking, Preston, you just don't know Rayland. If somebody is in a pickle, he'll help get them out. He's about the most helping out person I know. He's not going to leave you, or anybody else, stuck in the mud because you disagree on something." He pointed at Preston with his hat. "He's as good as they come. The gold standard for what a neighbor should be. He's the real deal, Preston. Don't you worry."

Preston raised his eyes skeptically, but agreed.

"Sit tight. I'll go get him," Jeep said climbing back, mud and all, into his vehicle.

"Sit tight?" Preston questioned. "Where do you think I'd be going?"

Star had been missing all morning. That's not like Star at all, Rayland thought. As he milked, he kept looking around for his friend. Maybe he got trapped in the house. He hates that when I'm out and he's in. I'd better go look.

When he finished milking, he went looking for the dog. He wasn't in the house. He walked around the outside of the house, checked the wood shed and the cold house. He looked up by the pond and found Champ, but no Star.

As he walked past the horse barn, he heard whimpering coming from underneath. He went outside and looked through a broken board into the crawl space under the barn flooring. Star lay there just out of reach, trying to lick his wounds.

"What's wrong, boy? What's the problem?"

He tried to reach the dog, but couldn't.

"Come on, Star. Come on, buddy. Let me help you out."

Star crawled toward him. Rayland could see the problem. He reached his arm in as Star got closer and petted him on the neck and talked softly to him, tried to coax him out. Finally, the dog started crawling out on his belly.

"Oh boy. You had a run in with a porcupine, didn't you? Come on out here, boy. Come on out so we can see what kind of trouble you got into."

The dog came to Rayland. He held him while he visually checked the quills. Not touching any.

"Well, the good news is it looks like you just gave that old bugger a good sniff and didn't bite."

A dozen or so quills protruded from around the dog's nose and mouth.

"The bad news is they've got to come out."

He carried Star inside and threw a horse blanket onto the barn floor for him. The dog lay down happy that Rayland had found him. Fourteen quills in his face. One in his mouth. On his tongue, actually. He got a pair of needle nose pliers, a clean rag and a half bottle of whiskey. He held the dog gently, but firmly, in his lap and talked to him. He'd done this enough times to know that it was imperative to get the entire quill out. The quill has a barb on the end to keep it embedded. It's got to come out to avoid infection.

Holding the dog still, he started cautiously. Star jerked and recoiled each time Rayland pulled a quill. He pulled two or three, took a break and dabbed the small wound with the alcohol. He repeated the process. The quill on the tongue was obviously bothering Star the most. “Let’s get that one out, Star, and then we’ll be past the worst part.”

Holding Star’s mouth open as best he could, he reached in with the pliers. The dog shied.

“Come on, boy. It’s got to come out. The sooner we get it out, the easier it will be for the both of us.”

Again, he opened Star’s mouth and reached in slowly with the pliers. He tried to hold the tongue flat with any available finger. He pressed it against the bottom of the dog’s mouth, reached with the pliers and firmly and steadily plucked the quill out.

Star was exhausted and needed a break. So did Rayland.

“Four more to go, Star, and then we’re done. Then you can relax.”

They looked at each other.

“Doesn’t seem fair, does it? Some strange critter comes into your yard ... your yard .... and you go check it out. You give him a little sniff and whap. You get a face full of quills. Unfair.”

He pulled another.

“You’ll remember it, though. You’re too smart to sniff another porcupine for a while, aren’t you?”

He pulled one more.

“Two to go.”

He set the pliers down and took a sip of whiskey.

“Life can be unfair at times. This highway stuff seems unfair to me.” He looked at Star and smiled. “It’s my porcupine.”

They sat for a moment.

“Let’s do another one.”

He pulled the next to last quill. Without much fanfare, he pulled the last one.

"That's it, Star."

He rubbed the whiskey on the open sores.

"A little rest and you'll be as good as new."

Rayland wrapped the blanket around the dog as they sat on the barn floor together. Star was comfortable but worn out. He may have been asleep, but Rayland continued talking to him.

"You know something, Star, when something like this happens you get angry. But when you learn that it was done to speed thing along or to save money, done with no consideration for who's involved or how it's going to affect them, you feel cheated. Yeah. I feel cheated. What the heck did I do to deserve this?"

He looked down at the dog sleeping with his head in his lap and pulled the blanket up around the dog.

"I'm frustrated. I'm left without any options."

He petted Star as he watched through the barn door as the clouds passed by.

"Star, when I realize that progress doesn't think about who gets hurt, I let these things get all balled up inside me, and that's when I get sad and messed up. And then I act like a jerk. Norman was right. I have been a jerk. Worst of all, it's my entire fault. They came to me as nice as can be at Kathleen's meeting. What did she call it? An intervention, I think." He paused to reflect. "They're all good friends. Wonderful people. And they ask 'Where you going to go, Rayland?' 'What are you going to do, Rayland?' That's when I act like a jerk because ... because, damn it, I don't want to talk about it. I want to tell them to shut up. Stop asking where I'm going to go, what I'm going to do. Lay off."

"Just shut up." He rolled onto his back. "I don't want to go anywhere. I want to stay where I was."

He bunched some of the blanket under his head for a pillow.

"I want to stay in the past."

He pulled his hat over his eyes to block the sun.

"I hate to admit it, but that's what I want to do. Stay in the past. Milk my cows. Enjoy my farm."

He stretched out and got real comfortable. A nap with his dog was coming on.

"But I know I can't do that. And that's when I get all balled up."

They lay there comfortably. Star sleeping and Rayland headed toward his nap.

"Rayland? Are you okay? What's going on? Are you drunk?"

Rayland sat up, somewhat startled by Jeep's entry.

"Why would you ask that, Jeep?"

"Well you're lying on the barn floor with a bottle of whiskey and your dog."

"Oh! Jeep," he laughed. "We had a run-in with a porcupine." He nodded to Star. "Someone is a bit under the weather. That's my antiseptic. Want a sip?"

"Did he bite it?" Jeep extended his hand and helped Rayland up onto his feet.

"No. No. Luckily. Only a sniff, I suspect."

"How many?"

"Fourteen. Plus, one in the tongue."

"Oh. Not good. Is he doing okay?"

"Seems to be."

They looked at Star resting comfortably. "What's up?"

"Got one of your neighbors stuck in the mud down the road a piece. Up to the frame on his car. I can't get enough traction. We really need a pull. Hoping you and your horses can help. I think they'll have better footing than my semi-balds. Think you can help?"

"Sure. Sure, Jeep. Can Star rest in the back of your mail car?"

"Well," Jeep hitched up his pants, "only U.S. government mail is allowed, you know."

"Jeep, for crying out loud, it's a dog who just had fifteen porcupine quills pulled from his face."

"Okay. Close enough."

Jeep got back to Preston first, Star resting comfortably in the back of the mail car. Rayland and the two big draft horses came walking down the road minutes later. When he reached the bogged-down vehicle, Rayland turned the horses and backed them toward the big Lincoln.

"Whoa. Whoa." The horses held their place. Rayland patted them on the neck then walked over to the vehicle in the mud. As he approached, he recognized Preston sitting behind the wheel.

"Hello, Preston. Wasn't expecting to see you up here. Got yourself in pretty deep, it seems."

"Hello. Rayland. I appreciate your coming to pull me out of this mess. I'm sure you've got better things to do than drag my fat ass out of the mud."

"No. Not really."

He carefully walked around the car surveying the situation. He came back and leaned by the open window.

"I'm going to hook the team to your front end. When we start to pull, give me steady, forward acceleration. Not too much. Just steady. Jeep will be in the rear pushing. Don't back up or you'll run him over. He smiled. "That wouldn't be good,"

"Will he be pushing with his four-wheel drive?"

"By hand. If we push with his Jeep, it's going to mess up the back of your car. Let's see what we can get done with just the horses first. They should be able to dig in and get pretty good traction. Let's see how far we get. Okay?"

"You're the boss."

He hooked the team to the car so they could pull from the front. Rayland loved this kind of challenge. To help someone out of a jam brought him alive. Preston. Star. A total stranger. Didn't matter. Helping out made him feel good. For a moment he wondered if Kathleen and Em and Norman and his friends felt that way about their intervention. He wasn't sure. But this made him feel good.

"Tck. Tck." He moved the horses forward a little to take the slack out of the rope. "Okay, Preston. Steady acceleration. Ready, Jeep? Here we go. HAW... HAW. The horses leaned into their harnesses. They leaned into their work and they pulled. Preston stepped on the gas. The tires spun. More gas. More spinning. Then even more gas. The horses strained, but made little progress.

Rayland stopped to reassess. He checked the rear tire ruts. He checked what lay in front of the front tires. Jeep walked over to Rayland. He lowered his head and raised his eyes to meet Rayland's.

"He doesn't know what he's doing, Rayland. If the frame weren't already on that ridge, we'd be going deeper."

"I know." Rayland wiped his brow with his felt hat. "I've got to get you behind the wheel."

He sloshed around to Preston again.

"Preston, I've got to get Jeep behind the wheel. We're not making any progress." He looked purposefully at the driver. "You know, Jeep was a driver in the Army and he's our mailman. He's on these roads all the time. He's a like a professional driver."

"Where do I go?" Preston asked.

Rayland looked at him without answering.

"Where do I go?" Preston asked again.

"You're a big man, Preston. We want your weight out of the car and pushing rather than inside adding to the burden."

"You want me out there?" He looked at the mud like he was seeing it for the first time.

"Rayland. Rayland, I've got on Italian leather wing tips, for crying out loud."

Rayland looked at him without expression.

"Do you know how much these cost? Do you?"

There was no answer. Just a steady look.

"They're imported, Rayland. From Italy."

Rayland continued to look at him void of any expression. Preston was slowly coming to terms with the situation.

"Aw, shit, Rayland. They're handmade."

Rayland opened the door.

Finally giving in, Preston turned to the side, slipped around and put his feet out into the mud and slowly stood up. He sunk in a couple of inches and muttered another, "Aw, shit."

"Jeep, take the controls. I want you to rock her real good and see if we can elongate this rut. That way we can get a better run out of here. Preston, stand over there for now."

Preston moved carefully to the side. Leather soles aren't very good in mud. He slipped more than once. He carefully picked his way across the muddy road.

"Okay, Jeep, it's all yours. Rock it good. The more room you can create the easier this is going to be."

Rayland was feeling good about the situation. Getting Jeep behind the wheel. The horses getting good traction from their forward position.

Jeep got in, adjusted the seat, checked the automatic shift and slowly started to rock the big car. Forward. Back. Forward. Back. Six or seven times. He kept a steady pace working with skills gained from experience.

"Okay, let's give it a try. Preston, move to the back of the car so you can push. We need everything we've got."

Rayland barked out the instructions.

"Push from the center of the trunk. Otherwise you're going to get mighty dirty. Jeep, you rock, nice and smooth. I'll count ONE... TWO... THREE. We go on three. Got it, Preston?"

"Rayland. I didn't dress for this occasion." Preston inched his way to the back of the car. Rayland readied the horses. Jeep started to rock. Forward. Back. Forward. Back. Rayland caught Jeep's eye and nodded. Jeep returned the nod. Preston was back by the trunk getting ready for he didn't know what.

"Okay, Jeep. ONE... TWO... THREEE. HAW... HAW... HAW," he commanded. The horses again leaned into their work. "HAW... HAW. "

Jeep was moving the car forward now, giving it all he could. It was sliding forward in a small zigzag, but it was moving forward. It was coming out. The wheels slid and spun a few feet forward but the car was coming out. It soon got up to the road level. Jeep backed off the gas quite a bit. The horses finished the job. The Lincoln Continental was back in business.

"Alright, Jeep. Nice work. We did it." Rayland smiled. "Yahoo!"

"Yeah, Rayland." Jeep was excited, too. "Those horses are impressive. Powerful, man. Really powerful."

As they congratulated each other, they failed to notice that as the car moved forward, Preston's shoes did not. The shoes remained stuck in the mud and Preston, unable to move his feet, had fallen forward onto his knees. Now he was slowly pulling himself up to standing. The other two men moved to help him but they were too late. Preston had a pained expression on his face as he wiped his hands on his suit. They stood looking. Preston looked back at them.

"Aw, shit."

Jeep snickered but tried to contain it. Then he laughed. Rayland tried to stifle his laugh, but couldn't. Jeep convulsed. Rayland quickly followed. As they laughed, damn if Preston didn't start to laugh, too. His big, full throated belly laugh. The three of them stood there laughing at the sight of themselves standing in the spring mud laughing at each other. It was like the funniest thing they'd ever seen. They roared with laughter.

Everyone felt pretty good about their accomplishment. Not much needed to be said. Finally, Preston spoke up. "So, this is what you fellas do for fun, is it?"

"Well, around here, we've got to deal with whatever Mother Nature sends us. Fun? I don't know about that, but it feels pretty good to help someone get out of a mess," Rayland said.

"Look at that," Rayland said, nodding toward the torn-up road in front of them. "Must be a spring under this part of the road. Mucks up right here every year."

Turning to Preston, he continued. "I'm sure these dirt roads are another reason you're pushing for that new highway. But you know something, if you had been on that new highway today, you would have roared right on by. Right past here and been on your way. Me and Jeep wouldn't even have seen you. We wouldn't have worked together. Wouldn't have gotten to know you better. We wouldn't have laughed together. You would have just roared on by in your big car and your Italian shoes. A little time in the mud and I feel like I know you better, Preston."

He gave him a big smile and his eyes sparkled just like they used to.

"I actually kind of like you."

"Well, if I had roared right by, I'd sure be looking a lot better when I get home this evening. But you know something? I'm starting to see that big changes, like the highway, aren't for everybody."

Preston brushed his dirty hands together to get the dried mud off.

"Anna keeps telling me that, but I'm kind of obtuse." Turning to Jeep, he said, "That's a fifty-cent word for a little bit stupid. She always says I'm kind of blind to country ways. Maybe she's right. I'm working on that. I'm starting to see that this process of change isn't to everyone's liking."

Preston pulled out his wallet.

"I want to give you boys a few bucks for all your help. You don't know how much I appreciate what you've done. I really do appreciate it."

He handed them a fifty-dollar bill.

"Put your money away, Preston," Rayland said. "We didn't do this for money. We did this because someone needed help. Glad we could be here for you."

They shook hands and he thanked them again. Preston got back into his car and drove away carefully. He blew the horn and waved out the window as he departed.

"Job well done, Jeep."

"Rayland. That was a fifty dollar bill."

Rayland put his muddy hand on Jeep's shoulder and gave him another big smile. "Jeep, you're a better man for not taking it."

Jeep looked at his friend, paused, and muttered, "You know what I've got to say to that, Rayland? Aw, shit."

They shared another good laugh.

Chapter 16

THE SHERIFF CALLS

Friday - June 5, 1964

Saigon, South Vietnam – *Henry Cabot Lodge, the U.S. Ambassador to South Vietnam, sent a cable to President Johnson recommending that the United States not send more troops into South Vietnam to fight the Viet Cong. Such a step, he cautioned, would be a "venture of unlimited possibilities which could put us onto a slope along which we slide into a bottomless pit."*

There is a day each spring when the robins return. A flock of thirty or forty swept in and land in the raw fields to peck for grubs and worms. You can hear them tuk and cluck as they discuss nesting, food availability and foliage. If the nesting area is favorable, the robins return every year. Some of the many move on. Others stay to build nests and families. As leaves appear, they spend more time roosting in the upper branches singing their songs to attract a mate. They build nests and lay their eggs and seem well at ease around humans. Spiritual folks will tell you that the robin is a sign that a deceased loved one is still with you. Rayland thought of Ma that way.

Everything was now on site. Dozers, excavators, loaders and graders. Dump trucks and bucket loaders to move dirt, materials, soil and rock. The sound of diesel engines warming up was soon followed by the high-pitched whirling of drills as they bore into rock ledge. When the whirling stopped, the siren soon sounded. Then explosions reverberated off the mountains and throughout the valley.

Boom. Three seconds. Boom. Three more. Boom. And, so it went all day.

Rayland had become used to the noise. It rattled the tranquility of the Green Mountains even from miles away. The sounds were creeping closer.

Shortly after the cows had been fed, he took off his barn boots and went into the family room to make notes on thoughts he'd had, notes that began even before he put pencil to paper. He walked to the desk and opened it.

Before he got started, he softly said, "Good morning, Ma. It's always so nice and sunny in here in the mornings. Hope you don't mind if I do a little work in here today. It's strange, Ma. Everybody has been asking me what are you going to do, Rayland? Where you going to go. Rayland?' Drives me nuts, Ma. It really gets under my skin. You'd be upset with me if you knew how I acted toward them. Not at my best. I'll start doing better, Ma. I will."

It didn't matter if he was writing or just ambling through his thoughts, sometimes out loud, sometimes on paper, sometimes simply in his mind. Something about the parlor and Ma helped him sort through his thoughts.

He looked back at the couch and began again.

"I think I have a plan now, Ma. I'm feeling better about things. The important thing is it's my plan. Everybody has a plan for me, but now it's my plan. Listen to this one, Ma. Remember Jeep, our mailman? Jeep's such a good guy. He comes by the other day. He bows his head down and looks up at me from raised eyes. Then he tells me, like it's a secret, that he's got a friend over in New Hampshire who would like to hire me for this business he's starting. He's building a place called Santa's North Pole. Yeah, Santa's North Pole."

He sat back and fiddled with the pen. He smiled, imaging how his mother would react to what he was next about to say next.

"He needs someone to care for the animals and then be Santa. I laughed. Oh my. Ma, I laughed. Jeep laughed too. Me as Santy Claus. Of all the ideas folks have come up with, that's the worst. But then I thought, maybe it's the best. What if that's the best plan for me? Playing Santy Claus at some animal farm? That got me sad again. Really sad. Really quick."

He sat and studied his stocking feet before turning back to Ma. "He's a good man. He means well. You've gotta love Jeep, Ma."

He sat quiet for a while, not thinking, not writing, just looking at the couch, as if remembering his mother and the predicament he found himself in,

"I guess I got off track. Thinking about being Santy Claus in New Hampshire got me off track. That would get anybody off track. Anyway, two days ago I was up by the pond. You know how folks say 'You can see the light at the end of the tunnel?' Well, I saw a light. I never have seen a tunnel. I've seen a lot of dark lately, but no tunnel. When I saw this light, I knew it was the light those folks were talking about. It was in the pond. I thought it was the reflection of the sun, but I'm not so sure."

He slid to the edge of the chair and leaned forward. His words came faster.

"It was so bright. Almost too bright to look at, but I saw something in that light. I saw something. It seemed to be a message for me."

He moved to a chair near the couch and began talking more quickly. It was almost like ... well, almost like really talking to Ma.

"I thought about that all day. I slept on it. Next day, after the chores, I walked back up to the pond and I saw the light again. Bright, bright yellow. He rubbed his brow. It was kinda cloudy that day, Ma. Lots of those long wispy, summer clouds. The sun was out, but it was behind those thin clouds. Yet there the light was reflecting out of the pond. The more I looked, the more I heard it speak to me. It wasn't a voice, but it was saying 'Rayland. You've got a plan. It's your plan, and it's okay. It's okay to have your plan.'"

He sat quietly. Thinking.

"Weird isn't it, Ma? I've gotta keep thinking on it, but I feel like my plan is okay. Only problem is Kathleen. She's not in my plan."

He rested his chin on his chest. It stayed there for a few moments. He looked up, and said, "I like her, Ma. I like her a lot, but I can't seem to fit her into my plan. I'm kinda lame when it comes to the ladies. Inexperienced, I guess. Pa wasn't much of a talker. When it came to the birds and bees, he'd usually point to a horse or two and say 'See?' That was it. I learned more from Anna when she came to inseminate cows than I did from Pa. I think I might have two plans. One with Kate and one without. The 'with' plan scares me, but not in a bad way. I like being with her so much. But I don't want anything more than that. Seems I've got to give up everything if I want her in my life. That scares the heck out of me, Ma. Not sure I can do that."

He turned back again and wrote for a long time putting down these thoughts.

"Mail call." Rayland looked up to see Jeep in the kitchen.

"What are you doing in there, Rayland?"

Rayland moved right past the question, he turned in his chair.

"You married, Jeep?"

"Yep."

He put the mail on the table.

"That's an odd question. Yeah, I got married when I was in Fort Rucker. Seemed like a good thing to do at the time. It seems so odd that we have known one another all this time and you didn't know that."

"How's it working out?"

"Pretty good, seems to me. Got two great kids, and Betty is a good companion. She feeds me. Doesn't rag on me a lot. Yeah. Pretty good, I'd say." He got himself a glass of water. "Why you asking me these marrying questions, Rayland?"

"I don't know, Jeep."

He got up and walked to the ell.

"I've been working on my plan. You know what I'm talking about. Anyway, for the longest time I didn't have any plan. Now it seems I've got two plans."

"You don't seem to be the marrying type to me, Rayland. But Kate would be a sweet catch."

"Jeep, for crying out loud. What are you talking about? Kate? She's...well...." He paused. "She is sweet, isn't she? And that's all I want, Jeep. Good company. And friendship. And ...,"

He paused with a further realization.

"And then I want to go home and milk my cows."

He looked at Jeep and shook his head.

"I can't seem to figure out a way to have both. The farm seems to be a lost cause. Kathleen is a fine lady. What does she want with an old farmer who's set in his ways? I'm afraid that of my two choices, I may end up without either one."

"Rayland, Rayland, Rayland." Jeep bowed his head slightly and his eyes looked up. "Rayland, lady problems and cows are not my strong suit. There must be something in those books of yours that can help." Jeep headed for the door. "I'll ask Betty. She seems to have advice on just about everything else. I'm sure she'll have some advice for you too."

"Let's keep Betty out of this, okay, Jeep?"

There was no reply.

"Right, Jeep? Let's keep your wife out of this," he shouted after the mailman.

It was early afternoon when Sherriff Moore pulled in next to the barn. He drove a semi-official police car. It was a 1960 Chevy with a portable blinker on top. He seldom needed the blinker, and it often didn't work. He parked, got out, put on his sheriff's hat, and walked into the barn.

"Afternoon, Rayland."

"Afternoon, Sheriff. You here on official business on this fine day?"

"I guess it's a little bit official, and a little bit not." He eyed a hay bale. "Mind if I sit a spell and talk."

"Be my guest." Rayland balanced on the milking stool. "What's on your mind, Mel?"

"Rayland, you know this is a part-time job for me. I'm a local constable who signed up to make a few extra bucks when I'm not at the sawmill."

He crossed his arms in a confident fashion.

"I've always been glad to drag a killed deer off the road or bust up beer parties down at the ball field if needed, but that's about where my enthusiasm for law enforcement ends."

He took off his hat.

"Of late, I've had to do some things I don't like at all." He looked down. "I don't think these things are right, but right or wrong, I get stuck with the duty." He looked up. "Let me get down to business, Rayland. I've got some good news for you, but it's not great news."

He sat up a little straighter.

"You know, you've got to be off the farm by the end of the month."

He let that sink in. He pulled some papers out of his back pocket

"You know that! I know you know that. But you got a stay in your proceedings," He waved the papers to prove his point. "That's a legal term. Think of it as an extension. The court filing now reads that you don't have to be out until September 12 of this year."

"Why'd that happen?"

"There's more." He looked at the papers. "The state's going to give you $13,500. Three thousand dollars more than the original offer."

"Wait a minute, Sheriff. What's going on?"

"Well, I don't know if I'm supposed to tell you this or not, but what the hell. It ain't going to hurt anybody. Just don't go blabbing it around, okay?"

"Okay. What?"

"If I tell you what happened, you've got to tell me that you won't go telling the others."

He looked at Rayland for an acknowledgement.

Rayland wasn't sure what he was agreeing to, but he nodded yes.

"Preston Jaffee."

Rayland looked at him with a blank stare.

"Preston Jaffee what?"

"I guess ole Preston knows somebody in the state capital. He went up and talked to Mr. Somebody on your behalf."

"Preston?"

"Yep. The one and only." He nodded. "I don't think he wants you to know it though. He just went and did it."

"Preston? Did that for me?"

"Yep." He smiled. "Surprise you?"

He slapped his thigh and asked again, "He did that for me?"

"Yes, he did. Now don't go running over there and give him a big kiss. You're not supposed to know. He don't want you to know it was him."

"No. No big kiss, but I've got to thank him. Don't you think?"

"No. I don't think. They don't pay me to think."

"He's a tough one to figure out. Tough one. Doesn't really matter. I've got to thank him somehow."

"Don't get all excited and emotional now. You still have to be out of here by September 12."

He looked sternly at Rayland. Then he lightened up.

"At least you got some extra money to get you going. That can't hurt."

Mel reached into his breast pocket and pulled out two pepperoni sticks.

"Want a Slim Jim?"

Rayland shook his head then sat back. His emotions were swinging from high to low. Nonetheless, reality was finding a seam somewhere between the two.

"Mel, I appreciate you're coming over to tell me."

"Hell, Rayland, it beats coming over to evict you."

He bit off a chunk of meat and with a full mouth said, "Please, Rayland, please don't make me come back in September to evict. Please."

"Sorry, Mel. I don't think I'm leaving."

The sheriff looked at him with disbelief. "Dammit, Rayland. What do you mean, you don't think you're leaving?"

"Not leaving, Mel." They looked at each other with blank expressions.

"You going to do one of those armed stand-offs?" He leaned in. "Don't do it, Rayland." He shook his Slim Jim at Rayland. "Don't you do it."

"Remember a few years back, that crazy couple up near Montpelier? The ones who tried to hold the Staties at bay thinking they could avoid eviction? They were foolish and stupid to think they could hold off the state police. They served them with papers and warrants and court orders, and they just stood their ground, guns in hand. But that ain't going to work." Mel shook his head. "They stockpiled months of food and all kinds of weapons and ammunition. They vowed they'd rather die than move out."

He spit out the door.

"Some of their friends and supporters came and made things worse. They camped out on the farm outside their home. They helped with the stand-off and morale, I guess." He pointed what was left of his pepperoni stick at Rayland, and said, "Well, they held off 80 state troopers for months. Six, maybe seven months. Finally, finally winter came. The

Staties pretty much froze them out. They cut off their oil and gas and food too, at least the best they could. Now they're doing five to seven in the pen."

His expression turned very serious. "Don't do it, Rayland. Don't you do it."

Mel looked over his shoulder. "Someone coming to see you. We'd best change this conversation." He hurried to finish. "I was sure that mess was going to end up with someone getting shot. Those Staties earn their money. For me, this is a part-time job so that me and Maylin can make a few extra bucks. No armed standoffs. I don't do armed standoffs, okay, Rayland? Don't you do one either. You're too smart for that. Okay?"

He popped the last of the pepperoni into his mouth. "Okay?"

"You're a good man, Mel. I'll make your job as easy as I can."

It was Otto who'd pulled in. He was already out of the truck.

"Oh boy." Mel didn't look toward Otto. "I've already spent too much time with Otto this week." He looked up as Otto entered the barn. "Hello, Otto."

"Hello, Sheriff. Thought I was done with you."

"Sorry, Otto. Nothing personal, you know. It ain't much fun working in Towsley these days. I'm just doing what they tell me do."

"Helma and I are out, Rayland. Thanks to Sheriff Moore and his pals. We're out of here tomorrow morning. I vanted to come by and say goodbye." Otto seemed unsteady. "And a goodbye and a kiss my ass to you, Sheriff Moore."

"I'm sorry, Otto. Where are you going to go?"

"Vee go back to Salzburg and start over, I guess. Why do you give a nickel bout me and Helma?" Otto seemed to be slurring his words.

"Well, I do care." He stood. "I've got to go, Rayland."

Turning to Otto, the sheriff said, "I wish you well, Otto. You're a good man."

"Ja. Dat don't get you far in dis state."

The sheriff put his hat on and made his way back to his car. Otto moved to the bale of hay.

"You like schnapps, Rayland?" Otto offered a small flask.

"No thank you."

Otto took a nip. "Vee call dis a knee bender. Helps mit de old bones. I know it's a little early for knee bender, but I'm celebrating my last day in Towsley." He studied the flask. "It makes me sad. Last day. Everything makes me sad. I sit at home and weep."

He bowed his head for a second, then looked up. "Helma gets mad and throws me out. Makes me go do something. She throws me out today and says 'Go say good bye to Rayland,' and I say 'Gut idea.'" He took another nip. "But, dat too makes me sad. I don't want to go, Rayland."

"The last time I am in Salzburg, I vas a kid. Sixteen. Since den, ders been war, I get married and I have kids. Twenty-four years go by." He looked again at the flask. "Now I go back. My father-in-law, he say 'Otto, what have you been doing?' 'Me? What have I been doing? Well, I build a nice farm. I start with nothing. I work until my bones hurt. 'Oh, dat's nice. Otto. You must be wealthy American.' 'No. In fact, I don't have shit. Dey throw me off my farm. Dat's what I been doing.'"

Otto shook his head and took a swig of the schnapps.

"Things will work out, Otto."

"Ja." He wiped his lips. "I hope day work out for you too, Rayland." Another sip. "I hope day work out for you, too."

They had a warm handshake. Otto lifted his flask. "To your health and well-being, Rayland." He sipped and departed.

Rayland pulled down a fresh bale of hay for the cows and thought, first the sheriff and then Otto. It has been a tough day. He was uplifted when he saw Kate pulling in. My goodness, he thought, must be call on Rayland day. He walked out to meet her and leaned into the open window on the passenger side.

"Hi Kathleen. I hope you're coming by so that I can apologize for the way I've been acting of late."

"No. No, that's not really the reason, but it's not a bad place to start."

"I'm sorry I've been so short with you. So short with everyone. I'm having trouble finding my way through this situation and it's not fair taking it out on anyone else. Especially the people I like the best."

"Hmm... what got you thinking about that?"

"It's hard to explain, but I've been thinking. About a plan and all. It's starting to come together."

"Want to tell me about it?" She looked at him. "You don't have to, but I'd be interested."

"I'm still feeling a little unsure of things, but it's coming together."

"Okay. When you're ready." She put both hands on the wheel. "Want to go someplace for dinner?"

"You mean like out?"

"Yeah. Out." She could tell he didn't want to go to anything close to fancy. "Let's drive down to Baker's and go to that outdoor place with the picnic tables that's across the road."

"Yeah. Good." He liked that idea. "Let me go in and clean up." He opened the car door for her. "I'll meet you on the porch."

Ten minutes later, a spruced-up Rayland arrived on the porch. Kate got up and together they got in her car and headed toward Baker's Four Corners. Along the way, they talked about everything. Everything except the plan he'd been thinking about. They enjoyed a simple summer meal together. She had barbeque chicken with a garden salad and he had fried clam strips with coleslaw. They both had an ear of corn.

"Must be from New Jersey or somewhere," he said. "Way too early for local corn, but I like corn."

"Me too," she said as she buttered the ear.

Rayland just went straight at the corn. No butter required. He inspected the corn slowly and quite deliberately to determine exactly where to start. And when he started, he went slowly, savoring the flavor, seemingly kernel by kernel. When he looked up, Kathleen was crying. Sobbing actually.

"What's wrong, Kathleen?"

"Nothing. It's nothing, Rayland." With that, the sobbing got heavier and she got up and left.

Rayland was dumbfounded. What happened? What's going on? Should I go get her, he thought, or just give her some space? Wow. This is a new one. He decided to go make sure she was alright. She was sitting in the car still crying. Crying hard.

"Kathleen, are you..."

"I'm okay. I'm okay." She sniffed. "Give me a couple of minutes, please," she said through heavy sobs. "I'll be okay."

She'd found an old Kleenex in her small clutch bag, but now it was wet and worn out. She wiped her eyes with her hand. "If you'd get me some napkins, I'd appreciate it. I just need to blow my nose."

"Sure, honey."

He went back to the counter and picked up a half dozen paper napkins all the time thinking it was surely his fault. Something he had done. And now, he'd gone and called her honey. He'd never called anyone honey in his life.

"Thank you," she said as he handed them to her. "I'll be okay. Give me a few minutes. You go have your dinner. I'll be okay."

She looked at him through red eyes. "I promise."

Rayland just stood there. She sniffled.

"I promise. You go. I'll be along."

Rayland made his way back to the table feeling useless and stupid having no idea what had occurred. Useless and stupid. He picked at his fried clams and kept his eye on the car. Soon enough, the door opened and Kathleen emerged looking somewhat composed.

When she got to the table he stood up. "You okay?" She nodded and sat down. "Yeah, I'm okay." They both picked at their meal as conversation died.

"Is it something I did?"

"No." She paused. "Well, yes, but really no. Nothing you did."

After a bit, he softly said, "Well, that explains it."

She smiled. Then chuckled and reached out and took his hand.

"It's the way you eat your corn. Two rows or three rows at a time. Very carefully. Vincent used to eat his corm the same way. We were married for 31 years. He's been gone four years now. The big things, like anniversaries, holiday, birthdays, they don't bother me anymore. But little things, like watching you eat your corn as he did. Sometimes little things sneak up on me." She looked up and added, "and then they tear me apart.

"Silly, isn't it? But just in that moment watching you eat your corn two rows at a time, a flood of emotion, love, sadness, happiness, everything, just rushed through my head. I couldn't handle it. I'm sorry, Rayland."

"Kathleen, don't worry about it for one minute. I'm sorry for you. For your loss. I'm sorry." He gazed upon her beautiful face. She gazed upon his. No words were spoken for a long time, until he said, "Let's not eat corn again."

She gave him the best smile she could muster at the moment. "Okay. That's a deal."

"I've got an idea. I'm going to make you dessert back at the farm. Sit right here. I'll be right back."

She watched as he crossed the street and disappeared into Barker's. A few minutes later, he emerged with a brown bag and his surprise.

"See that big old moon just starting to peek up over that ridge. That's the Strawberry Moon. That's what inspired my idea for your dessert."

'Strawberries?"

"Not yet." He gave her a smug look. "But you're on the right track."

When they got back to the farm, he unloaded his groceries. Two bottles of beer, a pint of vanilla ice cream and a Twinkie two pack. She looked at it and thought, well... I like ice cream.

"Come on. While we still have good light."

He started out the door with a small bowl in his hand and headed up the hill toward the pond. She followed.

"Where're we going?" She asked.

"This is it. You're standing in the middle of our dessert, so be careful."

She looked around, but couldn't figure out what she was standing in the middle of. It looked like field to her.

"See these plants?" He knelt and pointed out the shape of the leaf.

"This is a wild strawberry. Look underneath and you'll find the little red fruit. Hopefully, red. If it's not red, don't pick it. Not worth the effort. Let it go back to its mother." He pointed to a spot next to him. "You pick there and I'll pick here, and who knows, if we're lucky we might get enough to make our dessert."

Twenty minutes later they had enough berries for dessert. "These are the smallest strawberries I've ever seen, they're tiny."

"They're wild. Taste one." She did. Her eyes lit up.

"Wow. What flavor. I've never tasted anything like it. You can tell it's a strawberry, but it isn't like any strawberry I've ever eaten."

She ate another.

"Save some for my special creation."

When they got back to the ell, Rayland went right to work on his special creation. When it was ready, they moved back outside and sat on the porch. Ice cream with wild strawberries, she thought, pretty darn good. He drank a beer. She ate a Twinkie. Then he ate the other Twinkie. Rayland pointed out Jupiter, but had no luck finding shooting stars. The moon was high by the time they finished.

"That is also called the Honey Moon. Know why?"

"This is going to be a dirty joke, isn't it?"

"You've been hanging out too much with those eighth-grade boys, Miss Dirty Joker. No. It's because it coincides with the first harvest of honey. Strawberry Moon. Honey Moon."

They sat and enjoyed the summer sky.

"Well, it is more fun to hang out with you than those eighth-grade boys." She put her hand on his arm. "I'm glad I'm here with you tonight. It's like it used to be. I'm glad of that." She pulled back her hand slowly. "When you're ready to tell me your plan, I'm ready to listen."

"It's not that easy." He shifted uncomfortably in his chair. "I think it's a plan, but then sometimes when I'm with you, I get confused. Maybe it's not the right plan."

She looked at him quizzically.

"I like being with you so much, but I know…" He was struggling with how to proceed, "but I'm afraid it wouldn't be right."

Kate sat quietly not wanting to interrupt. Still, she couldn't help but think, what wouldn't be right. Where is he going with this? She knew he was struggling with whatever it was he was trying to say, so she pretended to look for shooting stars. Maybe Rayland wouldn't notice the confusion on her face.

"If I were to settle down…" he started slowly. She turned away from the evening sky and looked at him "If I were to settle down," he continued, "it might be nice. I don't have much experience with that kind of thing, and," he wiped condensation off his beer bottle and rubbed it into his hands. "And I might not be very good at it." Still groping for words, he added, "but I imagine it would be nice."

They sat in silence. Eventually he stood and looked off into the night. He turned back to Kate. "Kate, if I were to settle down with you, I'm not sure I'd be the same anymore. It makes me nervous thinking about it."

He rubbed his hands together. He took a deep breath. Rayland was clearly uncomfortable. "I like the idea, but it makes me nervous just talking about it."

He pursed his lips and exhaled. "I'm sorry, Kate." He stood. "I've got to get some air." He looked at her for sympathy. There wasn't any. Only confusion. Stepping off the porch, he walked to the water trough, stopped and splashed water on his face. With Star at his side, they headed toward the pond.

Kate sat for a moment looking at the porch floor as if there were something to see. Eventually she looked up and said to the dog, "Wow. That was confusing," she said. "I'm worried about him, Champ,"

The dog just looked at her and wagged his tail.

Chapter 17

A DUSTY FOURTH

Thursday - July 2, 1964

Washington, D.C. – *President Lyndon Johnson signed the Civil Rights Act of 1964 into law, abolishing racial segregation in the United States in public schools, public accommodations and travel, and in voter registration. Only one southern Democrat voted in favor of the bill.*

Early, early morning was the cleanest part of the day. Only a light haze of dust covered the rising sun. Crews arrived around six and machines started to move. From that point on, for those living anywhere near the construction area, dust was part of your life. It rose. It thickened. It settled. Machines pulsed above the town like a large advancing army. Windows were closed to keep out the noise, but more so the dust. It got through cracks around the windows, under the door jams, into the cupboards and closets. Windows, shut all summer against the blowing dirt, were tinted brown. After a light shower, they streaked with mud. Cars and trucks looked like they'd been in some sort of dirt storm. Front windshields were caked with mud except for the arc that the wipers could reach. Dust got in your eyes, your ears and nose. A good blow into a handkerchief revealed the dirt you'd inhaled. The dust caused coughing spasms, shortness of breath and asthma. In fact, it was a health concern for infants and the elderly.

Everyone in town had to live with it, but perhaps wives and mothers had it the toughest. Serving dust-free food was an achievement. Some women took to kneading bread under a bed sheet. If they set a pie out to cool, they'd better cover it. Town's people took to wearing a bandana over their mouths and noses if they went out for any length of time. Some housekeepers covered their windows with wet sheets. It kept the house temperature cooler without letting in dust. The women wiped and cleaned everything. A lot.

No one in town had ever seen anything like this. The huge earth-moving machines rearranged the landscape. Rock was blasted, old farms cut up and buried. Thousands of yards of fill were hauled in to raise the road bed where needed. Drainage ditches were lined with culverts and covered with more fill. Rolling meadows were leveled. Embankments were built. Screened dirt was used to level bumps and dips. Layer after layer of gravel was dumped to make the roadbed. Twelve inches minimum. Layers were added and compacted. Added and compacted until the roadbed reached the height called for in the design. Every step, every action raised more dust. By noon, the haze of dirt that hung in the air sometimes overshadowed the sun.

The scale of the project overwhelmed the little town. Everyone knew the highway was being built to speed Vermont along on a faster economic trajectory, but the thought of what was being left behind was now setting in. Towsley, like other Vermont villages, had the misfortune of being right in the path of the largest peacetime construction project in U.S. history.

The Fourth of July parade was scheduled for Saturday at 4 p.m. The town select board had petitioned the highway crew to knock off early on Friday and hose down the loose dirt at the construction area so the town could enjoy a celebration the next day without choking on dust. The workers agreed. Hosing down the loose dirt made a significant difference.

Families started staking out their spot along the parade route well in advance. They shared the shade of a tree or beer with friends and neighbors. The summer dust, better known as 'the damn dust,' gave them plenty to talk about.

Ron and Mazie Davies staked out an early site in front of the church. They gathered friends as they walked by. John and Ginnie Hurley spread a blanket, Steve and Julie Bryant brought their own folding chairs.

The first parade was always the parade of families walking by. Neighbors greeted one another and caught up on local news. Albert and Marie Tanner passed by, going about as slow as a Sunday afternoon. They were both dressed for a party.

"Albert, how'd you get an afternoon off? Did you run out of coffee and donuts?" John yelled out.

"Heck, I'm usually out of coffee and donuts by 7:30. Marie puts on the first pot at 5:30 and damn if they don't start coming in the door about that time. Coffee and beer are my retirement plan, Johnny." Albert raised his good eyebrow and waved.

"Good for you. Find a way to sell this dirt and you'll be a wealthy man."

"Are you bothering this good man and his wife, John?" It was Doris Regusta. She was wearing a red, white and blue top hat with two little American flags sticking out the top. It clashed with her floral print dress, but it was the Fourth of July, and so what?

"Doris, you look like a hundred bucks today." John pointed at her hat.

"John, I think that expression is 'You look like a million bucks,'" she corrected.

"Nope. A hundred bucks. That's as high as I can go." He laughed at his own dumb joke.

"You're awful, John Hurley." She frowned. "See you later, Ginnie." She waved and continued on to say hello to the next group.

The Towsley parade wasn't a big parade. There were about as many people in the parade as there were along the parade route. The ranks got inflated slightly by disgruntled travelers who had to wait for the parade to start and finish before they could proceed on their way. If you were headed north or south, there wasn't any way around Towsley. The new highway would soon change that.

Four o'clock came and went, but eventually five WWII vets in ill-fitting uniforms marched into view carrying the American flag and Vermont state flag or bearing an old M16 rifle. Dennis Gould, this year's grand marshal, followed. He was last year's grand marshal, too. And the year before that's. The grand marshal is always the oldest person in town. Dennis was 92, but he was obviously outlasting lots of other local citizens. He was chauffeured in a 1931 Ford Model A Roadster with Preston Jaffee at the wheel. Dennis waved to the crowd and tried to throw candy to the kids, but most of his tosses barely make it out of the car. Preston was waving, smoking a cigar, and enjoying his celebrity position.

Melvin Moore, the town constable, was in full uniform in the back of a red convertible driven by Mazie Davies. She was leaning back and explaining to him that Dennis Gould should not be the grand marshal every year, no matter how old he was. It was not unusual for people to live into their nineties these days, she lectured. Melvin looked a little bored with the conversation.

With the dignitaries out of the way, the procession of floats, town teams, bands, and fire trucks followed. The floats were mostly promotional in nature. There was Jon Johns Portable Johns, Helen's Beauty Salon, and the Community

Church youth group for starters. Aud Cairnes organized a float to promote the new community garden. Local ladies in overalls sat and displayed bushel baskets of early season produce that would all be given away after the parade. The 4H kids and their leaders strolled by with several heifers while young ladies paraded their well-groomed horses. Little League teams marched, as did the Cub Scouts, Boy Scouts, Girl Scouts and Brownies. The Windsor High School marching band made a prized appearance. The Marching Cougar band, 27 strong, was always a welcomed guest. The town coronet band, limited though they were, was a big hit nonetheless. Then came the grand finale. The big finish. The star of the show. The fire engines.

There were fifteen engines from towns near and far. The oldest was the 1890 hand-pumped antique wagon out of Springfield. Four local men in period dress pulled it. The newest machine belonged to the White River Junction Fire Department. The big, slick black engine was cleaned and polished. Towsley had two engines and a rescue truck. Rayland was riding atop the newer one. He was charged with throwing candy to the kids. He seemed to be having a heck of a time. As they passed, Rayland hurled a small Tootsie Roll and hit John Hurley squarely in the back of the head.

"Hey. What're you doing, you old fool?" John bellowed recognizing Rayland. "You're too dangerous to have that job."

Rayland laughed, waved and tossed a whole handful of Tootsie Rolls to John's gathering. He saw Kathleen further down the parade route, sitting with friends. She got two handfuls tossed in her direction. Rayland hadn't enjoyed himself that much in quite some time. He felt like he was out in the sunshine again. Dust and all.

The parade ended, but it was followed by yet another parade. Bumper to bumper travelers who could finally move and get out of town. Some townies stayed, had another beer and watched the traffic. Others started moving toward the ball field where the celebration would continue. There was the Little League championship game, a picnic dinner and fireworks yet to come.

The ball game was just something going on in the background while the adults partied. Kathleen had invited Norman and Aud along with Emory and Alina to join her. She hoped Rayland would be up to it as well.

"Hey, Em. Step on over here and have a dirt burger," John called from the food stand. "Support Rotary. Support Little League. Support dirt." He laughed. "You gotta eat a peck of dirt before you die, Em. Might as well get started and support Rotary while you do it."

Em offered a friendly wave and continued along. "There's Kathleen," he pointed her out to Alina. "Behind the center field, out by the trees." They joined her, said their hellos and set their picnic basket down on the edge of the blanket. Em was quick to his cooler as he opened a cold beer.

"Norman is over watching the game," Kate pointed out. "Take a beer and go join him if you'd like, Em. Aud is right back there." She nodded to the blanket two down from them. "She's just catching up. Pull up a seat, Alina. How's your summer been?"

Em wandered toward home plate where he saw Norman and Thomas Lumfield talking. "Hi, Em. Got a good one going here. Beavers 4, Crows 3," Thomas said looking dressed for the festivities in his American flag bow tie.

"Who names these teams?" Em asked.

"Somebody's mother, I guess," Thomas said raising his eyes and bobbing his head and smiling as he spoke. There was a hot grounder toward the hole, but the shortstop made a nice play and an out at first.

"Keep an eye on that kid." It was Rayland. "We could use that kind of glove on my Phillies, Tom." The shortstop, number 12, was Tom's son. "He's pretty good. Just like his old man, I'll bet."

"Well, Rayland. Let's just say your Phillies are doing darn good without him. First place in the National, I believe." He smiled at his own knowledge of Rayland's favorite team. "And that pitcher you added threw a perfect game a few days ago. Right?" He looked at the others. "Did you guys hear about that? Jim Bunning threw a perfect game. That's a no hitter with no walks. Nobody reached base. Don't see that often. If the Phillies keep playing well, maybe you can let Tommy finish seventh grade."

Tom chuckled.

"Just scouting, Thomas. Just in case." He shook hands with his brother. "How you doing, Em?"

"Good. Good. How about you?" They turned back to the game. "Got a surprise for you, Rayland."

"Oh man, Em. Surprises these days are killing me. Hope it's a good one." The Beavers retired the side holding their one-run edge.

"Ricky's home on leave. He's going to stop by to say hello and bring you up to date so you won't have to worry about the United States Navy." Em knew that would please his brother. He sipped his beer and smiled.

Rayland lit up. "That's great. Can't wait to see him. Hope he's going to wear his uniform."

"You sound just like his mother. He's not going to wear his uniform for crying out loud."

The Crow's pitcher tired. The Beaver's extended their lead. Actually, the Crow's pitcher was done. He couldn't throw a strike and his misses were wild. Walk. Walk. Walk.

With the game coming to a predictable conclusion, they all walked back past center field to join the ladies.

Em and Rayland walked along chatting and saying hello to friends as they went. Rayland felt free and unburdened. First time in weeks. Maybe months.

"Hello, Doris," Rayland greeted her. "Love your hat. You always get into the spirit of things."

"You do, too, Rayland."

He had no idea what she meant. She took hold of his sleeve with her thumb and forefinger. And held on.

"You and Em come by later and have a piece of pie with me." A beautiful apple pie sat on her wicker basket. "I call it my big boom special."

She obviously had a story to tell.

"I put that pie outside to cool yesterday and went to the store to get some stuff. BOOM. Damn if those workers didn't start detonating their dynamite. BOOM. By the time I got home the pie was covered with dirt. Covered."

She gave a sly smile.

"So, all I could do was brush it off and sprinkle it with powdered sugar. Ha. What do you think of that?" She released his sleeve and chuckled. "It will be great. You two come on by later and we'll have some pie. But, don't mention the details, okay?"

"You make the best pie, Doris." Rayland winked at her. "Always tasty. Always tasty. We'll catch-up with you later."

They wandered along, taking their time. When they arrived at the designated blanket, it was blankets. Friends had gathered.

"Hello, Rayland," Kate smiled. "Thank you for the candy today. I think I have enough for everyone." She offered one to Rayland. "Want one?"

"Hello, Kathleen." He smiled self-consciously and took a Tootsie Roll. "I feel like I haven't seen you in a long time." He popped the candy into his mouth.

"Not since our dinner at the Four Corners a few weeks back. That was fun. You're going to join us, I hope."

"I'm parked right there, next to Alina's fried chicken and spicy potato salad. She makes the best darn potato salad. Seems like a good place to be on the Fourth of July, doesn't it?" He threw his hat over onto her blanket. "Maybe after dinner we can go for a walk. Down to the river, maybe."

"I'd like that."

Ulmer Winslow was starting his Fourth of July speech. It was a good speech, but he made the same speech every year. People had lost interest five speeches ago. Fortunately, his speech was short, but he followed it with the Gettysburg Address. Before launching into Lincoln's address, he tried to gather all the school children around the gazebo. You could watch the older kids drift off finding something else to do. The younger kids gathered not yet knowing what to expect.

Ulmer cleared his throat. Then cleared it again. He looked left. He looked right. He looked out on the small crowd before him and he started.

"Four score and seven years ago our fathers brought forth, upon this continent, a new nation, conceived in liberty, and dedicated to the proposition that 'all men are created equal." Ulmer was in his element. The adults relaxing on the blankets lowered their voices to whispers. Perhaps it was with respect for Ulmer or maybe Lincoln.

Rayland relaxed on the blanket and watched the clouds roll by as he daydreamed about being with Kathleen. He looked forward to walking with her along the river pathway.

"Would you like a drumstick, Rayland?" Alina handed him a piece of chicken and whispered, "What do you think of Kate's new job offer?"

Rayland found this so unexpected he almost dropped his chicken.

"What job offer?" He was startled by his own concern. He felt like his life was finally getting back in order. Was he losing Kathleen? No. Don't throw that at me, he thought. Rayland was looking at Alina. She was speaking to him. He didn't hear a word she was saying. His mind was racing. He didn't know why. He wanted to think clearly, but he couldn't. What did this mean? What was going on? He needed space. He walked away, toward the river, his chicken sitting untouched on the paper plate.

Alina realized he was upset but sure didn't know why. Em saw him go.

"Em. I just told your brother about Kate's new job offer." She handed him a chicken wing. "He got all upset. It seemed unusual to me. Not sure why." She had a worried look. "You should go talk to him." She motioned toward the river.

There was a well-worn path from the ball field to a clearing by the river. The ball players swam down there on hot days. Fishermen and young boys walked it to go fishing. Older kids used it as a preferred place to make out. It was peaceful there. Rayland like to go there to sit and think, and maybe clear his head and get his thoughts in order. Em found him sitting on a log at the water's edge.

"What's the matter, bro?"

"Hi, Em." He tossed a stone into the river. "I don't know. I thought I had a plan, but Alina's news about Kathleen kinda threw me. I could tell. It threw me." He shook his head. "I don't know why, Em."

They sat still for a moment.

"I'm having trouble with change." He looked at his brother. "Any change." He tossed another stone. "I thought I was handling things better, but now, now they're throwing too much at me. My plate is full, Em. You know what I mean? My plate is really full." He turned to his brother. "I thought I had a plan. I was comfortable with my plan, but anything, anything throws me off. It just throws me off."

Rayland thoughtlessly threw stone after stone into the river. Em sat and watched while thinking, he's so fragile. He's up. He's down. Just when I think he's coming around, he goes into a fog. Then he walks back out of the fog only to disappear again. Eventually, he turned to Rayland and said, "That job might be nothing, Rayland. Let's go and talk to Alina and find out what's going on. You can't get all upset about something if you don't know what it is." He got up. "Come on. Let's go back."

A dejected Rayland followed along as if he were the little brother. There was a difference between being confused and being upset and he wanted Em to know he knew that. "I'm not upset," he said, sounding a bit obstinate. "I'm confused. I got upset at that surprise meeting you all had for me a while back. That was too much. That's why that upset me. It was too much. But now, I'm confused."

Alina saw her husband and brother-in-law as they approached. "Everything okay?"

"Honey, what can you tell us about Kate's new job?"

"I don't know. I don't think it's a job. It's a job offer. She's thinking about taking a different job. That's all I know. What the heck, Rayland. So what? People change jobs. Did you talk to Kate about it?"

He shook his head.

"Then what are we talking about? You don't know. I don't know."

Trying to lighten the mood, she added, "You want to take a poke at it, Em?"

After thinking that over, Rayland agreed.

They approached Kate who was deep in conversation with Aud.

"Kate," Em started enthusiastically, not realizing he was interrupting in his haste to get Rayland back to the good mood he'd been in just a little while ago. "Alina tells me you got a job offer. Nice. What's the news?"

Slightly embarrassed, she chose her words carefully. "Well, at this point, it's just an offer. It is a nice one though. I'm thinking about it. The White River Junction school union has offered me the job of over-seeing all the elementary grades. It's a big job. A big pay raise, too. All of which is nice." She wrinkled her brow. "I just want to be sure I can handle it."

"Wow. Sounds great." Alina pitched in. "If you take the job, do we lose you as a neighbor and friend?"

"Neighbor, yes. Friend? I certainly hope not."

Rayland's stomach fell. He didn't participate in the conversation. Nor did he hear much that was said. He'd heard enough, so he slipped out and went back to the blanket. Alina followed shortly. "Want that piece of chicken now?"

"Sure." He nibbled. Alina broke the silence.

"Rayland, it's a maybe. It's only a maybe." She reached for the potato chips. "A new job doesn't mean you're losing anything. And besides, Rayland, it's not like you've been romancing her socks off."

She offered him some chips. He declined.

"If you want to be part of something, you've got to work at it." She snapped a chip in half and ate it. "Come on, Rayland. If you want her in your life, give yourself a chance. Put a little effort into it."

"It's not that I want her." He looked at Alina. "Except, I do, but ... my life is too...my life is too much up in the air. I can't ever remember it being like this. I like her a lot. I hope she doesn't move away."

Rayland thought about that for quite a while. He saw Kate out in the field watching children chase each other with sparklers. He decided to confront her. She saw him coming, and looked over smiling.

"Remember how much fun sparklers were when you were a child?"

"Kate, can we talk?"

That seemed abrupt, she thought, but she nodded agreement. "Let's walk down to the river," she suggested. "Remember we talked about that earlier today?"

They walked across the grassy field, around the blankets that were spread for the picnics in progress. The woods ahead opened to a well-worm path to the river. Before they even reached the woods, Rayland stumbled right into it.

"Kathleen. Don't take that job. You can't leave."

She was surprised at his odd pronouncement. "Why, Rayland?" she asked, stopping and looking directly at him. He looked back to the field at the kids playing. They stood that way for a minute. She asked again. "Why, Rayland?"

"I don't know." He turned and looked down the path. "You just can't."

He was having difficulty finding the words he wanted. "It will leave a hole in me if you leave. A hole as big as can be." He looked at her. "When you smile at me..." He swallowed. "When you smile at me, I feel warmth. If you leave, the warmth goes too. A big part of me will die, Kathleen."

"Rayland, stop! Stop!"

She was startled by his comment. She searched for words. She took her time. "You barely talked to me for much of the year. And when you did, it was half conversations. Sometimes it felt like you had something you wanted to say, but never did. And now you're telling me a part of you will die... if I take a different job?" She was firm. "That's not fair, Rayland. That's not fair. In fact, it's absurd. You can't say that. I cannot build my life, or my career, around someone who only talks to me now and then. When he's feeling up to it."

"Kathleen, you know I care for you."

"No. No, Rayland. I *don't* know." She inhaled deeply. "I *think* you like me. I *think* you like being with me. But care? How would I know? You hide. You hide from me. You hide away from your friends. You hide yourself away. We try to help you find an answer to your dilemma and you push us away. Caring is a two-way street." She exhaled through pursed lips. "You won't take responsibility for your future. How can someone be in your future, make plans around you, when you won't talk about your future?"

She ran her fingers through her hair. "You talk about some plan but no one knows what that means, what you're thinking about. If you can't take responsibility for what comes next for you, how can you dare ask me to not to make decisions about my own life ... Yikes, Rayland, don't make this my fault."

Rayland stopped walking. "I'm scared, Kathleen. I'm scared." He looked at her with frightened eyes.

"Scared of what? Tell me." She started down the path toward the river.

"I don't know. I don't know." He walked beside her. "I don't know, Kathleen." He kicked at a stick. "Scared of what's ahead. Scared of what I'm leaving behind. I don't know. Scared because I can't see the future."

He looked at her sheepishly.

"Sometimes all I can see is nothing. It's black." He sighed and stuck his hands in his pockets. "Stupid, isn't it? I'm scared like a little kid in a thunderstorm. I'm not scared when I'm with you." He raised both arms in desperation. "Finally, I thought I had found a way out. And now, I hear you might be leaving."

He looked away.

"I'm afraid I'll slide back into the darkness."

His eyes pleaded.

"I don't want to be in the dark. I want to be out. I want to be with you. I want to be with my friends."

Kate methodically scratched her forehead with one finger as if it made her think better. After a bit. she said, "Rayland, you're very sweet. You're a wonderful man. Do you understand the concern and the feelings your friends have for you? Your friends adore you. That includes me." She paused. "But let us be your friend. Let us stay close. Let us help you."

They sat on the log by the riverbank.

"Things will work out, but you've got to share your thoughts and ideas for the future and make some plans before it's too late."

But Rayland said nothing. The quiet was loud and then it was just quiet. They watched the river roll by. In the quiet, they could hear voices coming down the path. It turned out to be Ricky. He was excited. Em was with him.

"Hey, Uncle Rayland." Ricky shouted as he neared. Just seeing Ricky lifted Rayland's spirits and lightened his mood.

"Ricky. Ricky. Ricky. How are you doing?" He gave his nephew a big bear hug. "You look great, Ricky. I can see the Navy is whipping you into good shape." He rubbed Ricky's head. "What happened to the hair? You used to look like a Beatle. Now you look like... well, you good, Ricky. Glad to see you. He said proudly."

Ricky was equally glad to see his uncle.

"We were getting a little worried about you two." Em said, explaining their interruption. "You've been down here a long time. Ricky stopped by specially to see his uncle, but he's got a hot date, or something, so he doesn't have a lot of time."

"No. No hot date. I'm getting together with Hannah tonight. She's back in school. Law school this time. We're still friends, so we want to hang out. I'm only in town for two days. I ship out Monday." He looked at Kate. "I wanted to catch up with Uncle Rayland. Might not see him for a while."

She smiled.

Em told Rayland he promised to get Ricky going before the fireworks started, and suggested they head back and talk along the way. As they started up the river path, Rayland asked about the Navy. Ricky was excited to tell him about his upcoming tour of duty.

"Monday night, they fly me to Rota, Spain to catch up with my ship. We're headed into the Mediterranean. Looks like I'll be in the Med for a while. I'm assigned to the USS Des Moines, CLG 9."

"So. So, what's all that mean? Where's Rota, Spain? What's a CLG 9?"

"Rota is a munitions depot somewhere in Spain. I'm meeting the ship there. That's all I know." Ricky picked up a light branch off the ground. "Then we shove off." He rapped the switch against his leg as they walked. "CLG means Guided Missile Light Cruiser. We carry nukes." He looked at Rayland. "Don't tell Mom."

"I don't want my nephew messing around with any nuclear bombs in some foreign country. What do you think, Em?"

"He'll learn how to handle the weapons. His mother is more concerned about the senoritas."

"Yeah, senoritas. I should learn something there, too, don't you think, Uncle Rayland?"

As they walked along, Rayland taught his nephew what he called his one and only Navy song.

"I joined the Navy to see the world,
And what did I see, I saw the sea.
I saw the Atlantic,
It was gigantic.
I saw the Pacific,
It wasn't terrific.
I joined the Navy to see the world,
But what did I see, I saw the sea."

It was the appearance of him acting normal again.

The path diverged. Parking this way. Field that way. Kathleen said good night to Em and wished Ricky good luck. She turned to Rayland. "We can talk any time you'd like. I'll see you back at the picnic. Good night, Em. Bon Voyage, Ricky."

They walked to the car where Alina was putting the blankets and lawn chairs into the trunk.

Rayland stopped short. Out of their hearing, he turned to his nephew and got serious. "Ricky, I'm so happy and excited for you. Off to see the world, Ensign Ricky Jensen. Yes sir. Ensign Ricky Jensen." He took a deep breath. "I'm so proud of you."

Rayland took his nephew by the shoulders and looked him in the eye. "Ricky, I may never see you again."

"Whoa. What are you talking about, Rayland? It's a two-year tour. I get rotated back to the states in two years. That's barely enough time to meet one of those senoritas. I'll be home before you change your underwear."

Rayland laughed and hugged him. Then he pushed back and whispered, “I love you Ricky. I’ll miss you.”

“I love you, too, Uncle Rayland. I really do.” He turned and joined his folks at the car. Rayland took the path back to the ball field.

Em noticed how the conversation ended. “Everything okay, Rick?

“Yeah. I think so, but that was strange.” He looked at his father, concerned. “He said he loved me. But it was the way he said it, Dad. It was really strange.”

Chapter 18

LABOR DAY

Monday, August 31, 1964

Biloxi, Mississippi – *Schools in Biloxi were integrated for the first time as 16 black first-grade students were enrolled, without incident, in the four elementary schools that had been previously all white. The twelve girls and four boys were protected from protesters by 20 U.S. Marshals supplementing local law enforcement officials. An emergency force of 1,800 members of the Mississippi National Guard was on standby in the event that 'federalization' needed to be ordered by President Johnson.*

"Where you been, Rayland? Haven't seen you in a dog's age."

"Hi Leo. I don't know. Busy, I guess."

"Doing what?" Leo was organizing produce in the bins while he talked. "You gotta eat." He sorted onions by size. "You're killing my business," he joked as he picked up a sack of potatoes. "Anyway, good to see you. How they treating you over on the farm?"

"Not so good, Leo. They're kicking me out, you know. Putting me out to pasture." He picked up a couple of bananas. "Only got two weeks left. No extension this time. The machines are working right up to the property lines on both sides. If they keep digging and moving dirt, my house is going to be buried before I can get out."

"I hate to hear that. What're you going to do?"

"I don't know," He put the bananas back. "But I'm not leaving."

"Well, sounds to me like you're not staying either." Leo poured potatoes out of a sack and into a bin. "I'll bet you're the last one standing. When they pave that highway, they should tip their hats to Rayland Jensen. One solitary old Vermont farmer who took them on and gave them a damn good go at it. I respect you, Rayland. I respect you a lot. You stood up for what you believe in. They just didn't treat you like we'd expect from a civil society. They didn't treat any of you very well in my opinion. Some of these folks have been devastated by this eminent domain stuff. I know some of those properties were bruised and needed some fixin' up, but hell, the valley's been home to some of you folks for generations. Folks like you. They had dreams of leaving their farms to their children," He inspected his vegetable display. "State didn't even offer to help resettling people. Damn shame if you ask me." He looked at Rayland and shook his head. "Damn shame."

"What do you think I should do, Leo? I'm confused. The confusion makes me sad. Sometimes I get too sad to move." He inspected a Macintosh. "Guess that's why I haven't been over here in a while." He shined the apple on his shirt. "I start walking over here, and someone always picks me up and gives me a ride. Then I'm stuck talking to them. Guess what they want talk about? Damn, Leo, sometimes it's just too much."

He checked the grapes.

"See what I mean? We're talking about it again. Drives me nuts, Leo. Drives me nuts."

He put the grapes down.

"I gotta get out of here."

"Do you mean the area?" Leo walked behind the counter. "Hope you don't mean my store. You're always welcome here. You know that."

"Thank you, Leo." Rayland started to pay for his provisions but interrupted himself. "Give me a container of that chop suey, also."

Leo wiped his hands on his apron, reached into the deli cooler and took out the bowl. He filled a small cardboard container, affixed the lid and handed it to Rayland. "Here you go. One pint of Cavatappi Pomodoro Ragu."

"No. No. No." Rayland was confused. "I want the American chop suey. I like that stuff."

"Mama's Cavatappi Pomodoro Ragu. Same thing. Don't tell. Somehow, between here and there, the name changed. Still tastes the same. Maybe better. And Rayland. Here."

He put a deviled egg into a waxed paper sack and handed it to him.

"Ten cents apiece? Two for a quarter?" Rayland asked.

"Not today. That's on the house."

"Thank you." He took the egg, saving it for later. "I probably won't be seeing you again, Leo. Thanks for being my friend."

"What the hell you mean by that? Of course, I'm your friend, and, of course, I'll be seeing you again." Leo hesitated. "If I don't, I'll come find you and kick your ass."

"Leo, I don't think you can get your foot up that high anymore. Not as young as you used to be, my friend. Not as young as you used to be." Rayland smiled, put the egg in his sack, tipped his hat and headed toward the door.

As he walked, remembrances whirled in his brain. His head was filled with good memories, but he was empty. He was filled with empty. It ate at him. He was sad. Everything made him sad. Leo made him sad. The deviled egg made him sad. Memories made him sad.

As he walked along, friends passed and offered a ride. He turned them down. How many times have I walked to Leo's and back? He smiled and said to himself, not many, actually. Everyone always gave me a ride. Everyone. That made him sad. He wanted to go back to the farm and talk to Ma. She was the only one who really listened. No, he thought. They all listen. She's the only one who heard. She's the only one who cared. The others are always nice to me, but Ma cared. He stopped himself. No. that's not true. Norman cares. So does Aud, and Emory and Kathleen. It's me. He walked and thought. Maybe it's me. I care too much.

Confusion filled his mind. It fed his sadness. At times, a single unknown voice filled his mind as he tried to sort out his feelings. Whose voice was it? The voice reminded him of things he loved. The voice made him think about those things. The thinking about those things made him sad. He didn't know why. They are all things he loved. These were things that made him happy, but damn if it didn't soon change to sad. I can get to a point where I no longer know how to feel happy, he thought. Then Leo gives me an egg, and it's like a summer's breeze. It seems like a small thing, but it makes me happy. Then it makes me sad. I'm supposed to be making a plan but you can't make a future different than your past when your past is all you've ever known and loved.

Without realizing it, he was nearing the river. He looked across the bridge. He took a long look, and thought, 174 paces from this side to that side. How many times have I crossed this bridge?

Today was different. Today he was afraid of the other side. He looked into the river hoping to find the light. The river just rolled on by. There was no light. "I've got my plan. I don't need a different plan. I've got my plan," he repeated to himself. But the blackness was setting in again. It whirled in his head.

He stopped when he got to the center of the bridge. Feeling dizzy, he leaned against the metal fencing. He thought he was going to vomit into the river. When he didn't, he sat down. Staring through the mesh fencing, he watched the current race by. He was afraid of something. Was it something in front of him? Or behind him? Was it at this end of the bridge? Or that end? The river just kept moving along.

He had no idea how long he'd been sitting there when he was startled by Aud, who gently shook his shoulder. "Rayland! Are you alright?"

He looked at her but didn't comprehend. In his confusion he thought, what is Aud doing here? Where'd she come from? How long have I been here?

"Aud, what are you doing here?"

"I saw you slumped over. I thought you might need help." Her car was idling alongside the bridge walkway. "What's wrong, Rayland?"

"I don't know. I can't figure out where to go."

He looked to one end of the bridge. Then to the other.

"It's like something has a hold on me. I'm just riding along. I thought I was getting better, but I'm just riding along. Going nowhere."

He waved his hand in the direction of the farm. "If I go that way, I see nothing. It's gone. It's all black and gone." He turned. "If I go that way, it's a place I've never been. I can't see what it is. All I see is the river." He looked up at her. "The river doesn't care." He lowered his head. "I feel lost, Aud. I'm in control of nothing. I might as well be adrift on that river."

He looked down at the water again. "And that river doesn't care. I could be drowning down there. right next to the shore. That river just doesn't care."

"Oh, Rayland."

She sat down beside him.

"Oh, Rayland. My sweet Rayland. Let me help you."

They sat for a minute.

"Come on. Let's get you off this bridge and back to my house. I'll make you a cup of tea, and we can talk." She got up, and helped him to his feet. "Do you want your egg?"

The deviled egg and waxed paper were sitting on the bridge walkway.

"What's it doing on the bridge?" He studied it for a moment. Then with the toe of his boot, he pushed it under the rail and watched it land in the water and disappear. All five foot two of Aud helped walk Rayland to the car. She opened the door and he slumped in.

They rode in silence. "Let's go in through the mud room, Rayland." He followed. They entered the mudroom where she suggested, "Why don't you sit on the bench and take off your boots? Put on Norman's slippers."

She handed them to him.

"Come into the kitchen when you're ready. I'll put some water on for tea."

He looked haggard and worn out as he walked into Aud's kitchen. He sat at the breakfast table, and she put a cup of tea before him. He reached for the sugar bowl and put a big spoonful into his mug. Then another.

"Norman is in Brattleboro for some sort of meeting about cattle. He should be back in an hour or two. When you've done with your tea, why don't you to go up to our guest room and rest until he gets home. Will you do that for me, Rayland? You look exhausted."

He nodded.

Eventually, Rayland shuffled up the stairs and stretched out on the bed in the guest room. Aud cleaned the table and looked through the day's mail. She sat and read the letter addressed to her from Helma. Shortly after five, Norman pulled into the driveway. Aud met him at the door with a prolonged hug.

"What do I owe that to?"

"I'm so glad you're home, honey. Today has been awful. Just awful."

He sat to remove his boots. She started telling about finding Rayland on the bridge. "He was just sitting there. Confused, but I don't know what he was confused about. He didn't make a lot of sense." She took Norman's jacket and hung it up. "He wasn't angry or out of sorts like he's been. He was just babbling on about the river, and not making much sense. He said he was confused about which way to go."

"Do you think he was thinking about jumping?" He looked for his slippers.

"No. He was more like an animal out of its habitat. Lost. He couldn't figure out which way to turn. Where to go."

She watched him search for his slippers. "They're upstairs. On Rayland's feet. He's taking a nap. I told him I'd send you up to wake him when you got home."

She noticed his big toe sticking out the front of his sock.

"Leave that by my sewing basket and I'll darn it. But, not today." She smiled. "Tell him dinner will be in about an hour, but no hurry."

"Don't need it today." He stood. "I'll go wake him."

Norman returned almost immediately, his big toe still protruding. "He's gone." They looked at each other not sure what to do. "My slippers are gone, too. Guess I'll have to wear my boots." He tickled her quickly and said, "Only kidding. Only kidding."

"Not a good day for kidding, Buster Brown."

"After the problem on the bridge with Rayland, Jeep came by and dropped off this letter for us," Aud said as she slid the letter across the table. It was airmail stationary so he knew it was from a foreign country. Switzerland, he assumed. Something from her parents. He picked it up and noticed it was from Austria.

It was the letter from Helma. In it, she wrote that Otto had been drinking more and more. She finally asked him to move out. Living with her mother and father and a drunken Otto had been a nightmare. Norman read aloud. 'Tell the others to move in little steps. We made one big step coming back to Austria and leaving everything we know and love in Vermont. It is too big a step. Tell then to make their changes in little steps. Moving away is very hard. I am sad and very unhappy. I love Otto and hope he gets help, but it is so hard living under one roof with my parents. We talk, me and Otto, about getting our own place, but then Otto drinks and then he cries because we just don't have the money or energy to build a new farm from scratch again. Please tell the others we think of them and wish them well. Warm regards, Helma."

Norman finished reading, but sat looking at the letter without saying anything. Finally, he looked up and said, almost to himself, "Tell the others?" He looked up at his wife. "The others are gone, Aud. Gone. Only Rayland remains and we don't know where he is. We certainly don't know where his head is."

He looked at the letter without expression.

"Coming back from Brattleboro this afternoon, as I drove on the new highway, I thought, This is beautiful. It's a magnificent, four lane highway cut through farm lands and valleys. Woods and meadows. The shoulders of the road have been planted with grass and wild flowers. There are places where you don't even see the southbound lane as you come north. You drive around a curve and there, right before you, is a beautiful vista of the mountains. It's stunning. Prettiest highway I've ever seen. Hands down prettiest."

Aud brought him a cup of tea. "But then I thought about how much pain and suffering has gone into building that road. Things no one will see. Farms plowed under, houses knocked down, families uprooted and scattered. No one will see that. No one will know about that. But the families know. The Struckins know. Rayland knows. The others know."

He sipped the tea.

"Some of those folks will land on their feet, because some always do. But others? Who knows?" He slid the letter back to Aud and continued. "They got scattered in the wind. Where are they? What are they doing? How did their kids handle it? This road is built atop broken homes and government-imposed hardship."

A quick sip, then he continued. "What did we get in return? We got a beautiful, shiny new highway that will soon roar from one end of the state to the other. It will roar right past Towsley, for better or worse. It will roar right past." He looked at his cup. "What did those whose lives were wrecked by eminent domain, what did they get? They got a little bit of money."

He seemed to be coming to a conclusion. “Money can’t buy roots, Aud. Money doesn’t buy family roots.” He fiddled with his cup. “We have an abundant community garden, filled with the Lord’s bounty, but no one to give the vegetables to, because so many of the families in need are gone. Families who helped make this a community are gone. Dispersed. Chased away by some damn highway. Gone.” He sat with his head down, staring at the tea as if there was something there to see. “Gone.”

Aud got up and started to fiddle with dinner preparation. “Why don’t I fix up a dinner that you can take to Rayland? Bring him back if he wants. You can pick up your slippers, too.” She looked at him and smiled. “Before he walks through his barn in them.”

Chapter 19

SEPTEMBER SONG

September 11, 1964

Associated Press – *North Korea's President Kim ll-sung announced today that "From now on, all new major plants must be built underground instead of on the surface" in order to protect the Communist nation's industry from aerial bombardment. Strategically important industries, such as munitions and chemicals, would supplement the factories on the surface "making North Korea the world's most heavily fortified country."*

By Labor Day, the highway pressed in on the Jensen farm from all sides. Rayland was truly the last man standing. The old house sat quietly by the big maple while the meadows to the right and left were bulldozed down to road level and turned into piles of dirt and stone. Blasting was close enough to rattle windows and occasionally break one. A parade of earthmovers, bulldozers and dump trucks passed by the barn and raised havoc with the dust it kicked up. Dust in the water trough, the feed and even the milk.

When they first rolled up to the property, Tom-John and Marty and a few other crewmembers went to pay their respects to Rayland. His farm was the next site on their demolition list. They respected the stand the man was taking even though it made their job that much, much harder.

"Rayland, I'm sick about this." Marty offered. "If there is anything we can do to make this easier on you, you let me know. Let any one of us know." Marty extended his hand. "You're a man who stood up for all of us." He paused. "We're all Vermonters. We love this land, too." They shook hands. "Damned sorry I got stuck with the job of, well..., of mucking it all up for you." He stepped back. "Sorry, Rayland."

Each man, in turn, came forward to shake Rayland's hand. It was obvious they were genuinely sorry.

"Thank you, guys." Rayland had a hard time getting those few words out. "Thank you."

The workers may not have liked the job they had to do, but they went back to work and kept at it. It seemed wrong that the day was so beautiful. A perfect blue sky day. The noise, the dirt and occasional explosion didn't add to the beauty, but it was a pretty day nonetheless.

Rayland was writing at his mother's desk when Norman entered.

"Okay if I come in, professor?" Norman asked softly.

"Hi, Norm. Sure, come in. Better yet, I'll come out. Too nice to be inside today."

"Got some stuff you might need as you pack up. We bought new desks for the sixth, seventh and eighth grades and they were delivered yesterday." Norm was the head of the school board. "Look at these cardboard cartons. They'll be great for packing." The boxes were in the back of the pickup. "What do you think?"

"Yeah. Thanks, Norm."

Truth was, Rayland hadn't given packing a minute's thought. Norm started to unload boxes, handing them out to Rayland. "No sense leaving them in the barn," Norman said. "Let's put them right in the house. That's where your stuff is."

As they unloaded, Norman asked, "You doing okay, Rayland?"

"Yeah. Sorry about last week. I'm sorry to put Aud out so much."

"She was glad to be there for you." He looked at him seriously. "What do you think it was?"

"I don't know." He shook his head. "I watch these big machines tear up the land. That yanks at me hard. This is land my Ma and Pa worked from scratch. They walked here from New York State. Did I ever tell you that? Built the farm by hand. These big wheel excavators roll in and tear it apart in minutes. It's tough to watch. It hurts me deep inside."

Norman was lost for words. They stacked without conversation. Rayland added, "Memories kind of hurt, too. I've got so many good memories of this place and the life I've lived." He looked at his friend. "Between the memories and the hurt seeing what's happening... I get really torn up."

After a few more trips, the boxes were unloaded and stacked. Some pieces of furniture had already been removed, but there was much more to go.

"What are you going to do with the rest of the furniture, Rayland? Give it to your sisters?"

"Yeah, I guess. Anything Aud might like?"

They stood quietly surveying the room. "No. We're in good shape. But thank you." Finally, Rayland said, "Can I catch a ride down to Tanner's with you? If you're going that way."

They rode along without much conversation, glad to be out of the dust and noise for a few minutes. Norman tried again to learn something about Rayland's plan, to nail him down as to where he might go in the next few days. All

Rayland came back with was, "Well... I'm living' now, but I won't be living long."

"What's that mean?" Norman snapped. He was pretty tired of Rayland's cryptic remarks but every time he lost his patience with Rayland, he'd feel guilty about doing so. Still, there was no time left and he was as frustrated as anyone else. Did the old fool think the state would build the road around him? Did he think some solution would miraculously appear? When it came to so-called progress, no miracles. Just what had already been ordained. He repeated his question: "Rayland, what exactly do you mean, I won't be living long. None of us will live forever."

"Just sounds right," Rayland said and smiled. "Don't you think?"

"Sometimes I don't know what to think with you, Rayland. One minute you're laughing and joking around and the next minute you say the strangest damn thing

"Well, it's like the song says, 'How you going to keep 'em down on the farm after they've seen TV?"

Norman paused, "It's Paree."

"What?"

"It's Paree." Turning to Rayland, he laughed. "It's Paree, Rayland. As in Paris. Paris, France."

"What are you taking about?"

Norman shook his head and chuckled. Was the old goat just singing a different tune, or did he just change the topic in mid-stream? Or maybe he had lost his ... He didn't finish that thought, just sat in his vehicle until the silence got too awkward, then asked, "You want me to wait and give you a ride home?"

"Thanks. No, Norman. I'm good to walk. It's a nice afternoon for a walk."

Tanner's old screen door banged shut behind him as he entered. Albert was at the cash register. Albert was always at the cash register. Rayland looked below the checkout area where they kept the candy. "Hello Albert. Got any more of those Sky Bars? Oops. Never mind. Here they are." He helped himself. "And Albert, I need a can of beans and a gallon of kerosene. Where you keeping the kerosene these days?"

"Look over by the kindling. Maybe behind the windshield wash."

"Got it." He picked up a gallon jug and waked back to the counter.

"Everything okay up at your place, Rayland?"

"Well, they're about to tear it down, bury it under the new road, and kick me out." He picked up an apple "Other than that, things are great."

"Well, that's a stinker." He checked Rayland's provisions and tallied up the tab. "You must have some sweet tooth. Four Sky Bars, two apples, bacon, a can of beans and a jug of kerosene."

"No. Actually the candy bars aren't for me." He bit into the apple. "Macintosh. Mighty tasty this time of year." He paid his bill, put his wallet away and said, "I won't be seeing you again, Albert. I want to wish you well."

"You going over to Claremont? That would be a good place to be, by Jeezum."

"Nope. Back to the farm." He picked up his sack. "I'm not leaving, Albert. Not leaving now. Not leaving ever." Albert raised his one-and-only eyebrow and gave Rayland a confused look.

Rayland just smiled, tipped his hat and was on his way.

Melvin Moore was waiting in his police car just outside the barn quietly eating a Slim Jim as Rayland walked up from behind. Rayland leaned in the open driver's window surprising the sheriff. "You here to see me, Melvin? I see you brought your posse."

He acknowledged the two other men in the car. "Afternoon, gents. Expecting trouble?"

Just then, Star ran up to greet him with a big stick in his mouth just in case Rayland wanted to play. Star was acting as if the world made sense, that life as he knew it was going to stay the same forever. Maybe not knowing is the best way to get through this, Rayland thought.

"Hello, Rayland. No. No. Not suspecting trouble. I got a court order for this visit. Here it is, if you want to review it."

He handed it to Rayland.

"No. I trust you, Mel. Do what you gotta do."

He tried to pull the stick away from Star, but Star won and went off wagging his tail.

"This would be a lot easier, Rayland, if you were a prick."

"Sorry, Mel. Guess I just wasn't in school that day."

They walked toward the barn. The two deputies followed

"You can come along if you want. It's your tools and wagons. At least until tomorrow."

"No," Rayland said and headed to the house. "Give a yell if you need me."

"I'm sorry, Rayland."

"Not your fault, Mel. Just a part time job to make a few bucks. Remember?" He turned to go.

"Rayland." There was purpose in Mel's voice. Rayland turned and the sheriff extended his hand. "I'm really sorry, Rayland."

Rayland looked at him and smiled, and they shook hands. "It's okay, Mel. It's really okay." He smiled and his eyes shone with the old sparkle. "You're just doing your job. See those guys knocking down the meadows? They're just doing their job. Everyone is just doing their job. Man's gotta have a job. It's okay, Mel."

Rayland walked over and sat in the sunshine on his dusty porch. Star lay at his feet chewing his stick. They watched as the sheriff and crew entered the horse barn. They emptied it. The harnesses, plows and the wagons. They dumped tools into a pile. Next to it, another pile. Old bridles, blinders, and saddles. Then the sleigh. The sleigh brought back so many memories. Riding across the fields and meadows through the snow with the kids all bundled up. Riding into town to see neighbors and friends. He loved that old sleigh. He couldn't help but wonder what the heck they were going to do with the sleigh. But Melvin was just doing his job. A job the court had ordered. He knew Mel. He knew Marty and Tom-John.

Who exactly is the court, he wondered? Were they just doing their job? They don't know me, and I don't know them. Rayland got up and went inside. Enough was enough. Melvin and the deputies finished and departed without much ado. Rayland wandered back to the parlor, and sat down and wrote late into the afternoon. After a supper of beans and bacon and biscuits, the cows were milked and put out to pasture, what little pasture remained. As Ida Mae, always last, left the barn, he opened a Sky Bar. Ida Mae stopped and then they all stopped, like a bunch of second graders coming back for their treat. He looked every cow in the eye. They looked back with an emptiness that lacked understanding.

Nonetheless, it lifted his heart to feed them the little square of chocolate. He let the horses out. They each got a half of an apple and were happy to get out into the warm, end- of-day sunshine.

Rayland sat on the beaten up porch and watched contentedly as the sky faded from daylight to dusky, milky blue. As the sun slipped over the western ridge of the mountains, Rayland looked for Venus. The sun set and Venus appeared, as it always did. The sky darkened and more stars and planets appeared, accenting the crescent moon. He marveled at the night sky. Deep, dark blue filled with stars and planets. Ursa Minor. The Little Dipper, the North Star, the Milky Way. Magnificent. He smiled. He was happy. He'd found the North Star. Polaris. Now he knew where he was. This is where he belonged. He was home.

Norman woke in the middle of the night to the distant sound of the town fire siren. Before his feet hit the floor, through the window, he could see the orange glow in the night sky. He knew immediately the location of the fire. "Aud. Aud." She was startled awake by the rush in his voice. "The farm's on fire. Rayland's." He slipped on his trousers. "I gotta go."

The alarm sounded at 2:50 a.m.. It could be heard for miles. The entire sky glowed orange as volunteer firemen rushed to help in a fleet of pickup trucks. The town fire engines weren't far behind. The house, barns and sheds were ablaze. Even the piles of harnesses and tools were burning. Flames gushed toward the sky. George Davidson, one of the first firemen to arrive, quickly surveyed the scene.

"There could be someone inside. Come on." Karl Zalewski was already at his side. They rushed to enter the house through the front door. It was nailed shut. Karl had an axe.

He knocked the door down. Karl, George and Star rushed in. Heavy smoke knocked them back. They retreated. "We just can't go any further," Karl coughed out. "No breathing apparatus. Try the other side." Others rushed to the other side. The porch was about to collapse. Star was frantic, eager to stay on the heels of the fire fighters.

Ron Davies and Jeep tried to enter the ell, but found that door nailed shut as well. They knocked it down, but it was too late. The ell was crackling, and about to collapse. Chief Spaulding ordered everyone back.

"Hold the dog. Hold the dog," he barked out orders. Star wanted in as much as anyone. The fire was extremely hot. It melted a plastic pail 80 feet away. The engines got as close as they could, but with only 100 gallons of water each, they weren't very effective against the roaring blaze. An engine from Windsor arrived, but it was too late. They were all too late.

Norman was one of the first on the scene. Without protective gear, mask or helmet, he was relegated to pulling hose and helping where he could. Melvin asked him to hold Star. He was happy to do so. It's possible they held on to each other. Both needed calming down. Aud appeared next to him. "I brought your boots." Norman was wearing his slippers.

Thirty or so volunteer firemen fought the fire because that's what you did, but a terrible feeling of hopelessness was setting in. Ralphie arrived as did most of the neighbors. "Dad. I'm going with the search party to look in the woods and upper meadow. Maybe he's hurt or hiding," Ralphie said, then ran off. Norman stood and stared. He was unable to turn away. Softly, he said to no one, "He's not up there, Ralphie." He wiped a tear from his eye. "He's not up there."

Aud put her arms around him and held him close. The search party spent two hours looking for Rayland, hoping to find him. Just hoping. The house and ell were blazing in a full-throated roar.

"Norman. Look." Aud noticed the secretary desk sitting under the maple tree a good distance from the house. The light from the fire lit it up as if it were a spotlight. Firemen had been running back and forth past it all evening, but amid the scurry and confusion, no one questioned its reason for being there. She walked toward the tree. Norman recognized it immediately, and he followed. They stood looking at it.

"It belonged to Rayland's mother. He loved this old desk." He reached out and touched it gently. "He put it out here for some reason. Look around. Nothing else here. Just a desk. Probably filled with memories."

Norman sat and opened the drop down desk using the skeleton key still in its slot. A letter was placed carefully, front and center. It was weighted down with a little music box so it wouldn't move. Norman spent a long time reading the letter through teary eyes.

"What's it say, Norman?"

"It says 'I love you,' Aud. It says 'I love you all.' Let me finish reading, then you must read it, too."

It was part last will and testament, and part a letter to family and friends. One by one, he told every one who mattered to him how much they had meant to him. How much they were a part of the life he loved. He thanked each one for being his brother or sister, or friend. He thanked them all for sharing his life with him.

The letter tore at Norman's heart. Aud watched from a distance and left him to these private moments with his friend. Finally, he put the letter away. She walked over and put her hands on his shoulders.

"He left the cows to us. Emerson and Alina get the desk, and they also get you, Star." He gave the dog a happy scratch on the head. "Kate gets this." He picked up the little music box to show his wife.

"Oh, it's lovely. She will cherish it." Aud carefully cranked the little handle and played the soft, romantic piece. The fire raged in the background.

By dawn, hundreds stood around looking at the smoldering ruins and sharing their grief. Some had been there all night. Others were just arriving. Some were crying. Some were hugging. Anna saw Norman and went to him with tears running down her cheeks. They hugged and Anna buried her head against his chest.

"I'm sorry, Norman. This is awful." She looked up. "I'm so sorry this mess got so out of hand. He didn't deserve this. None of them did." She wiped her tears with her hand. "I'm so sorry."

Preston stood next to them in silence, looking at what had been the farmhouse. Many just stood silently and looked at the smoldering ruins.

Doris Reguska made many, many peanut butter and jelly sandwiches. She passed them out to the firemen.

John Hurley told her, "Best damn peanut butter and jelly I ever tasted, Doris. Thank you." Both had teary eyes. "Thank you so much."

"Why would he do such a thing, John?"

"Pride, I guess. Just too much pride to pack up and quit."

The fire chief found Norman and beckoned for him to come over, out of earshot of others. "Thought you'd like to know, Norm. We found the iron bed frame." He looked Norman in the eye. "Rifle next to the bed."

He swallowed hard. "Thank you, chief." Norman walked away crying. He saw Kate through his teary eyes. She was crying, too. They hugged and consoled each other. Once he could talk, he told her about the desk. He wanted her to read what Rayland had written to her.

She sat and read the letter. She cried again. Once she'd regained some composure, she picked up the music box he'd left her. Cranking the handle and listening, she looked up at Norman and smiled.

"Debussy." She looked back at the little box and played the tune again. "He was such a sweet man." Wiping her tears with both hands, she sobbed, "He was such a sweet man."

Chapter 20

I KNEW HIM

September 12, 1964

London – *The Daily Herald published its final issue. The first issue of The Sun newspaper, which supported the Labour Party, was published to supersede The Daily Herald. Its inaugural editorial commented that "steaks, cars, houses, refrigerators, and washing machines are no longer the prerogative of the 'upper crust."*

All weekend, hundreds visited or drove by the site. When the construction crew arrived for work, they were sick about what had happened. They joined in and did what they could to help the firemen. Friends, neighbors and complete strangers came by to express their feelings. The *Claremont Daily Eagle* sent a reporter to cover the fire and the aftermath. He interviewed the fire chief and various volunteers, but found that those who came to observe and mourn had a deeper story to tell.

He interviewed a woman in her twenties. "When I was a kid, he taught me how to ski and ice skate," she sobbed. "I never said thank you. He was the nicest, kindest man." She wiped her tears. "I never said thank you."

"I feel like I know him even thought I don't," a middle-aged man from Windsor offered. "I totally understand his love for the land and a simple way of life. I totally understand. The law told him to leave his home. His land. But he wouldn't. Wish I had met him. He sounded like a fine man who just lived at the wrong time. I came to say goodbye to the past."

The young reporter spoke with a short, dark-haired man who shut down his market across the river and came as soon as heard the news.

"He wasn't a protester or a trouble maker." The man spoke with emotion and a bit of an accent. "He was a farmer. Minding his own business. Progress came and found him and snapped him in the rear end. His way of life stood in somebody's way, and they took him down. I know progress is necessary in this country, but at what price? My hat's off to Rayland. I'll miss him. Be at peace, my friend."

A neighbor added, "We live up the road. My father and Rayland were friends. As a kid, he was always so kind to me. I blame the state. Think of it." He pointed. "This highway is going to cost a million dollars a mile. A million dollars a mile and they couldn't make a slight curve to take care of an old man who lived on his family's farm?"

"A beautiful farm and a beautiful man. I knew him all my life," another neighbor piped in. "He had the blessing of living here and the misfortune of living in the path of Ike's highway."

A local farmer with a woodsy accent said, "Ya know. Ya pick a spot. Ya break the ground. Ya build a home and raise some kids on it." His grey eyebrows went up. "That's gotta count for something." The eyebrows came down. "Don't ya think?"

The young reporter heard over and over again -- kind, jovial, gentle, beloved. Others used words like happy, friendly, and generous. This had been a simple farmer. Kind and gentle. And this was his farm.

By late afternoon the gathering had thinned. It grew again the next day.

When Monday morning rolled around, the big machines chugged back to work. First, they bulldozed the smoking cellar hole. Then huge earthmovers tore into the remaining meadows. Dump trucks were loaded with dirt and fill from the pasture and dumped the soil where ordered to get the road up to grade.

The farm, a lifetime and a way of life were buried under Route 91, Exit 8 and a dirt Park 'N Ride.

About the author:

A graduate of Pennsylvania State University, Richard Lechthaler served three years with the US Navy's Sixth Fleet in the Mediterranean, attended the London School of Economics and worked on New York's Madison Avenue before life in the Big Apple soured and he moved to Vermont in 1968. He was delighted to discover that, while the state was going through a dramatic change, precious remnants of the old Vermont remained. Lechthaler was director of marketing for Stratton Mountain for six years before joining the regional planning firm Northeast Planning Associates. He and his wife Carole have three grown children. He retired in November 2019 and sat down to write a book. Here it is ...

CPSIA information can be obtained
at www.ICGtesting.com
Printed in the USA
LVHW020559010821
694125LV00003B/226

9 781605 715438